I0595423

Campbell Praed

Affinities

a romance of to-day

Campbell Praed

Affinities
a romance of to-day

ISBN/EAN: 9783337348519

Printed in Europe, USA, Canada, Australia, Japan

Cover: Foto ©Andreas Hilbeck / pixelio.de

More available books at **www.hansebooks.com**

AFFINITIES

A ROMANCE OF TO-DAY

BY

MRS. CAMPBELL-PRAED

AUTHOR OF "NADINE," "ZÉRO," ETC.

LONDON
GEORGE ROUTLEDGE AND SONS
BROADWAY, LUDGATE HILL
NEW YORK: 9 LAFAYETTE PLACE
1886

AFFINITIES.

CHAPTER I.

MAJOR GRAYSETT and Colonel Rainshaw had been in the same regiment in India. They had gone out there together; but Major Graysett remained on service some time longer than Rainshaw. The latter went home on sick leave, married an heiress, sold out of the army, and settled himself very comfortably in one of the Midland counties, on a property which had been bought with his wife's money. He did not, however, lose sight of his friend; and when, three or four years later, Graysett found himself in England, almost the first invitation he received was to Colonel Rainshaw's place, Leesholm.

The visit was arranged under what seemed attractive conditions—good pheasant-shooting, a small party of pleasant people in the house, and a hunt ball in the neighbourhood.

Graysett travelled down by an afternoon train. It was almost dark, therefore, when he arrived at Leesholm; and a raw evening, with a blustering wind and snowy clouds. The building seemed, as he approached it from the back, to be large, rambling, and of the Tudor style of architecture, with low mullioned windows and irregular gables. It was built of pallid grey stone, which in the dim light gave it an almost spectral appearance. The east front looked out upon a prim pleasure-ground, bordered by a high yew hedge, cut at the corners into pyramidal shapes, which stood out sombrely against the leaden sky. An apparently unused, three-aisled avenue stretched in a straight line beyond the ha-ha ; but a bend in the approach, bringing the visitor to the principal entrance, showed him an addition to the structure, of later date and more imposing pro-portions. On the west side might be seen an extensive prospect of smooth lawn and trimly· kept shrubbery, and beyond, in the hazy distance, lay a flat, well-timbered park, over which the grey mist was stealthily creeping.

An owl hooted from an old tree near, as Graysett drew up before the portico. He shivered. Though not impressionable in every day social matters, his temperament was susceptible to atmospheric influences, and to those of scenery and surroundings ; and he was struck now by a certain weirdness in the aspect of the place and of the evening. Possibly, he reflected, this might arise from the fact that he had for long been un-familiar with the details of an English wintry landscape.

He got down from the fly in which he had

driven from the station—for, the time of his arrival being uncertain, he had requested Colonel Rainshaw not to send for him—and paused for a minute before ringing. Again the eerie feeling seized him as he looked along the broad carriage drive, above which the naked boughs interlaced, spreading a misty fretwork against the sky. The ground was covered with a light sprinkling of snow, whiter upon the turf than where an array of empty flower-beds stretched in a fantastic pattern upon the lawn. There was a dampness in the air which told of a coming thaw ; and the wind blew in fitful gusts, moaning plaintively through the trees, and round the grey spire of a church close by. Ghostly white patches lay upon the evergreen shrubs and the funereal yews, against which the snow had drifted ; while every now and then a flake, loosened by the blast, would hover for a moment and noiselessly fall. A watery moon had just risen, cold and round, concealed at intervals by driving clouds, and shedding broken reflections upon the gleaming ground, and on a stretch of ornamental water shadowed by drooping beeches.

The windows of the house were closed and shuttered, only here and there a light twinkled ; but he caught a faint sound of melancholy music, a waltz air which he did not know, played dreamily and in uncertain time, two long notes quivering in suspense as it were, and then an impassioned turn in the melody, swelling louder and gracefully dying away, like some magic strain of mysterious import. The music, which had indeed a certain wildness and beauty, due perhaps to the manner in which it was played, impressed Graysett so powerfully that he lingered in the porch till it had ceased, hesitating to break its charm. Then another gust swept chilly round him, driving a branch of dripping ivy against his face, and almost drowning the bell's muffled peal.

The outer door swung open, and he was ushered into a hall, warm and harmonious, and flooded with soft light from a great blazing fire and several rose-shaded lamps—a pleasant contrast to the glassy paleness and wintry desolation without. The hall was of the conventional type—old oak carving, deep window seats, Chippendale tables, willow-patterned plates, brass dogs on the wide hearth, palms, bulrushes, and peacocks' feathers in tall blue vases, screens of faded leather, and tapestry *portières*. It was like a dozen other halls of the same design, and almost oppressive in its want of originality but for the traces it gave of recent occupation—library books, newspapers, crewels, a sketching-block, and an easel on which rested a canvas with a lightly dashed-in girl's head. Just now the place was deserted, but the sound of voices and of grown-up people's laughter, and again snatches of that pathetic, mysterious waltz air, floated down from some upper room or corridor. The servant withdrew and Graysett waited, enjoying the luxurious warmth, and reflecting that his friend had made for himself a very comfortable nest.

"If the wife be only in keeping with the good things her money has purchased," he thought, " I might be tempted to follow Rainshaw's example, and give up the fancy I've had all my life, that a twin soul is wandering about the world waiting till my mine claims it as a mate."

He gave a little laugh, and stooped to caress the Dachshund which came rubbing against his legs. Then he looked at the drawing upon the easel, and while thus occupied became aware of steps upon the stairs, and went forward to meet his host.

"Well, Rainshaw, I'm glad, indeed, to be with you again. You see I've managed after all to get down in time for dinner. One forgets how easy travelling is in England, and what a distance one can fly over in a day if trains fit. One forgets, too, what a dreary, ghost-like effect moonlight and snow produce, and how horribly cold a winter's night may be. In fact, there is so much forgotten in all ways, that it is pleasant to find oneself remembered by an old friend. You are looking well."

There was a great contrast between the two men. Rainshaw had a thoroughly English face and physique ; he was broad-shouldered, muscular, and ruddy-complexioned, with blue eyes, and light hair and moustache. Graysett, though not less athletic or soldier-like, was dark and sallow, with refined features, deep-set brown eyes, and a more thoughtful expression of countenance. He looked worn, and his skin was transparent, as though he had been for some time out of health.

Rainshaw shook hands delightedly with his friend.

"I am sorry to say that I cannot return the compliment, old fellow. What has been the matter with you? Jungle fever?"

"Something of the sort," answered Graysett carelessly; "but I have quite got over it. I am perfectly well."

"Well, if not, we will soon put you all right. Let me introduce you to my wife."

There came forward a handsome, "well-got up" young lady, who had followed Colonel Rainshaw down the stairs. Her hair, of the fashionable bronze, was touzled in front, and drawn upwards from the nape of her neck. She wore a very mediæval-looking tea-gown, and carried a great fan of peacocks' feathers. But her dress, her designedly dreamy gaze, and affectation of deep earnestness, were in odd contrast with a briskness of movement, solidity of form, and frank address which would have suited a young English country girl to whom life was a very pleasant and material fact.

Mrs. Rainshaw greeted her husband's comrade with flattering warmth, offering him tea, sherry, and seltzer, and all kinds of refreshment.

"You've had a long journey, haven't you?" said she. "Of course I don't mean from India— that's too far to think of. *I* never got any farther than Nice; and it was while we were wintering there that I met Tom, and my mother persuaded me into marrying him, by promising me as many dresses for my trousseau as Queen Elizabeth had in her wardrobe. I wonder why mothers want their daughters to marry as soon as they are out of the school-room. I'm sorry I had so many dresses, for I might have considered that I should have been able to buy them for myself afterwards. Now all that I can do is to buy things for Tom—at least he buys them and I pay for them,"—and her girlish laugh and frank smile at her husband, as though the whole affair were an excellent joke, prevented Graysett from thinking then of the bad taste of the remark, though afterwards it occurred to him that there might be drawbacks to the pleasure of marrying an heiress.

" I daresay that you heard us laughing," continued Mrs. Rainshaw. " We have been behaving like a pack of children, playing at games in the Long Gallery. It began most seriously with thought-reading : and each person willed that somebody else should do something extraordinary. And I must say that Lady Romer did make an impression upon Mr. Margrave, and he looked decidedly queer when she told him what he was thinking of ; but I said that I'd have nothing to do with mesmerism and mediumship and all that horrid stuff—I know one man who was turned into an atheist by it—so we played magic music instead. I'm going back to start a paper chase, which will give us all a little exercise before dressing time. Now, Tom, it's all very well for you to frown and call me hoydenish ; but if you had married straight out of the school-room, and if you had to entertain a set of county frumps this evening, and to ask them how their children are, and to talk about clothing clubs and mothers' meetings, and all sorts of dank subjects till you felt like a fly in a honey-pot, you'd be glad enough to fortify yourself by a romp beforehand. I suppose that you're used to county people and to being improved, Major Graysett, or were before you went to India, and that you would be too sedate to join us."

Major Graysett assured her that such was not the case, but declined the invitation as he was evidently expected to do ; and then looked round with a view to making some appropriate remark upon the adaptability of the house to such amusements.

They had gone upstairs and were standing in a quaint kind of ante-room, into which several doors opened. Through an archway Graysett caught glimpses of more oak carving and blue china, and of a tortuous panelled corridor. He saw that Leesholm was an old and irregularly built house, which had been furnished according to modern lights by some one terribly nervous about anachronisms. As at least two periods seemed clearly indicated, the task could not have been without its difficulties. This he observed to Mrs. Rainshaw.

"Oh!" she exclaimed, "it's despairing to any one with a sense of harmony—not that I am harmonious ; but, as everybody seems to think so much about their houses and their furniture being in keeping with a period, I thought it would be the correct thing to get up an enthusiasm about. I didn't know that I shouldn't have everything clear before me till after I had begun to fix up the old place. I fancied that, as long as a house was ancient, all the parts were bound to match, but that doesn't seem to be the case. One had an idea, you know, that people in those times kept to their century, and didn't try to go backwards or forwards. That's all a mistake; they jumbled up their centuries just as much as we do; and as we've got more to choose from, why, we have decidedly the advantage of them."

Mrs. Rainshaw stopped and laughed in a way that was infectious.

"I had set my heart upon being Queen Anne and nothing else," she went on. "The front is all right; it's this part that is mixed. I did this room myself; do you like it? But I must have a Grandfather's Clock for that corner. I suppose it ought to be inlaid; what do you think? I know that I've got out of my period."

"Isn't everything just what it ought to be," said Graysett, "I am sure all looks delightfully harmonious."

"Yes," she assented doubtfully, "except, perhaps, those two arm-chairs. Spindle-legged seats are beautifully early—though that's rather out of fashion now; but they are so uncomfortable."

More peals of laughter floated down from a higher level.

"They are waiting for me," cried Mrs. Rainshaw.

"Good bye! I am sure, Major Graysett, that, although you look rather severe, you'd like me to have my little bit of play before I do my lessons this evening. If you come down early I'll tell you who everybody is." She ran away, but came back to say, "Tom will show you where you are to go, and will take care of you for the present, Major Graysett; I'll put myself in charge afterwards. I must consider while I am dressing who I shall send you in to dinner with. I could not decide how you were to be paired till after I had seen you. I promise to give you some one nice. You sha'n't have a frump."

"Now that you have seen my wife," said Rainshaw, as the pretty vision finally disappeared, "you will be less surprised that I did not want to go back to India. It is hardly fair to ask your opinion."

"She is charming," replied Graysett warmly. "As frank and unaffected as a child. I congratulate you upon having got a real good thing out of life's lottery."

"I knew you'd understand her. She is a child. I begin to think that I was rather a brute to take advantage of her innocence. But I fancy she is very happy, and I always let her say just what comes into her mind. I like her to be perfectly natural."

Colonel Rainshaw conducted his guest along some curious passages which apparently belonged to what Mrs. Rainshaw called the mixed part of the house, and left him in a cheerful bachelor's apartment where a bright fire burned, and an arm-chair stood invitingly near the hearth.

"I hope, old fellow, that you will forage for anything that you want. I see that they have unpacked your portmanteau. That's all right. You'll hear the first gong presently. As you don't know your way about, I'll come round after I've received my marching orders for dinner, and pilot you down."

It was, however, earlier than they imagined, and before the first gong sounded Graysett was already dressed. He seated himself in the arm-chair by the fire, and, leaning back, fell into a reverie. He was tired, and was conscious of nervous excitement unusual with him. He had travelled from Scotland that day, and though to Rainshaw he had made light of his recent illness, it was certain that the fever had left traces, both physical and mental, upon his constitution. Among its effects of the latter kind were a vague sadness and dissatisfaction with the world, a keener susceptibility to music, and to the in-fluence of Nature, and some romantic and poetic tendencies, to which he had heretofore been a stranger. He had now a curious illustration of this fact. The melody of the waltz which he had heard upon his arrival had lingered with extraordinary vividness in his memory, and seemed at this moment to reproduce itself in the air of his chamber.

Slowly, with expression.
p
cres.
dim.
cres. . . . dim.
rit. . . . .

CHAPTER II.

COLONEL RAINSHAW knocked twice at Major Graysett's door before he received permission to enter. As soon as he went in, it became evident to him that something strange and discomposing had occurred during the interval. Graysett was standing by the chimneypiece, his head bent and his face very white. He looked up. There was a dazed expression in his eyes, and he started violently, seeming at first almost unable to collect himself, when Rainshaw spoke:

"Are you ready, Graysett?"

"Yes," replied the other in a dreamy way. "I have been ready for some time."

"Sit down then, and let us yarn for a few minutes. You don't catch me in the drawing-room before it's absolutely necessary to put in an appearance. It's the English country gentleman's privilege, which he gains as soon as he marries, to be let off hanging about doors and saying civil nothings. We had a dose of that sort of thing in our aide-de-camp days—eh, Graysett?"

"We had indeed," rejoined Graysett mechanically.

"I tell my wife that I have had enough of the 'superior footman' business, and that she must manage social arrangements for herself. Pulling the bell, ordering the carriage, acting valet upon occasions, and doing master of the ceremonies generally—that was about it, wasn't it? Do you remember how his Excellency used to funk taking in old Lady Whalley at the dinner parties; and how he swore at the table of precedence?" Rainshaw laughed at the recollection. "I feel much in the same mood when we entertain what my wife calls the county frumps. However, my lines are cast in pleasant places this evening. Aren't you well, Graysett? Knocked up, perhaps, with walking over the moors. Let me send for a sherry and bitters to pull you together."

"Nothing, thank you. I'm detaining you; don't mind me. I shall be myself in a few minutes, and will follow you downstairs."

Graysett made an effort to resume his usual manner. He waived Rainshaw's offers of restoratives, and to some extent succeeded in allaying the anxiety of his friend, who, however, refused to leave him.

"There's plenty of time. I met Judith Fountain on the landing going up to dress—your destiny for this evening by the way. She will be the last to appear. It is a fashion of hers to keep every one waiting while she is in one of her dreams."

"Do you believe in dreams, Rainshaw?" asked Graysett abruptly.

"About as much as I believe in the manifestations at a dark *séance*. You don't know Lady

Romer? She is staying here. I made her very angry not long ago by telling her that her spirit faces were no more than phosphorised bullocks' bladders. It's a fact, I assure you. A medium once let me into the trick."

"But one has heard and read strange things about dreams," persisted Graysett. "It is known that they have foretold events."

"I only know that I once lost a considerable sum of money through backing a dream event which didn't come off in reality," said Rainshaw. "I have fought shy of dreams ever since. I don't remember you of old as going in for that sort of thing, Graysett. But you will be quite in harmony with some of the ladies here; and I see that Molly showed more discrimination than I gave her credit for, when she coupled you with Miss Fountain."

Graysett made no reply. He seemed to be thinking deeply.

"Haven't you any curiosity about your destiny?" said Rainshaw. "I felt inclined to pity you, for in my opinion Judith Fountain is one of the most stupid girls for whom I ever tried to make conversation. She has no go in her whatever. Yet she is sought after, because, in the first place, she is good-looking, after a rather uncanny style; and, in the second, as some one puts it, 'A vast fortune doth buy for her consideration.'"

Graysett made two or three sudden paces up and down the room, then halted before his friend,

Rainshaw, surprised at something strange and excited in his appearance, exclaimed—

"What is wrong with you? You don't look in the least like yourself. Have you seen a ghost? I'm not aware that the house is haunted, but we'll make inquiries. There hasn't been time for you to fall asleep and dream a dream."

"That's the curious part of it," said Graysett. "That's what baffles me. It's altogether strange, and I suppose my nerves have been a little shaken by that fever. Look here, Rainshaw," he added excitedly, "I can't make out your house—I can't make out whether I have been dreaming or not. Just come in here for a second."

He crossed to the opposite wall and threw open a door, revealing a small narrow room panelled in oak, with a writing-table, a few severe-looking chairs, and two or three old-fashioned cabinets. It looked something like an oratory, and did not appear to communicate with any other part of the house.

"Has this room any outlet except through mine?" asked Graysett.

"No. That's the nuisance of it. We can only use it as a sitting-room."

"There's no *portière* painted in imitation of modern tapestry, with a representation of the sleeping Endymion, concealing a door—— ?"

"Certainly not. The only hangings in the room are those window curtains of crimson silk."

"The door leading into an oblong sort of ante-room, lighted from above, the wall covered with

Japanese figures, as far as a dado which runs all round, and is formed of Japanese plates sunk in a dead gold ground—— ? "

" A dado of Japanese plates !" exclaimed Rainshaw. " My good friend, we are nothing if we are not Early English. As for the ante-room, all the walls of this little excrescence are outer walls, except that which divides it from your bedroom."

" I'll go on with my description. I want to know if there's any part of your house which answers to it. At the end of the oblong room are double doors, one of them inlaid after the Japanese style ; there are also some fine Japanese bronzes ; but the other furniture is utterly incongruous with the prevailing style. The cabinets are Florentine, and scattered about are pieces of *bric-à-brac* which might have been chosen haphazard in the shop of any London curiosity dealer. The incongruities, however, don't end here. The outer door opens into a sitting-room panelled in white and gold, each alternate panel a painting of wreaths of flowers and Cupids after Boucher. Here everything seems intended to correspond with the rest, but utterly fails. Forgive me if I wound your susceptibilities. Several of the pieces are glaringly out of harmony. There is a Pompadour cabinet, a so-called Marie Antoinette writing-table, a Chippendale writing-table, a Tottenham Court Road couch drawn up by the fire, with a satin *couvre-pied* embroidered in wreaths of roses——"

"My dear Graysett," interrupted Rainshaw, "what does all this mean? You are describing the boudoir of some heroine in a French novel; assuredly nothing that you will find in this sober English country-house. Come, what is the mystery? Is it a dream or an hallucination? Out with it."

"I believe that it is a warning," said Graysett solemnly.

"Let me hear it. Perhaps you are not aware that there is a society in London devoted to the investigation of all branches of supernatural phenomena. I will introduce you to Lady Romer when we go downstairs, who will be happy to place you in communication with the secretary to the committee of inquiry into dreams and portents."

Graysett laughed. "I have never considered myself a subject for phenomena. Seriously, I have had a dream or a vision—I can't say which —that has made a most uncomfortable impression upon my mind. I don't know of anything which ever before laid such a grip upon my imagination. I cannot get over it. I'll tell you exactly what I saw or fancied; and if by laughing at me you can drive away the queer, squirmy sensation that has taken hold of me, I shall feel grateful to you."

They went back to the bed-room. At that moment a gong echoed through the corridors.

"Go down," said Graysett. "I'll tell my tale another time. Mrs. Rainshaw and your guests will be impatient."

"No, no. The butler knows my ways, and

always allows me ten minutes' grace, and Judith
Fountain is good for another ten.   Go on."

"I suppose it was a dream," began Graysett ;
"but I don't remember feeling in the least sleepy,
and I am not in the habit of napping in an arm-
chair.   I dressed directly you left me, and was
sitting here by the fire waiting for you to come
back, thinking about you, your wife, and your
home, and how pretty and cosy your hall looked
when I came into it out of the snow and moonlight.   I kept fancying that I heard a waltz
some one was playing upstairs when I arrived—
a melancholy, fanciful thing.   It was curious
how the tune stuck in my memory, for I had never
heard it before."

"Ah!" said Rainshaw, "Judith Fountain's
waltz !   Yes, I know.   She was playing it just
as you came, for a sort of thought-reading,
'magic-music' game.   An odd connection of
ideas !   She always declares that she did not
compose it, but that she heard it in a dream.
Anyhow, it has become very popular, and you
will probably dance to it at the Holmborough
ball on Wednesday evening.   Coote and Tinney
have got hold of it.   Well ?"

"Some one knocked at the door," continued
Graysett.   "Supposing that it was you I called out
'Come in, Rainshaw.'   But, to my surprise, there
entered a man I had certainly never seen before,
though I should recognise him again in an instant,
under any circumstances or after any lapse of
time."

"What was he like?" asked Colonel Rainshaw with a practical air.

"A large man, very tall, and of great breadth of chest, with a way of tossing back his head so that attention was called to his statue-like throat. He had a smooth-shaven face, rather classical features, and sensuous, Greek lips. He reminded me of a statue in the Louvre, I think of the young Alcides. There was a good deal of intellectuality in his face, and of fire in his blue eyes when he opened them fully, which did not seem to be his habit. The most striking thing about him was his hair. It was not red and it was not gold, but something between the two; and he wore it very long, and brushed back from his forehead. It was curly, and stood out at the ends like——"

"Tail of a chestnut cob in full gallop," coolly interjected Rainshaw; "I know. You have described Esmé Colquhoun to a *t*. And now I have got the clue to the whole thing. But let us have your story to the end."

"Who is Esmé Colquhoun?" asked Graysett with interest.

"Have you been living quite out of the world? Punch's Platonic poet," returned Rainshaw drily. "He has been down in his luck lately. Surely you must have seen the correspondence in the newspapers a little while ago. Don't you know how, when sensation is slack, the public and the press have a way of lashing themselves into a fury of excitement over a mere nothing? Some social personages fancied they had been gibbeted in a

novel. It might have been you or I—a perfect
storm in a teacup. But that gave an impetus
to the pendulum ; and a reactionary movement
generally goes beyond the mark. Then it was
discovered that our poet had lost all his money in
a rotten investment—a bubble scheme floated by
a pair of knaves, who made Esmé their dupe.
The saw-mills were burnt down, and the whole
thing exploded. I need not enter into particulars.
You will hear rather too much about Esmé
Colquhoun presently from the ladies who are
staying here. He is still a god to a certain set of
worshippers."

"Whoever the man may be, he had in my
dream a strange and most unpleasant power of
fascination," said Graysett gravely. " He crossed
before me to the door of that inner room. I felt
constrained to rise and follow him. We passed
through the Japanese room which I have described,
and into the Louis Quinze boudoir. I seemed to
halt for a few moments on the threshold of the
door, and while I did so the scene photographed
itself, as it were, on my brain. The apartment
was evidently that of a refined and luxurious
woman. All sorts of knick-knacks were scattered
about. On a chair lay a mantle of some rich
material, apparently not long taken off. There
was a bunch of yellow roses upon the carpet,
crushed and drooping, and giving out the strong
perfume of dying flowers. At one end of the
room there was a raised alcove—a window recess,
approached by a step, and draped with curtains of

blue satin, the borders embroidered like the cover-
let on the sofa."

"But the woman, the woman!" cried Rainshaw.
"Skip those details, though your dream must
have been singularly vivid to have taken in all
such particulars—the pattern of a cabinet, the
embroidery upon a curtain, the perfume of roses."

"It is this which gave the whole thing such
ghastly reality," said Graysett, shuddering slightly.
"The woman was lying upon a sort of divan in
the window recess. One arm supported her
head, which rested against a pile of cushions. It
was thrown back, showing her throat, and her
eyes were closed. Her form seemed tense, and
her whole attitude had the abandonment of one
not mistress of herself. Don't you know how in a
dream a fact forces itself upon one's intuition?
You don't reason, you *know*. I *knew* that the
woman was dying some horrible death ; that this
man was her husband, and that he had killed her."

Graysett paused, and lifted his hand to his
forehead, which was damp with perspiration. "It
is horrible!" he ejaculated. "I feel as though I
had seen a murder."

"Describe the woman," said Rainshaw, now
deeply interested.

"She was dressed in a kind of brocaded robe, of
a curious yellow colour, the reflection of which on
her face made it look corpse-like. She moved
her head a little, and opened her eyes, looking
first at him and then at me. They were very
large, unearthly, grey eyes. The face altogether,

apart from its lividness, was remarkable, and had a beauty difficult to define ; it was terrible, and yet angelic. A great quantity of golden-brown hair was gathered up above the forehead. I should know that face if I did not see it till my dying hour. I hope the look she gave me will not haunt me till then. I never saw such eyes. They seemed to be gazing into another world. . . . But, great heavens ! the horror, the tragedy of them ! It is indescribable. I had not the power to speak or move ; I seemed under a spell. I knew she was in deadly peril, and I could do nothing to save her. I fancied she was entreating me. The sense of helplessness was frightful. A clammy sickness came over me ; my very bones quaked. The feeling was something more awful than can be told or imagined. Then in a moment everything had gone, and I was here alone, shaking and faint. It was a ghastly dream—if, indeed, it was only a dream."

"What else do you suppose it could have been ? A dream, and one very easily explained," said Rainshaw, putting on a didactic and practical air. "I told you that I had a clue. Isn't it in a novel by Wilkie Collins that a most weird and portentous dream is traced back, link by link, to the impressions made upon the dreamer's brain by the day's events ? I'll trace your dream in the same way. To begin with, your nerves are shaken by that fever, which has altered you, Graysett—I see it now—more than you are perhaps aware of. You dropped asleep when in an uncomfortable position, chilled with your drive, cramped by railway travelling, and probably fasting.   This is quite sufficient to account for the nightmare-like feeling of clammy horror.   Judith's waltz had turned your imagination into a melancholy channel.   On your way down you read this evening's 'Globe,' in which there is a long article upon Japanese art. The same paper contains an account of the De Brissac sale, which suggested your Louis Quinze room.   You dreamed of Esmé Colquhoun—no one could mistake your description.   He is a noted man, and, although you don't remember it, you have heard him talked of, or you have seen his photograph in the shop windows, or—why, of course—one of Pellegrini's caricatures or Du Maurier's society pictures has stuck in your memory. Now I think of it, there's a cabinet photograph of him in the hall, and your eyes unconsciously rested upon it while you were waiting till we came down. As for your lady, if you rack your brain sufficiently you will find her in another or the same shop window as Esmé Colquhoun, or in some picture gallery through which you have been lately strolling.   Now, have I satisfied you ? "

Graysett shook his head.   But he moved to the door with the manner of one who, having unburdened himself upon a certain subject, wishes for the present to have done with it.   " At all events," he said, " there's no use in arguing out the matter.   I have kept you too long already ; 'let us go down.   I admit that your explanation, from the materialistic point of view, ought to be satisfactory. I begin to suspect that I am rather a fool, and that you are right in attributing the alteration in me to the effect of my illness. I *have* changed during the last few months, and I never realized it so strongly as I have done since I entered your house. This is a bad prelude to my visit. I'll try and forget my dream, and be a more agreeable companion. But I can't shake off the impression that sooner or later I shall come across that man and woman."

"Nothing more probable in the case of the man. You may meet Esmé Colquhoun any night of your life in London. As for the dream-lady—now what sort of thing should you do if you identified them both?"

"I can't say. Probably warn her against him."

"That would make rather a good 'Hard Case' puzzle," said Rainshaw, thoughtfully. "What should a fellow do? It would depend upon how far he believed in that sort of thing, wouldn't it? Belief or no belief, *I* shall hold my tongue, watch events, and reason. For, you see, if it is fated that a certain thing is to happen, warnings and botheration cannot prevent it from happening. That's the philosophical way of looking at the point. And, hang it all, you know," cried Rainshaw energetically, "you wouldn't think much of a girl who was ready to give up the man she loved because a stranger had dreamed something unpleasant about him. At any rate, it would take something more than a dream to turn a good many women against Esmé Colquhoun.　He's 'a dealer in magic and spells';" Rainshaw softly hummed a few bars from the " Sorcerer "; "platonic attachments so-called, and that sort of thing.　I am not saying anything against the fellow.　Some people declare that he has a fine and unusual talent for virtue."

Graysett laughed mechanically.

" But I suspect," continued Rainshaw, " that Esmé Colquhoun is sufficiently worldly wise to prefer a reigning sovereign to one discrowned. That's a practical sort of philosophy.　Well, when your vivid imagination identifies your dream-heroine, as it assuredly will do, with the first good-looking girl to whom you see him paying attention, I'll pull a grave face and refrain from chaffing you.　In the meantime let me give you a hint.　Talk to Miss Fountain about your dream, and you may perhaps find her more interesting and more interested than my experience has proved her to be.　I am told that she has queer theories about affinities, presentiments, psychic force, and all that rot, and that these are the only subjects about which she ever gets up any excitement."

CHAPTER III.

A CHEERFUL hum of voices filled the drawing-room when the two men entered. They were not the last, though, as Rainshaw perceived, Miss Fountain had been before them. The butler was awaiting the arrival of a spinster from the neighbourhood in order to make his announcement. Mrs. Rainshaw had already marshalled her guests, and with the exception of one gentleman and two ladies, all the couples had been told off for dinner.

These exceptions were a young married woman and a young girl. The former was thin and willowy, with a rather long face, a pathetic smile, big intense eyes, and reddish-brown hair, of which the tint was unmistakably artificial. She resembled one of Rossetti's models. The younger lady was slender also, and the poise of her neck was very graceful. She stood with her head lowered and her face turned to the fire. She was not speaking, but seemed listening in a preoccupied manner to a triangular conversation between Lady Romer—as the Rossetti lady was called—another pretty girl, and a sandy-haired, distinguished-looking man.

Lady Romer turned and addressed her host,

but her large eyes wandered in the direction of a bountiful-looking matron—placid, upright, decorous, whose smooth hair was drawn straight down from her forehead, and who wore black velvet and the family diamonds. This lady, the very type of a well-conditioned British squiress, was evidently studying the fashionable beauty with curiosity and disapproval. Lady Romer talked slowly, in a sweetly modulated voice, with an appearance of extreme candour and some pretty gesticulations.

"Colonel Rainshaw," said she, with innocent audacity, "Miss Geneste and Mr. Margrave are trying to persuade me that I looked better when my hair was black. What is your opinion? I don't know whether you have a good eye for colouring, or perhaps you are one of those people who think Nature can never make a mistake."

"I am liberal all round in my views, Lady Romer, and don't conform to the dogma of infallibility either in the case of Nature or the Pope," said Rainshaw, diplomatically, with a comprehensive bow and a series of greetings to various guests who were not staying in the house. "The standard of beauty must always be regulated by a charming woman's taste."

"Or that of a man to be charmed," murmured Lady Romer, with a little shrug of her shoulders. "That's so nice of you," she added aloud; "but you take care not to commit yourself. You have not the courage of your opinions, Colonel Rainshaw. Now, I am unfashionable enough to be loyal to my old faiths and my old friends. Six months ago Esmé Colquhoun's verdict would have been generally satisfactory."

"Ichabod! how are the mighty fallen!" said the sandy-haired gentleman.

"Oh!" said Lady Romer plaintively, "it's all the jealousy of those horrid newspaper editors. They can't bear us to get rich except by inheritance. If *I* were to try and increase my income by taking shares in a dressmaking company, there would be a satirical article in one of the weeklies, called 'Bombast and Bombazine,' or something equally ridiculous. Poor Esmé! I sent him 'Sonnets and Sawdust' to America; I thought it would amuse him. I can't see why he should be laughed at because his stock of timber caught fire —or what the burning of the Champion Road saw-mills—by the way, where is Champion Road?"

"Follow Buckingham Palace Road to its bitter end, Lady Romer, and in due time you'll reach Champion Road and the site of Colquhoun's saw-mills," replied Rainshaw.

"I don't see how the Champion Road saw-mills can affect the abstract question of what is beautiful and what is not. Isn't it the highest art to idealize Nature? Well, I'm Nature idealized. Therefore—— That's a syllogism or something like it, Miss Fountain. I know you are nothing if you are not philosophical."

"Oh, yes! Judith is a great deal besides being philosophical," said the pretty girl, who had a remarkably vivid face. She was half foreign, and was noted in the little set to which she belonged for her clever impersonations of well-known people. She gave one now, which, however, was lost upon Major Graysett as far as its application went, though he listened eagerly. "I have heard Esmé Colquhoun say"—she put her head back slightly and rolled out her words in a liquid loose way, with a good deal of emphasis and expression —"'Miss Fountain is complex; she is a harmony of contradictions; she is everything but crude.' And then he added with a sigh, as though it were an after-thought : 'Nature is crude.' One felt so sorry for poor Nature."

Every one laughed except the girl with her face to the fire.

"That's exactly what I'm trying to prove," said Lady Romer, "but you will find it all exhaustively explained in Mr. Colquhoun's new book. I've read parts of it in manuscript. It is to be published anonymously in America and judiciously puffed here. Everybody will rush to the libraries, and admire it on the strength of its being American. Then the critics and the public will discover that their Transatlantic star is Esmé Colquhoun, the despised prophet."

"A phœnix rising from the ashes of the saw-mills," said Mr. Margrave. "It was stupid of Colquhoun to try and combine trade, fashion, and poetry. He didn't show his usual cleverness there. What should a young fellow, who has been educated at Eton and Oxford, who writes impassioned sonnets, and proclaims himself the Apostle of the Beautiful, know about sawing wood ? It isn't in reason. For instance, if your husband, Lady Romer, bought up Marshall and Snellgrove ; how should he know when bombazine was riz ? You'd expect a smash-up, and a laugh at your expense."

The door opened. Miss Cromlin was announced. There was a little flutter and a good deal of apologizing on the part of the late arrival.

"Lady Romer, allow me," said Colonel Rainshaw offering his arm. "And, Graysett— Miss Fountain, let me introduce Major Graysett."

There was a general movement and dispersion. The young lady by the fireplace turned and bowed. Graysett came forward and also bowed. Their eyes met. Involuntarily he recoiled a step. He turned very pale, and stared at her for a few seconds with a kind of wild wonder. She observed his emotion, and her eyes dilated with surprise ; but outwardly she was perfectly composed.

There was nothing startling in her appearance except a sort of spirituality, which was perhaps her chief attraction. Her features were delicately cut. Her hair—golden-brown, with ruddy shades here and there—was not cut and curled about her brow, but fell back in natural waves from her half-oval forehead. She had singularly lucid eyes, and rather thin, melancholy lips. Her smile was distant but engaging. Her air, though rather dreamy, seemed that of a woman accustomed to society, and her white dress had no affectation of peculiarity, and was perfect in all its details. Graysett beheld in her the woman of his vision.

The recognition was instant and convincing. There was no possibility of doubt, even making allowance for an overwrought imagination. Though in his vision the face had worn an expression of tragic horror and appeal, every feature was identical with the countenance before him ; and the great grey eyes, that now returned his gaze, had in them something of the same pathos and unearthliness as those other eyes which had mutely entreated him.

He gave her his arm, and they moved on ; but he was too stupefied to utter any of the tentative remarks which pave the way for more intimate conversation at the dinner-table. They filed in the procession across the hall almost in silence ; and it was not till the soup plates had been removed that, roused by a reproachful glance from his host, Graysett rather abruptly turned to address Miss Fountain, and found that she had bent slightly towards him, evidently with the same intention.

"You have come from Scotland to-day, have you not ?" said she.

He answered vaguely, with the usual reference to the weather. "I left it snowing heavily up North. You seem to have been more fortunate. But it was an odd sort of evening. I thought it very weird—the sprinkling of snow, the moonlight and everything—when I arrived."

"You got here late. I think I understood from Mrs. Rainshaw that you are an old brother officer of her husband's, and that you have not been long in England." She began to play with the illuminated card upon which her name was inscribed, and added, " Don't you think that it would be useful if a short biography of the person were written here under the name, for one's guidance in conversation—at all events at a London dinner party ? "

" I suppose it would. But some people like giving play to the imagination. One can always conjecture a good deal."

" Well, there's some amusement in verifying one's conjectures," said she languidly. " But, to take an interest in making frames for your fellow-creatures, you ought to be very fresh and sym-pathetic. I think that I like best to find the frames ready made."

Graysett hazarded the remark that a good many portraits were hardly worth framing.

" I agree with you," said Miss Fountain. " In a county collection, for instance, there would be several duplicates. But I must say this for London : you get more types there, and occasion-ally you can plunge straight into deep water without taking soundings. I'm rather confused in my metaphors," she added, with her soft smile ; and then it struck him that there was a suggestion of cynicism about her mouth.

" At all events," he answered, "you appear in my case to have taken a few soundings—suppose, if I'm worth it, that you plunge straight into deep water."

"I might strike against a rock.   And I'm not sure that you have not an advantage over me.   I fancied when you were introduced to me, that you thought we had met before.   I don't remember it, however."

Graysett evaded the implied question.

"You were playing, I think, when I arrived—a waltz, was it not?—very pretty and melancholy. And Rainshaw, when I remarked this of the air, told me a curious thing.   He said you composed it in your sleep.   Is that true?"

Miss Fountain hesitated a moment, and then replied, "Not strictly so.   I did not compose the waltz.   I heard it in a dream.   The air seemed unknown to me; but possibly I had heard it before."

"A dream which left a very vivid impression on your mind?" asked Graysett eagerly.

"No," she answered, "not particularly vivid. It was the impression of a very pleasant waltz, with a partner whose step suited mine, but who in all other respects was vague.   The dream has been realized," she added laughing.   "People have got hold of the waltz through hearing me play it, and I've danced to it several times."

There was a little interlude, during which Major Graysett tested the capacity of his friends' cook, and Miss Fountain, after toying with a morsel of sole, pensively observed the decorations of the table.   Presently Graysett said suddenly—

"Are you a great friend of the gentleman whom they were talking about in the drawing-room just now—Mr. Esmé Colquhoun?"

Judith turned her head swiftly, and looked inquiringly at her companion. "I have met Mr. Colquhoun very often in London."

"You know him, then, intimately?"

Judith smiled in a manner which made him feel that he had put his question more persistently than was becoming.

"Of course," added Graysett, "intimacy doesn't imply friendship."

"Aren't you adopting your own suggestion," said she, "and plunging straight into deep waters?"

"I beg your pardon," he said. "I thought we had tacitly agreed to skip the preliminary process. We might try the experiment, for one evening."

"I should not wonder if we made some curious discoveries," she replied; "I agree. And now there's the ocean before us. You have not made a very bold excursion, though; it's rather the fashion to talk of Mr. Esmé Colquhoun. We are not friends," she added with an appearance of candour. "He is only interested in people who cause him an emotion. I don't. I do not affect him in any way."

"Your opinion does not seem to reconcile itself with his criticism of you."

"Oh! if that remark had been a little more clever, I should say that he wanted a peg upon which to hang an epigram. The fact is, that he has studied me only in the most superficial way, and has probably talked more *of* me than *to* me. I am outside the circle of his sensibilities."

"The circle must be a narrow one."

"On the contrary, it is immense. Now I am going to say a spiteful thing. Mr. Colquhoun lives two lives : one is spent in cheating the world, the other in cheating himself. Do you suspect me of finding fault with grapes which are too high over my head ? He has never immortalized my hair in a sonnet; and he has written dozens to that of—a great many other ladies."

"I am rather inclined to suspect you of a sarcasm, which I am too ignorant of the subject to appreciate."

"You know Mr. Colquhoun, don't you ? " she asked in a matter-of-fact way.

"No. It is only a few weeks since I came home from India. I don't remember ever having heard his name mentioned before this evening."

"Yet it appears to interest you very much. That seems strange, since you are not acquainted with Mr. Colquhoun even by reputation."

"Has he a great reputation ? "

"I suppose so. In the literary and artistic worlds."

"Ah ! to those I am a stranger. But I daresay that at times some name, casually spoken, has struck a chord in your imagination, and you have felt a strange presentiment that you would shortly meet the owner. That was my case, and the reason of my questions."

"I have had presentiments," said Miss Fountain gravely; "some strange ones. Yours does not strike me as being very extraordinary," she added. "Several people here are friends of Esmé Colquhoun, and sooner or later you will meet him in their company."

There was another brief interlude, and Graysett became aware that Miss Fountain was examining him attentively.

"I fancy that you have a leaning towards occult subjects," said she. "Isn't it so?"

"What makes you think so?" he asked, without directly answering her question.

"Sympathy perhaps," she said, with a little laugh, which he thought very charming. "See" —she held her hand, with the back upwards and the fingers extended, before him for a second. He saw that it was very long and more tapering than is usual, the point of the third stretching considerably beyond that of the index finger. "I have the hand of a mystic, so have you. That's a sign of freemasonry between us."

"I am glad of that fact at any rate," said Graysett, "though I must confess that any mystic tendency which I possess is in an early stage of development. In what way does yours show itself?"

"I have intuitions. Seers say that I am clairvoyant. They tell me that I have psychic power. I am bound to believe them, though in honesty I too must acknowledge that no one has succeeded in testing my power."

"How have people set about attempting it?" asked Graysett, not quite sure how far she was in earnest.

"Oh, no one in a really serious way. Lady Romer and one or two of her friends have tried to mesmerize me, but, although these persons have assured me that I am an admirable subject, they have never been able to do anything with me."

"Is Lady Romer occult? That is the word, is it not? I should not have imagined it."

"She dabbles in everything that is mysterious and exciting. They—the seers—say that she has strong physical magnetism; certainly she contrives to make people do very foolish things."

"I wish you would tell me who 'they' are to whose authority you refer so mysteriously," said Graysett.

Judith waited a moment before answering. "I don't think you are likely to meet them. They don't court notoriety. 'They' is a little set of wonderful people who have come—some say from India, some from America. I really don't know. They see—what we cannot see. They have a curious religion of their own, and are under the orders of a mysterious brotherhood. They have strange clear eyes and a downright way of talking—as though they could not be contented without absolutely getting at your soul, and judging you by the sort of stuff it was made of. It was they who told me that I had psychic power. I wanted to join them—to be taught how to exercise it. But they would have nothing to do with me. In fact they solemnly warned me against laying myself open to influences from the spiritual world."

"You listened to and obeyed the warning, I suppose."

"No. My curiosity was rampant. You'll think it strange that I should be at once a materialist, and a spiritualist, but it is so. I can't believe in arbitrary agencies of that kind, nor can I get up any becoming awe of the supernatural. I am convinced that everything which happens in that world is a question of cause and effect, just as it is here. We are not afraid of material things because we can reason about them. If we knew and could reason about what they call supernatural things, we should not be afraid either. I immediately joined Lady Romer's *séances;* but it was no use. I am not cosmic enough for that sort of magnetism to affect me."

At any other time her odd talk and the curious expressions she used, which were uttered without affectation, would have amused Graysett, and he might have analyzed with considerable zest this, to him, new specimen of the occult young lady. But the hold she took upon him was too serious for the play of humorous fancy. He was groping his way among mysteries, and all that she said deepened the impression of glamour and unreality which had been steadily creeping over him, making speech and action seem for the moment automatic.

"I wonder what sort of magnetism would affect you," he said, falling into her vein.

" I don't know."

She leaned forward as if meditating. It was quite curious to remark what a change had been wrought in her by the fascination of a subject which evidently engrossed her mind. Her eyes had the bright flash which indicates enthusiasm, and her manner had lost its little touch of artificiality and flavouring of smartness. Graysett felt sure she was not now thinking of him as a person, and that she had lost any curiosity she might have had at first as to how she should impress him.

" I don't know," she repeated. " It would be something not quite spiritual and not quite physical, but both. I'm not to be approached directly from either side. In fact I begin to fancy that I'm neither fish nor fowl nor honest red herring. At any rate, I couldn't be swayed by the power which works miracles on platforms. I only know one person who I think might open the door for me. And I'm not sure whether it would be wise to trust him. It's an intuition only. I have a curiosity, however, to test his power."

" That might be a dangerous experiment," said Graysett, in the leisurely way with which people commence an anecdote and an *entrée* at the same time. " I'll tell you why I think so. You were talking of mesmerism, which seems to be the recognized high road to that undiscovered country."

CHAPTER IV.

"I DON'T suppose it's the only one," said Miss Fountain, "though it seems the easiest. But tell me why you think the experiment might be dangerous. Were you generalizing, or—you could not guess to whom I referred then?"

There was something childlike in her frank curiosity, which contrasted almost grimly with the tragic suggestions that crowded Graysett's imagination.

"You do not know anything about me?"

He looked at her sadly. "I wish that I did," he said, with an odd kind of earnestness. "I wish you'd tell me whom you meant."

She laughed softly and shook her head. "Go on," said she, "this is a very interesting conversation; but I am afraid that I prevent you from eating your dinner. Still, time is long at a dinner party. There's a good deal before you. Tell me what *you* meant."

"Oh, it is nothing in reality," said he; "an intuition on my part. Only this. I once went to an exhibition of the sort in India. A woman was the biologist. She was a great, coarse, muscular creature. I shouldn't have fancied that there was much of the spiritual about her. I suppose it was what you call physical magnetism. She brought people up from the amphitheatre to the platform by a look, as it appeared, and when she had them there, her command over their bodies and souls seemed complete. At one minute they were yelping and barking round her like so many cats and dogs, into which she had in imagination transformed them. At another they were stretched, a dozen rigid corpses, on the stage. In a second, at the order 'Each one to his trade,' they were up and doing, all in a fever of excitement —climbing imaginary masts, shoeing imaginary horses, hammering, weaving, plaiting straw, digging, gesticulating, and cutting the most absurd capers. This was the ludicrous side of it. There was a tragic one as well. A poor boy, very slight and delicate, with strange dreamy eyes, who had shown a strong repugnance to mounting the platform, was made by his employer to go up. She was a long time operating upon him, and seemed very much exhausted by her efforts. She succeeded at last, however, in getting him off; but—he never came to again. You have eyes like that boy."

Judith gave a little shudder. "Poor boy!" she murmured softly. "Well," she said, after a few moments, "lest my death should lie upon any one's conscience, I depute you to bear witness that I have been duly warned, and have encountered the risk of my own free will. There's something wonderfully fascinating in the idea of that 'undiscovered country.' I have an intense desire to explore it ; I should like to pass the barrier to-night."

"Better keep on this side of the fence," said Graysett earnestly. "There is safety where no mystery lurks."

"Ah !" she exclaimed, "don't you feel, as I do, that everything is a mystery ? What can be a greater mystery than dreaming, for instance ? Isn't thought a mystery ? Isn't memory a mystery ? "

Judith's voice, though low, was penetrating, and rose clearly in a sudden lull which had fallen upon that corner of the table. The foreign girl with the vivacious face, who was sitting next Graysett, laughed and bent forward to attract his attention.

"This, at least, is no mystery," said she touching the menu—" *Cailles à la royale.* Major Graysett, when you are out of cloud-land you'll find them at your elbow. They've been there for some time."

Graysett apologized and mechanically helped himself, while he addressed some trite remark to Miss Geneste. But presently the buzz of the dinner-table increased, and he again turned to Judith Fountain, who took up the conversation at the point where it had dropped.

"Sympathies, affinities, and antipathies are mysteries—the most interesting of all," said she. "I am sure there are certain laws which govern all those things. Think of the strange way in which people affect you—no two alike ; well, there must be some current, force—I don't know what to call it—in people, which when they are brought together operates according to the given conditions. It's a kind of spiritual chemistry, and we are like the contents of a test tub." She laughed again in her soft fashion. "Don't you know there are liquids which won't combine unless a connecting medium is introduced into the tub? I think that must be the case with human beings sometimes."

"How do you mean?" he asked in a startled manner.

"Why, imagine two persons who might influence each other in the most powerful way, held apart by a spiritual antagonism! A third person appears, and some element in him or her forms the connecting link between the other two. There's a great deal in my idea, if it were worked out scientifically. And how glorious to have the knowledge which would enable one to direct the hidden forces in one's own and in other people's natures!"

"One might be burned as a witch or a wizard. That would not be glorious," answered Graysett.

"You forget," said she smiling, "what Mrs. Rainshaw is always trying to impress upon us: that we live in the nineteenth century, and that the mistakes of all previous centuries are so much clear profit to us."

Graysett laughed, not so much at her remark, as at his own thoughts.

"I know what is passing through your mind,"

said she. "Somebody—Colonel Rainshaw probably—has told you that I am stupid, and it
occurs to you that I am perhaps less stupid than
is supposed."

"It appears," said Graysett, "that you give
occasion for controversy."

"I see," she answered, "my intuition was a
correct one. I am getting into dangerous waters,
however; and perhaps we have been long enough
off the conventional track. Shall we talk about
something commonplace, and plunge into every-
day life again?"

"I beseech you, no. I feel in a mist of strange
impressions. Anything might happen to me—
except the commonplace. This is dreamland."

"A comfortable substantial dreamland," said
she, glancing down the table. "And the figures
opposite us look particularly solid. Am I the
only phantom in your dream?"

"That may be the case in a more literal sense
than you imagine," answered Graysett in a serious
manner.

She looked at him wonderingly, but did not
reply; and there was a pause, during which
Graysett's champagne glass was emptied and re-
filled. The stimulant seemed to him a necessity,
and braced his nerves. He was conscious of
talking with more animation than was his wont,
when an appeal from Miss Geneste drew him
into a discussion upon Buddhist philosophy which
à-propos of a criticism upon "Mr. Isaacs," had
been started upon his other side. There is

nothing more illustrative of the medley of life than the froth of truth and falsity, earnestness and flippancy, comedy and tragedy, which may be skimmed from the conversation at a dinner party.

Mr. Margrave, sitting opposite, had apparently alighted upon a barren pasture in the shape of his companion—the spinster who had kept everybody waiting. He was eyeing the others affectionately across the table, and had pushed up his flaxen imperial as if ready to contribute his opinions to the mass generally. He rather affected transcendental speculation, though he professed a cynical contempt for the supernatural; and he had a dry, colourless way of expressing himself, that suggested a reserve of something worth hearing, which however never came to the fore.

"What interests me in that line of thought," he said, "is, that at any rate it argues from analogy. Granting that there is such a thing as spirit at all, if you admit the physical evolution of the species you may logically infer the evolution of the soul also. And since every seven years one is supposed to change the tissues of one's body, may it not be conjectured that the 'soul stuff' changes likewise? Twenty years ago I believed in a God. My idea of Him was of an old man with a long grey beard and a very large eye, who was always on the look-out to punish me for what I particularly liked doing—always, so to speak, watching round corners. Well, that has passed. My soul is now, as I am well aware, on intimate terms with my digestion, and has no fear of the conventional deity whatsoever. Can any one tell me if this soul is the one I possessed twenty years ago ?"

Mr. Margrave looked round with the air of one propounding a conundrum, and then helped himself to an olive.

" H'sh," murmured Mrs. Rainshaw, darting daggers at him, her consciousness of the presence of a neighbouring rector overcoming her sense of the humorous, which, as a rule, was very easily titillated.

Mr. Margrave asked innocently, " Does anybody know Micky Frere ?" But his attempt at a diversion fell somewhat flat, for the rector had perpetrated a ponderous joke, at which all who heard it thought it their duty to laugh.

" Micky Frere generally says what he thinks," pursued Mr. Margrave reflectively, taking another olive. " When I ingenuously stated that I liked visiting my friends in the hunting season, he remarked, 'My dear fellow, you are five years older than I am, and you go to stay in a country-house, where you can't get what you want to eat, and you can't grumble when you are put upon !' There's something in it."

All the time this banal talk was proceeding and even while with his voice he joined in it, Graysett's mind was occupied with Miss Fountain, and her fanciful suggestions which chimed so curiously with his own mood. He could hardly keep from looking at her, though at the moment he might be conversing with others. Every movement she made and every passing expression upon her countenance, roused him to almost painful interest. The fascination she exercised over him was of a weird kind, and seemed quite independent of her personal attractions. He had hardly considered the question of her beauty, and when gazing into her eyes he had not been conscious of admiring them. He could not criticize her from any ordinary standpoint. His feeling for her was too subtle to be analyzed. It was as though he had met her upon another plane than that of social intercourse, and that in this rarefied atmosphere conventional limitations could not be observed, so that a glance, a smile, a word, seemed commensurable with hours, days, even weeks of intimacy. It struck him that she also might be possessed with the same fancy, and might be sensible of being acted upon by one of those mysterious forces to which she had half-jestingly alluded. While he was thus thinking, she turned suddenly upon him.

"Tell me," she said, "why did you look so taken by surprise—or was it by horror? I could almost have fancied so—when Colonel Rainshaw introduced you to me. Had you been dreaming of me?"

"I'll tell you the truth," he answered impulsively. "Your guess is a correct one. I had seen your face in a dream not long before I saw it in reality."

"Oh, this is very interesting, this is very

curious!" she exclaimed, in a low tone, her eyes dilating, and her whole face lighting up. "Perhaps you can help me. Did anything of the sort ever happen to you before? Perhaps you are a seer?"

"I am a most distinctly prosaic person, Miss Fountain, and I know nothing of the subjects you are interested in. I am not sure whether I should have treated them with proper reverence a little while ago; but I confess that I feel now less inclined to scepticism."

"And did you never have an experience of this kind before?" she asked again, looking disappointed.

"Never in my life."

"Yet you look—I feel almost certain—" she began thoughtfully; then added, "Here is an illustration of my theory of spiritual chemistry. You have come under the influence of my magnetism, and I have developed in you some latent occult faculty. May I not hear your dream?"

"Not now. And see, in a few moments you will be leaving the dining-room."

"You will tell it to me later?"

"I don't know. I am not sure," said Graysett confusedly. "I wish you would let me make a bargain with you, and that you would exchange secrets. I wish you would tell me who the person is, that you fancy might magnetize you. Then I will tell you my dream."

Miss Fountain's expression altered for the

moment.   Her smile had a suggestion of haughti-
ness, and she replied with dignity, "I have no
secrets in relation to these matters which I would
hesitate in telling to any one who looked upon
them in the abstract light that I myself do.
Certainly I agree to your bargain. We will
talk about it by-and-by."

She rose as she spoke, in obedience to Mrs.
Rainshaw's signal, and the ladies trooped from
the room.

A little later, they were scattered in knots
about the drawing-room. Lady Romer, Miss
Geneste, and one or two others of the more
fashionable sat together ; Mrs. Rainshaw heroically
entertaining two county matrons, whose conversation was not exhilarating.   Judith Fountain sate
somewhat apart; and between the two first groups,
though belonging to neither, was a little round-
faced lady—she who had been allotted to Mr.
Margrave—with a small *retroussé* nose, and fair
hair rolling in large waves over her forehead.
She had very round blue eyes, and a surprised,
innocent sort of look, and a little pucker about
her lips as though she were only just realizing the
fact that she had passed her first youth, and had
not yet adjusted herself to altered conditions.
She listened with great attention to Lady Romer's
lively cackle, and evidently considered herself
qualified by experience to join in the discussion of
London frivolities.

"The world is very bad ; yes, indeed," she was
saying in her small voice.   "But don't you think

it is getting better?　Now I have a friend in
London with two daughters, and they belong to a
society.　It's called ' The Society for Moral and
Social Reform among the Upper Classes.'　Oh,
nothing to do with the poor!　I assure you it's
quite beautiful to hear them talk of Humanity,"
added the surprised-looking lady, unconsciously
emphasizing the capital H, " and the Aspirations
of Women, and the Final End of the Race.　And
then the work they do is quite prodigious."

" Well, tell us, Miss Cromlin, how they set
about reforming the Upper Classes," said Mrs.
Rainshaw, welcoming the prospect of a diversion;
" though I don't think that I should support the
movement, for I always think the wicked people
are the most amusing.　I wish we had a few more
wicked people down about these parts.　At least—
I mean—I wish hunting wasn't looked upon as a
sacred duty, or that Tom didn't think it my
sacred duty to stay at home and mind the baby.
Tell us what these Reformers do."

" They have meetings, dear Mrs. Rainshaw; I
can't quite say what they talk about, for I was
never admitted to one.　The fact is, they always
said I hadn't realized the greatness of the sphere,
which I am sure was not the case, for the more I
see of life, the more I'm struck with the bigness
of it.　It's quite bewildering I'm sure.　Then they
write things and have a secretary, and they go
into society a good deal in order to improve its
tone.　Oh, they went out a great deal, and people
might have thought they were frivolous; but they

always said that their object was to elevate the tone of fashionable parties, and that from any other point of view London life was utterly vapid and unsustaining. Do you find it so ? " innocently added Miss Cromlin, turning to Lady Romer.

" London vapid ! " cried the latter. " ' The pulse of the world ; the mirror of life,' to quote Esmé Colquhoun. Why, if you want intellectual food, you have only to stand still like the Israelites at Sinai, and manna will drop into your mouth."

Judith Fountain, who had been listlessly turning over the leaves of a " Punch," and whose eyes were in dreamland, rose abruptly, and stood irresolute, as though debating how to occupy herself.

" Sing something, Judith," said Mrs. Rainshaw.

" My throat is relaxed, dear, and I have a headache."

Then there was a stir among the dowagers, for this raised a point upon which each had a right to be heard.

" Salt and water," suggested Miss Cromlin, sweetly.

" Sal volatile," spoke a meek-looking clergyman's wife.

" There's nothing like strong coffee," said a cheery-faced woman, who rode after the hounds. And Miss Fountain remarked languidly that the best cure for a headache was to let it wear itself out.

" That depends upon the kind, my dear,"

observed the stout, decorous matron, whose diamonds were to be envied. " If it is neuralgic, let me recommend three belladonna pilules—we are homœopaths, you know; but for a bilious head-ache, nux vomica, &c."

Judith sat down desperately to the piano. She played very prettily, in a fitful manner, but at times with crisp precision, and occasionally a passionate intonation that lent contrast to her fugitive style. It was a Bohemian dance which she sent ringing through the room, a wild fantastic thing of which each phrase suggested a fresh movement and a fresh emotion—now coy and inviting, now reluctant, now crashing and dashing in a phase of mad excitement, anon plaintive and reproachful, and again in stately minuet time, evoking visions of our powdered grandmothers, and of the ballet in " Don Giovanni." She was still playing when the gentlemen entered the drawing-room. Her head was bent slightly forward, her grey eyes shining and darkened, her lissom form curved. Graysett noticed, for the first time, the fine moulding of her shape, her cameo-like profile, and the dark masses of hair which crowned her head. There is no charm in a woman more subtle or suggestive than the back view of a well-poised neck, from the nape of which the hair grows upward in luxuriant waves, and which curves inward and downward and melts into the soft contour of throat and shoulder. It was to be noticed that Judith Fountain's claims to admiration lay rather in those rare indefinable charms than in any robust and striking beauty of feature, form, or colouring. To be strongly attracted by this girl seemed to imply the possession of a sense not commonly developed among men. She appealed not to the herd: some electric current must be established, some chord struck, before her influence could be felt. When once felt, it quickly became irresistible. She was then more than interesting, she was absorbing. This Graysett instinctively realized as he watched her.

By the same intuitive eye he perceived that, notwithstanding her undoubted individuality, she was extremely susceptible to impressions from her companions or surroundings. He now partially understood why Rainshaw had called her stupid, and could conceive of conditions under which her brightness would be completely dimmed, and her responsiveness to a congenial companion become stolid indifference when the topic mooted was not in accordance with her own bent. While playing she seemed to breathe an atmosphere which her music had created, and for the time to have forgotten her surroundings. When, however, she left the piano and dropped into the circle of country neighbours which Rainshaw had now joined, he observed that the very expression of her face changed. All brilliance vanished from her eyes and smile, she looked dazed and preoccupied, and appeared either to have lost the faculty of conversation or not to care about exercising it.

Presently a striking-looking woman, with short golden hair, fine blue eyes set wide apart, a clear creamy skin, and that sensitive nose curving slightly upward at the point which is supposed to indicate dramatic genius, took Judith's place and sang a little Venetian boat song, with the most charming air possible. She was dressed in dull-red velvet, with a high collar and ruffles of old lace. She had a full beautiful throat and neck like ivory, quite unadorned, and her whole appearance was what is generally termed artistic. There was something delightfully fresh and Bohemian in her voice and air ; but it was evident that she had all the *savoir faire* of a woman of the world. When she had finished her song she sat still, one arm resting upon the music-desk, the lace falling back and thus leaving its shapely outlines disclosed—it was a very beautiful arm and in its way eloquent. With the other hand she picked out little suggestive passages of different melodies which seemed a sort of running accompaniment to her talk. That too was picturesque and vivacious. A small group was gathered round her. She had created a little movement, and, as it were unconsciously, had broken up the stiff knots into which people had formed themselves.

"Venice!" she was saying ; "I have just come back. I went there to paint my 'Consuelo ;' that is my ideal city. The charm of old-world associations is in the very atmosphere ; but it is exhilarating, not oppressive. You are not weighed down by a sense of your deficiences and by the gloom and grandeur of the past as in Rome. In Rome you must know the history of every stone and you must study every master-piece; but in Venice you breathe history and art unconsciously; and to live is to be happy."

CHAPTER V.

"Who is that lady?" asked Graysett, glad of the opportunity to address Miss Fountain.

"Don't you know?" she answered. "That is Christine Borlase, the painter."

"I am an outer barbarian. But candid confession brings its advantages. You sum up characters so epigrammatically. I wish you would describe—Miss or Mrs. Borlase?"

"Mr. Borlase is the British Consul—at somewhere in Asia Minor. Mrs. Borlase goes out to him for a month in the winter, and he comes to London for a month in the summer. It is a very good arrangement when people's tastes clash; don't you think so? Mr. Borlase had delicate lungs, which, however, don't seem to prevent him from collecting and deciphering hieroglyphic stones, and otherwise amusing himself after his peculiar fashion. He is an Oriental scholar—an antiquary. Both in manners and climate the East suits him better than England. He dislikes London society. In fact, Mr. Borlase is not artistic—in our sense of the word."

"I see. The term 'artistic' implies a great deal in modern life."

Judith laughed. "And, like charity, covers a

multitude of sins. Not, however, in the case of Mrs. Borlase. She is perfect. She has no sins. But, apart from particulars, I prefer artistic to Philistine society, and so will you, if you have not already made your choice."

"Please go on describing the lady in question. I would not for the world miss a word of the biography."

"You must go to Miss Geneste for biographies. I am not generally suspected of being brilliant. Mrs. Borlase speaks for herself. She is a child, an artist, and a woman of the world all in one. She is equally devoted to friendship, amusement, and work. She is very spontaneous. She is so frank that no one could for a moment imagine her designing. Her studio is delightful, and her Thursday evenings more popular than any in London. Ill-natured persons say that is because cigarettes are allowed. It is there that you will meet Mr. Esmé Colquhoun, whom we both seem to have got on the brain this evening."

She moved as she spoke towards an archway, heavily draped with Oriental stuff, which led into a dimly lighted window recess. Here were some low divans and lounging chairs. Into one of these she sank.

"I am very tired," she said ; "I feel as though virtue had gone out of me. Now let me hear your dream."

"First, if you have no objection, I will call upon you to fulfil your part of the bargain."

"I have no objection," she replied, after a

moment's consideration ; "though it seems rather soon to begin making confidences about one-self. Yes, I'll tell you. I lay myself open, however, to a charge of inconsistency. But—it is a case of honour among thieves, isn't it, Major Graysett?" she asked, looking up at him suddenly as though to reassure herself. "We have made a sort of convention—haven't we?—to take each other and life in general from the abstract point of view, and to get what entertainment we can out of that way of looking at things. I am very abstract myself. If I speculate about individuals, it is in an impersonal fashion. I criticize them as I would a picture. I could not condescend to petty curiosity. But there are a good many people who would be interested in out-of-the-way subjects, and yet who are not abstract—Lady Romer and Mrs. Borlase for example. Colonel Rainshaw may be put into another category."

"Oh, yes, I understand," said Graysett ; "that all goes without saying. I hope that I have been trusted often enough to have learned that discretion, even in unimportant matters, is an accomplishment to be cultivated, and that a whispering gallery is best avoided whenever it is possible to do so."

"I am afraid that in such a case one would have to escape from civilization altogether, and live in noble and primitive simplicity," said Judith. "You may be surprised to hear, after what I said at the beginning of dinner, that Mr. Esmé Colquhoun is the person who I think might seriously affect me, if our natures could ever be made to act upon each other. I don't fancy that is likely. The two *won't* be brought into contact. There's an innate antagonism—unless indeed you, Major Graysett, turn out to be the connecting medium."

Graysett looked at her in a startled way, but did not answer. He seemed disturbed, and she became pre-occupied for a moment.

"I talk flippantly, I know," she said, with another little laugh, as was her way; then, as though impelled to frankness, she added, "I think it is that I don't want to be serious about that feeling—that intuition I had when I first met Mr. Colquhoun."

"Do you mind telling me how you felt?" said Graysett. "Please don't think that I ask from petty curiosity."

Judith's eyes took back their far-away expression, and her voice changed.

"Oh, no, we are serious inquirers. I don't think that we frivolous, excitable, modern people are so very different from the Athenians, who spent their time in hearing and telling of some new thing. It was spiritualism and the planchette till that got vulgar. One day it is mesmerism and will-power; another, thought-reading; and now India and America have set the fashion to a school of occultists."

Graysett smiled.

"You have no sympathy with that phase of Indian life?" she inquired.

"It hasn't come in my way. But—I asked if you would describe your feeling with regard to Mr. Colquhoun."

She shook her head decidedly. "No, I had rather not at present. Perhaps I may by-and-by. I have fulfilled my promise to the letter. Now let me hear your story."

Graysett narrated his dream in almost the same words as those in which he had told it to Rainshaw. Miss Fountain listened very attentively. When he reached the point at which the stranger entered his room, and described the appearance of his unknown visitor, she uttered a low, eager cry of interest, but made no comment till the tale was ended. Then she said—

"You recognized in me the woman of your vision? Don't you think that in reality the face might not have been so clearly defined, and that your excited imagination may have caused you to fancy that it resembled mine? You saw me very soon afterwards—and people say that there is something rather dream-like about me."

"Impossible," said Graysett. "There was nothing indistinct about the vision-face. I wish that I had drawn it before I went into the drawing-room to meet the original. I would show it you. That would be a convincing proof."

"I don't doubt you," she said thoughtfully. "It is only what a matter-of-fact person would say."

"It was *your* face," he continued. "I could have identified it with that of no one else."

"And the man?" she asked. "In his case the

impression was equally vivid.   But you have not
yet identified him."

" Rainshaw told me that I had exactly described
Mr. Esmé Colquhoun.   Now you see the connection of ideas.   Does this also strike you ? "

Miss Fountain did not reply.   She looked
troubled and at the same time excited.

" Tell me what you think of it all," said he.

" It is very strange !   I should like to ask
Madame Tamvaco."

" Who is Madame Tamvaco ? "

" One of those queer people I told you of.
But she has gone away.   I don't know where.   I
had rather give no opinion," she added.   " I daresay that you will meet Mr. Esmé Colquhoun
before long, and then you will be able to judge
for yourself.   Thank you for the story.   There is
one very curious thing about it which I will point
out to you."

" What is that ? "

" You have accurately described part of a house
which belongs to me ; and you are quite right, by
the way, in saying that it is in bad taste.   You
would be confirmed in your opinion if you could
see the outside—all stucco, and miniature turrets
—a horrid suburban villa.   I have only been
once inside it, but no one could ever forget the
odd contrast between the Japanese corridor and
the Louis Quinze boudoir.   I am surprised that
you should have pictured it as inhabited by me.
It is in a neighbourhood of London that I don't
like, and where I should not care to live.   The

uncle who left the place to me built it, half after his own taste, half after that of his wife who was a French actress. Between them they certainly did not arrive at unity of style. Well, now you will admit that dreaming is a mystery."

"If all this were a dream," exclaimed Graysett, "I must have gone to sleep and awakened in an incredibly short space of time."

At that moment Mrs. Borlase advanced towards the recess, and an introduction ensued between the artist and Graysett. She seated herself beside Miss Fountain.

"Forgive me for interrupting you," said she with her frank smile, which drew attention from the alert glance she sent from one to the other. "You seem very much interested."

"We were talking of my monstrosity of a villa," said Judith composedly.

"Give me a commission, dear, and I'll engage to make it charming."

"You are clever enough to do even that," said Judith, "but as no one is going to live there it would not be worth while. Since I am forbidden either to sell or to let the house, I shall allow it to go quietly to ruin. Have you come to tell us that it is bed-time? I am quite ready."

"My message is that, the frumps having departed, all so disposed may adjourn to the billiard-room for cigarettes and pool. Judith," she added, holding forth a square sheet of thick note-paper inscribed in a peculiar handwriting, "you are not going to be like the rest of the world—are you?—

and buffet a fallen giant. The evening's post brought me this. Read it if you like. I want to enlist your sympathies. You know that Esmé and I are true art comrades and faithful friends ; and that the licence of friendship is allowed him."

Graysett, whose faculty of observation had been quickened, fancied that Mrs. Borlase's peculiarly melodious, rich-toned voice trembled. It occurred to him that, underneath that impulsive manner and candid exterior, unsuspected depths might lie. But the woman herself disarmed criticism. There was about her nothing snaky or feline. He felt drawn towards her rather than repelled. She seemed to him like a prisoner facing the world behind a screen of bars, with eyes that clearly said, " It is a necessity that I should be still and bow to the authorities which are set up ; but if I were free I would be a law to myself. I would never stoop to dissimulation."

Judith took the letter and read :

" Is thy servant a dog that he should do this thing ? You are wise, noble, devoted. Your arguments are admirable. Your cold reasonableness is unwomanlike. For answer I will refer you to a novel by Octave Feuillet, which doubtless you know already, and for the hero of which I have some sympathy and some contempt.

"I have seen your ' Consuelo.' It is strong and pure. It is a poem. You could have painted the picture nowhere but in Venice. I took with me to your studio one Vanstone, an American millionaire. He will buy the painting. But he has one or two crude suggestions to which, perhaps, as a sop to Mammon you had better attend. You were right, Christine. Rose wreaths often turn into fetters. You will have seen the reports of my reception. It is a curious experience to be lauded as an Apollo on one side of the Atlantic, to be denounced as Society's last plaything, discarded and penniless, on the other. John Bull is a noble fellow, who never can resist kicking the fallen. An artist must needs be the sport of knaves and fools. But the Balzac temperament has its privileges—the choicest one that power which only such as he possess, of closing the door upon love, defeat, despair, and of passing as it were into another room. Life offers an endless variety of chambers, and in each sits the ideal woman, who will murmur with the tenderness of an angel, 'Thou hast suffered much. Be comforted and forget.' And so I pass on.

"I have engaged to see you concerning the 'Consuelo.' How long do you remain with the Rainshaws, and what is your destination afterwards? I shall be at the Holmborough Hunt Ball; and De Burgh mounts me the next day. Should you fail me there, I will ride over to Leesholm and claim a welcome from some of my old friends.

"I am yours till then, and ever,

"ESMÉ COLQUHOUN."

Graysett observed again that Mrs. Borlase

watched Judith closely while the girl read Colquhoun's letter. The two faces were a study. Repressed emotion was visible in both. It was a little drama below the surface to which he had no clue. He would have given much to know the thoughts of both women.

"Well?" asked Mrs. Borlase, as Judith handed her the letter.

"Thank you. It is characteristic. It is interesting : but I don't know why you should have supposed that it would especially interest me."

"It does, does it not?"

"Yes," replied Judith negligently. "I always like to be truthful when there is no obvious reason for being otherwise. It interests me."

"You will be kind to poor Esmé?"

"Why should I pity him?" said Judith. "He is not the only person in the world who has lost money or written one book below his level. There will be neither necessity nor opportunity for offering him my sympathy. Mr. Colquhoun never dances. He is not likely to break through his rule at the Holmborough Ball."

"Ah, but he is coming here. Colonel Rainshaw has promised to write to-night."

"That won't make any difference," said Judith. "Mr. Colquhoun will be overwhelmed with offers of consolation."

"Consolation from you is rare enough to be a sovereign balm."

"It has only become so during the last six months, Christine," said Judith calmly.

Mrs. Borlase flushed. "Judith, you are hard. You are incomprehensible. You are a sphinx."

"No, dear," answered Judith. "I am only stupid and indifferent; and prosperity has made me cynical. They are waiting for you in the billiard-room; and as I am very tired, I will say good-night."

When Graysett handed her a candle, she said to him, "You must get my biography from Colonel Rainshaw, and then you will understand about the London house. But please do me a favour. Don't tell him that I am connected with your dream."

"I had already decided not to mention the subject again to Rainshaw," replied Graysett.

"That's right. Thank you. Good-night."

Accordingly Graysett parried the attack which Colonel Rainshaw made upon him when they were alone by professing a far deeper interest in the Leesholm coverts than in psychological problems.

"At all events," said Rainshaw lightly, "you seemed to find Miss Fountain interesting, to judge by the manner in which you devoted yourself to her; and I begin to think that she is a problem in her peculiar way. I watched her at dinner. She talked—and appeared to talk brilliantly. I have been told that she can say smart things upon provocation, but I am not the only person who fails to get anything out of her but the flattest and dreamiest remarks."

"By the way," said Graysett, "she told me that I might ask you for her biography."

Something in his voice seemed to rouse Rainshaw's attention.   He looked at his friend as though considering an idea which had only now presented itself to his mind.

" Why was that, I wonder!   Judith is considered a reserved person.   She objects to being talked about, and is too indifferent to give any information about herself.   Does she wish you to understand that her income is something over 7,000*l.* per annum, and that she may be won by any daring fellow for the asking ?"

" I don't think that is likely.   She wouldn't have to go far if she wanted a suitor."

" Do you feel disposed to become one ?   You admire her ? " asked Rainshaw.

" Yes," assented Graysett ; " at least she attracts me.   I won't answer your first question, for I have never thought about what it would involve."

" A man is usually supposed to be beginning to think about possible consequences, when, just after having been introduced to a marriageable girl, he talks to her straight off for several hours."

" In that case," said Graysett, " I should be certain of your approbation."

" No, I'm hanged if you would ! " exclaimed Rainshaw," eyeing him with a half-grave, half-comical expression.   " I forbid the banns."

" That's hardly necessary at present," said Graysett.   " Notwithstanding your opinion, my dear Rainshaw, one doesn't commence laying siege to the heart of an heiress at two hours' notice."

"Doesn't one? I did," replied Rainshaw frankly. "I made my plans at once. That's half the battle. I know your state of mind exactly. You are feeling just as I felt when I came home. It arises from being out of sorts. Liver in my case—the same thing, complicated by jungle fever, in yours. Liver very often means love. You are dissatisfied with yourself. You take a loathing to steamboats, flirting married women, hill stations and clubs. You can't help thinking how pleasant it would be to settle down comfortably in England with a nice income, good preserves, and a string of hunters. You like the notion of a well-dressed, sweet-tempered, fresh, candid-faced girl, whom you could honestly love, always about you— and children and all the rest. It's respectable, clean, healthy, and altogether the proper thing. But I don't call Judith Fountain healthy or fresh. I should not like to see you married to her. I should expect that something uncanny would happen."

" You don't reflect, my friend, that the type of woman which you admire so much might not suit me. I might prefer something more subtle. But tell me about Miss Fountain, for at present I am quite in the dark as to the cause of your objections."

" Here is her biography. Judith is the daughter of one of the Fountains of Latchett, in Bedfordshire. Her father died some years ago, and his brother, the Radical Fountain, who is member for Scratch Hill, gave her a home.

Molly tells me that the poor girl had a rough time of it with Mrs. Fountain, who has the devil's own temper, and two plain daughters to make her jealous of the pretty niece. They would have kept Judith in the background like a Cinderella, but Fountain interfered, and she has been going out with them for the last three or four seasons. She has not been a success, however, though people have admired her. There was always something odd about her, and at her best she looked like Ophelia in the mad scene, without the dressing up. The men with money haven't wanted to marry her, or she hasn't wanted to marry them, and has never got the credit of refusing a good offer. Or else Mrs. Fountain always put a spoke in the wheel. But now we have changed all that. Fortune makes great fools of people. Six months ago an uncle on the mother's side, whom no one had ever heard of, died, leaving Judith a quarter of a million in the Funds, and a brand-new mansion somewhere in the north of London. So the poor Cinderella has now everything her own way; and we all koo-too before her, and fight for the honour of introducing a husband to her notice. She receives these attentions with blank sweetness, and a spice of sardonic humour, which is the only thing in her with which I have any sympathy. It is just when I see this, that I am puzzled and inclined to recant. I feel sure that I am the only man intimate with her, who has the honesty to declare his conviction, that her apathy is not the cloak of talent, or a sign of moral superiority. It is a sign of weakness of intellect. Yes, believe me this is so. That strange interest in ghostly things—that unpleasant trick of staring into vacancy—her long fits of silence, and sudden flashes of liveliness, as to-night for instance—and a certain cunning which she has in divining people's thoughts and motives, are all accounted for by something wrong here."

Rainshaw significantly touched his forehead.

Graysett looked horrified.

"I see no sign of it," he said. "God forbid that this should be the case in one so young, and so attractive!"

"I am afraid my supposition is not unreasonable, when one considers hereditary tendencies. I don't think I'd risk it even for a quarter of a million in the Funds. Now don't say that I haven't warned you. I shouldn't tell this to any one but an old friend, for it is not fair to run down a girl and betray the secrets of her family. Still she sent you to me for her biography, and I am bound to give it without prejudice."

"I fancy that you have a dislike to poor Miss Fountain," said Graysett.

"There's no reason for it. I have every inducement to wish her well. She is a connection of my wife's and Molly is very fond of her, and anxious to see her happily married. But I must candidly confess that I have never taken to her. She is not to my taste. She comes of an unsound stock. She gives me the creeps. That reminds me, you'll have an opportunity shortly of comparing your dream-hero with the original. Christine Borlase and Lady Romer have insisted upon my inviting Colquhoun here after the Holmborough ball. Mark my words—trust a woman to stick to you when you are down, and to lend you a helping hand up. They mean to marry him to Judith Fountain."

CHAPTER VI.

GRAYSETT had neither dream nor fateful vision
that night ; but he lay awake for many hours,
deeply occupied with Miss Fountain and the
extraordinary change which had taken place in
himself. He had always believed that his temperament was not one to be swayed by transcendental influences, or to yield rapidly to feminine
attractions. A man of six-and-thirty, who in the
course of many varied experiences, has never
seriously compromised himself in his relations
with women, and whose emotions have been
always more or less under the control of his
judgment, has a right to consider himself
hardened. It was a shock to him now to find
that his mind was completely engrossed by a
girl whom he had met for the first time that
evening. He had not looked upon himself as
likely to fall in love, though Rainshaw had been
right in conjecturing that the idea of marrying
had already presented itself to him. In fact
Rainshaw had drawn a prosaic but tolerably
correct picture of the state of Graysett's feelings
in regard to this question. Marriage seemed the
natural and orthodox future for him to contemplate. He had perhaps deferred it too long,

and had thus missed a sweetness which otherwise life might have given him ; but this he could not regret in the face of existing circumstances, and of the fact that, since the rupture of an early engagement, he had not seen any woman whom he would have cared to make his wife.

Though ready in action, ardent in sport, and keenly enjoying pleasure, he had been indolent and lymphatic in all that concerned the fiercer life of the emotions, perhaps not so much from temperament as from a lurking feeling, which he had always cherished, that fate held in reserve for him a passion and an ideal. He had been once or twice almost in love ; yet somehow or other the chance had slipped by him, and he had come out of two or three dangerous flirtations with married women a little disgusted, and rather bored by the atmosphere of intrigue in which they involved him, but not seriously injured.

It seemed to him now that, without any design on his part, he had been drawn suddenly into an exciting drama, of which the cast had been already arranged and his own *rôle* prepared for him. He had only to listen to the prompter, follow the cues, yield to the strange excitement which possessed him, and which partook of the nature of enchantment, and go steadily through the scenes till the tragical crisis was reached. The rapidity of the action bewildered him, but the play was as real as his own existence, and the weird touch of the superhuman, which had been brought into it by his vision of Judith, intensified the fascination it wrought. His theory of some occult connection between himself, Judith, and Esmé Colquhoun, whose appearance on the stage was being heralded by the by-play of that evening, was firmly fixed, but to reason upon it was impossible. He could not think out the situation. Never at any time had he been given to analysis. He only knew that he was under a spell, and that a woman, a dream, and an unknown man had suddenly upset his mental balance, and changed the current of his ideas and feelings.

He tossed about for some time in a curious tumult of mind, expecting that something would happen, yet unable to imagine what could possibly now take place. He lit his candle, but the light irritated him. He got up and paced his chamber, then went into the ante-room, and threw open the shutters. The moon flashed out from the driving clouds, and shed quivering beams upon the little mere. The snow was melting fast, and only a thin white sheet lay spread upon the earth. Water dripped from the naked trees, and the tall cypresses looked like menacing figures emerging from their shrouds. The night seemed full of trouble and mystery. There was no warm breath of life anywhere—all was spectral and silent— all was strange.

Graysett shivered and closed the shutters again. He went back to bed, and lay awake with nerves throbbing till a streak of daylight penetrated through a rift in the curtains. He fell then into a deep sleep and awoke refreshed. With clear morning and the commonplace sounds around him—the barking of a retriever, and the echo of voices along the corridor—revulsion came, and he almost laughed at his sinister and fantastic thoughts of the night. While dressing he assiduously cultivated a rational mood, and had fairly succeeded, presenting himself under quite a different aspect to the party assembled in the breakfast-room, who had mostly begun by looking upon him as somewhat removed from their sympathies, and were not prepared to find him as enthusiastic a sportsman as Rainshaw himself. Graysett discovered that he was taking the most cheerful interest in the day's prospects, and in the vexed question as to whether pheasants and foxes could by any possibility be reconciled. His pleasant illusions were, however, half dispelled when Judith Fountain put in a late appearance, and quietly nodded to him across the table. There was a curious smile upon her lips as though she partly divined what had been passing through his mind. He scanned her closely, and observed with a qualm of anxiety how absent and inconsequent was her manner. He watched for her voice, and noticed that she scarcely joined in the conversation, and that her eyes for the most part rested upon vacancy. Rainshaw was right: she did look strange—she was uncanny. But at that moment a remark of Mrs. Borlase elicited from her a reply so curiously to the point, that it appeared as if all the time she had been quite aware of the underplay of thought in the circle.

Her smile was now so sweet, and her appearance so altogether charming, that he could not help looking at her in wonder and admiration. She was dressed in a downy sort of white serge, which enhanced the limpid clearness of her grey eyes and the extreme delicacy of her complexion ; her long slim hands looked hardly human, her willowy frame scarcely equal to supporting her height. He thought of a flake of snow, of a white lily, of several other things which suggest purity, and unlikeness to all that is sensuous and earthy.

A little later, when the gentlemen were loitering about, inspecting guns, and making ready for a start, he saw her by the fireplace in the hall, buried in a deep arm-chair with a book in her lap. He came and stood near her, resting one elbow upon a piece of projecting oak. He looked very tall and rather masterful in that attitude. As a matter of fact he was a handsome man, and his bronzed yet refined face and soldierly bearing gave him an air of distinction.

"You are cold ?" he asked.

"I am always cold," she answered, with a little shiver. "There's something in me that will never let me get warm. Shall you like shooting pheasants as well as killing tigers?" she asked abruptly.

"I'm afraid that I have not shot many tigers," he answered. "I like all sport."

"Killing anything, in fact ?" she said. "That's a man's instinct. Women have it sometimes, but they are obliged to keep it under. I hope you will shoot a great many birds since you like doing it. I think that we are coming out to luncheon with you, and then I shall hear what you have done."

She looked down again at her book; but he still lingered. Presently she glanced up. "That was a strange talk we had last night. I think we had better forget it, and the dream too. The dream was very curious; I wish it had gone a little further—revealed something more. You are sure that there was no catastrophe—no explanation? There was only my look of terror, and the feeling of cold horror—no end?"

"That was all. There was no end."

"Well, we had better not think of it—that is, after the Holmborough ball. You shall tell me then whether it was Esmé Colquhoun who came into your room and took you to my house. Should you like to come with me some day, Major Graysett, and see the house?"

"I should, very much indeed."

"Then I will take you some time when we are in London together. You are not going back to India yet, are you?"

"I hope that I shall not go back for a year or more. I have been in harness a long time. I want a holiday."

"I suppose," she said in a listless voice, "that it is not necessary for you to remain in harness. I hope not."

"I have some money of my own, if you mean that," he answered bluntly, "but not a great deal."

"Do you see," she said, after a pause, "those two little blue flames leaping up, one on each side of that black log?"—she nodded towards the fire—"almost joining each other, and in an instant dying down to nothing. They will never blend till the wood is burned away to ashes, and then it will only be for a second. After that, they'll have disappeared too."

"Well?" he asked, for she said no more.

She looked at him intently. "Nothing. I have only said one of the things for which people call me stupid. Major Graysett, do you think it is wise, when you have a very strong impulse, to obey it unquestioningly?"

"Surely it depends," he replied, "upon whether the impulse is for good or evil."

"It is so difficult to define what is good or evil. My theory is that people ought to be true to themselves whether in goodness or in what the world might call badness; to follow the law of their own nature which is settled by some higher authority than their weak will. Some flowers give out a sweet perfume, others a disagreeable one. Some animals can be made pets of, others are ferocious and bloodthirsty. A strong love, a strong hate, or an overpowering impulse towards a particular course of action, implies strength and individuality. It means that you are not merely a mirror reflecting what is before you. I always obey an impulse when it seizes me ; but *I* follow *it;* it is never strong enough to drag me. I'd give anything to have a very strong impulse. I would yield to it gladly. It might do what it would with me."

"That is a very dangerous doctrine," said Graysett. "But you would be safe in one respect. I don't think you would ever have an impulse to do what was wrong, and perhaps your truest guide might be your own nature."

At that moment Rainshaw appeared.

"Come along, Graysett. This loafing is against all my principles; but it is next to impossible to get Fred Romer under weigh. Miss Fountain, you are coming out to lunch with us at the keeper's hut by Brindly Wood. I am sorry to interrupt so improving a conversation. You can continue it there."

They went off, leaving Judith to her book. The guns made a great deal of noise that morning; and by two o'clock long rows of brown and gold plumaged birds lay stretched beside the dark line of wood. There was much stir and merriment round and within the keeper's cottage, where ladies, hot Irish stew, brown sherry, and other good things awaited the sportsmen.

Judith Fountain was there, having exchanged her white dress for close-kilted cloth, and wearing a seal-skin hat in which she seemed less like the creature of another sphere; Lady Romer in dark red; Mrs. Borlase in a picturesque costume quite different to that of anyone else, carrying her sketching-block; the rest in order. It was a pretty scene, the men like most Englishmen looking their best in shooting gear, hungry, hearty and excited. Wine and chaff flowed freely. A great blazing fire threw gleams into the dark corners of the hut, which was lined with wood, and ornamented with stuffed birds, arms and woodland trophies. The windows were wide open, and the clear frosty air rushed in. Here and there outside in the shady places lay a sugary coating of snow, while the wintry sun, a pale gold orb, shone through naked interlacing boughs, down upon keepers and beaters, and into a small rivulet which, swelled by the melted snow, brawled in miniature cascades over a bed of stones.

At three o'clock they were in line again, and the wood was alive with the noise of beaters and dogs. Each lady, with the exception of Mrs. Rainshaw, who was too tender-hearted to witness the massacre of innocents, and Miss Geneste, who bore her company, had attached herself to one of the guns. Judith Fountain stood beside Graysett, to whom had been allotted one of the best positions at the end of the covert.

And now shot rained like hail, and then there were excited cries of "Ware hen!" and a succession of quick, sharp volleys, almost drowning the rapid whirr with which the startled bird rose, only to fall again. Graysett was shooting well, and felt some elation at the thought that Judith must remark his skill. She looked a little pale, but during the first lull congratulated him upon the certainty of his aim. A woman may profess horror at such indiscriminate slaughter, but she always admires the man who excels in it.

"I'd rather shoot tigers," said she. "You would have the satisfaction of feeling that you were destroying an enemy to mankind. It is wanton cruelty to kill these pretty, harmless things."

Nevertheless at the second onslaught she grew excited, and her quick eyes and ears marked the p-r-r and flight of several birds, which might not otherwise have fallen to Graysett's gun.

They two walked home together, the party dividing into two detachments, one of which chose the way through the village, and the other a longer round by the unused avenue. Graysett and Judith were among the latter. They lagged somewhat, for Judith's movements were not energetic. The dead leaves and moss made a springy carpet to their feet, and the winterly wind, fresh but not violent, blew chill in their faces. At first they did not talk readily. Judith was in an abstracted mood; but Graysett felt that their thoughts were running in the same groove. They paused for a moment, and turned with their faces from the wind, and their eyes met. The sympathy between them seemed expressed by her smile, which appeared to answer his inward reflection upon the rapid strides of their intimacy.

"I thought that you looked ill and worn at breakfast this morning," said she with her usual directness, "much more so than in the evening. Did you sleep well last night?"

"No," he said simply; "I was awake nearly the whole night."

"I can't bear to lie awake," she said, "I get so cold and so frightened—as though there were things round me. I want, then, to say my prayers; but I can't pray well, I have never been taught. My uncle, you know, is a disciple of Herbert Spencer. It is one of his favourite speeches that he will never do anything which might strengthen the hands of the clergy; and so none of us ever went to church. My father was the same, consequently I don't know much about the Christian religion in a practical way—so I have had to make out a religion for myself."

"How did you set about doing that?" asked Graysett, feeling a profound pity for this young creature, whose melancholy frankness touched him to the soul.

"Oh, I read all the books of philosophy I could get hold of. You would be amused if you could imagine the jumble in my mind at one time. I have never had much education, in a solid sense. I have always wished that I been taught science and Euclid, and that sort of thing. It would have given me something to fall back upon. I think my mind is logical to a certain extent. Why do you smile?"

"I should not have thought from my very slight knowledge of you that you are exactly logical. I should have fancied from what you have said, that you form your opinions rather by intuition than reasoning."

She seemed to reflect.

"At any rate," she said, after a pause, "I am

very fond of philosophy, and of things which most people consider dry and uninteresting. I remember when I was a quite a child poring over a book called " The Art of Reason," and trying to resolve life into Aristotle's categories. But I very soon left off the Aristotelian method, and took to the Platonic instead. I read all I could of the old Greek philosophers, and then I studied the German ones, and became transcendental for a time. After that there was a phase of Herbert Spencer, and Comte, and Protoplasm. But Protoplasm would not satisfy me, or prevent me from waking up cold and terrified, and longing to pray to something ; and I could not pray to Protoplasm. And then I read Swedenborg, and afterwards many other mystical books ; and then———" She stopped suddenly and walked on for a few paces silent.

"And then ?" he repeated.

"Oh, do you care to listen to my nonsense ? It is all nonsense, you know, and just my fancies, nothing else. It seems to me that the people who are searching for God look into a mirror, and see nothing but their own hearts and minds. The only truth in the world is in ourselves—a tiny flame which grows and grows, and penetrates all through us, and warms and fills us with a wonderful peace, the more we go on *feeling* prayer. That's my way of praying when I'm alone, cold and frightened, and when it's dark—I am never afraid in daylight. I can't *say* anything. I can only *feel*, and fancy a great glorious sea of light and truth and joy, upon which I'm rocked and warmed, and from which all bad, base things flee away, all evil thoughts and influences that are not pure.   I don't care whether Things "—she laid a peculiar emphasis upon the term, as though she meant more than an abstraction—"are what people call good or bad.   I only think whether they can live in that light.   It's softer than the sunlight and it's so gentle.   Oh, I like looking straight into the heart of electric lamps !   That is something like what I mean if you can imagine a universe of it."

"My poor child !" Graysett murmured almost below his breath.

"No, I know what you are going to say ; but don't.   I could never have any other religion than that one.   I like my own.   It is abstract, impersonal, just what I am myself.   Well, *I* slept very soundly and sweetly last night.   Tell me, what did you do while you lay awake ?"

"I thought a great deal about our conversation, and of the way in which you affected me."

"How do I affect you ?" she asked.

He laughed.   "I can't be analytical like you. I don't know.   There is something strange and not quite natural about my feelings towards you. The whole thing is strange.   There was my vision, and then our talk last night."

"I dare say that you have a very vivid imagination," said Judith.

"I never suspected it till I met you.   Since then, everything has become vivid, and a great deal seems to have happened.   I can hardly believe that we met for the first time yesterday."

" Perhaps it means that we are going to be friends."

" I don't fancy that friendship comes on in that way. It does not take possession of one all at once, nor is it ushered in by portents and visions. It is a much more commonplace and better behaved sort of sentiment."

Judith laughed. They had reached the end of the avenue, and were standing in the shelter of an old ivy-clad wall. There was a stone bench in the angle, well protected from the wind.

" Let us rest here for a minute or two," she said, "I am very tired. I get easily tired."

They sat down, Judith remaining for some moments perfectly still, her hands resting in her lap. These attitudes of complete repose were a peculiarity of hers. Presently one of the retrievers which had followed them from the keeper's cottage came close, fawning upon Graysett, who patted him carelessly. Judith made a gesture of disgust.

" Send the dog away," she said.

" Do you not like animals ? " asked Graysett in surprise.

" No," she replied. " They—I'm not human enough, I suppose," she added abruptly.

Graysett led the dog to a little distance, and gave him into the charge of one of the gardeners. When he returned, Judith had risen.

" I feel it damp," she said. " We will walk on

by the yew trees for a little way. It is dry and sheltered there."

They moved down a side path in the shrubbery, and presently emerged upon a sort of raised terrace leading towards the church. It was roughly paved and shadowed on one side by funereal yews, from which the moisture dripped to the ground beneath. Judith walked on for a few minutes silent and abstracted. Suddenly she said, but without turning towards him—

"I'll tell you, if you like, about the curious feeling I had the first time I saw Mr. Esmé Colquhoun."

Graysett felt almost shocked at his own eagerness. But he restrained it, and said quietly, "Please do. You interest me intensely."

CHAPTER VII.

JUDITH began——

"I was full of the mystical books I had been reading at that time. The American woman I told you of had roused my desire for occult knowledge, till it had become a craving. She told me, when I pressed her, that I was a sensitive, *a clairvoyante*, and that I had psychic force. I could not understand why she refused to help me in developing the power. I wanted to do so. I cultivated Lady Romer, who goes in for new sensations, and went constantly to Mrs. Borlase's Thursdays, where one meets people out of the common. It was there that Esmé Colquhoun was introduced to me, though of course I had heard of him and had seen him at parties."

"Is he inclined to mysticism?" asked Graysett.

"Oh, no. At least he was not then. He wrote very impassioned verses and raved about the worship of the beautiful——so they told me. He was a disciple of Théophile Gautier; and began talking to me then about the French school of literature, as though he were giving a lecture. It struck me that he was talking very well, and

intended to make an effect. I think he fancied
at first that I was worth impressing, and was
disgusted with me because I seemed to listen so
apathetically. But in reality I was keenly alive.
He had produced such an extraordinary effect
upon my nerves that to recall it sets them
quivering. I can't describe it in words—a kind
of eerie, excited sensation, like being galvanized,
or as if electricity instead of blood were running
through one's veins. I seemed to be out of my
body, and yet perfectly aware of everything that
was going on in the studio. It was being awake
and dreaming at the same time. I had an overpowering presentiment that he was destined to
influence me. It was as though unknown forces
in me were being put in motion. I felt as if his
double and mine were acting together in some
thrilling scene which involved my very existence ;
but what it was, or what it meant, I could not
tell. I could see nothing. I felt only the vivid
consciousness and thrilling excitement. It was
very weird and terrible ; but it only lasted a
minute, like one of those flashes of previous
existence which one has sometimes—lengthened
and infinitely more intense. Then, though I felt
dazed, I was myself again, listening to him,
criticizing him, and certainly far more repelled
than attracted by him. That is all. Tell me,
what do you think of it ? "

" I believe," said Graysett solemnly, " that this
strange feeling of yours and my vision are
warnings from some higher intelligence. I be-

lieve that your destiny and that of this man are mingled for evil ; and that it is in my power to save you."

Judith's eyes, in their clearness, and with no trouble or passion in their depths, met his full.

"I knew you would say that; I can read your thoughts—at moments quite distinctly. I can see how interested you are in me. You are good and loyal. I am sure that you would be a faithful friend, but I am sure also that it would be much better for you not to care what happened to me."

"That is quite impossible," he replied. "I will guard you from injury, as far as lies in my power. It is a charge which has been committed to me. This is how I interpret my vision."

"But you cannot yet know whether it is of Esmé Colquhoun that I must beware. Certainly my acquaintanceship with him so far does not warrant your belief."

"I shall know to-morrow evening," he answered.

She turned, shivering slightly. "Let us go in ; I am cold."

"Have you ever had any return of the feeling? " he asked, as they strolled round by the little lake into the carriage drive.

"No. What I said to you last night is perfectly true, I am outside Esmé Colquhoun's circle. I don't cause him an emotion—nor has he caused me one, since that night," she added, laughing softly. "I have only a sort of curiosity about him. It is mixed with contempt, I think, although I admire him, and can realize the fact of his influence. I fancy that, if he were in earnest about his life, he might seriously impress me. As it is, I seem to see through his artificiality, without in the least getting at his real nature. I have tried by way of experiment to read his thoughts, as I can often read those of other people, but have always failed. His mind is a blank to me. I think that he has a strong magnetic power, and feel almost sure that it would operate upon me under certain conditions, but I don't know what they are."

They had reached the house, and Judith left him.

Coming out of her room half an hour later, she saw Mrs. Borlase in a recess of the gallery which overlooked the hall. Judith's soft white draperies made no noise upon the carpet.

Mrs. Borlase was rapidly dashing in an harmonious bit of background. She was very intent upon her work, and looked singularly handsome as she bent over it, her thick curly hair falling upon her forehead, and her long lashes contrasting with her creamy cheek. She was dressed in a brocade tea-gown of some rich nondescript colour, which might have been taken from a wardrobe of centuries back. Her capacity for combining earnestness with the picturesque was marvellous. There was about her an extraordinary mental strength and vitality. She reminded one irresistibly, though why it would be difficult to say, of

George Sand.   She put out her hand and detained Judith.

"I've just finished.   You see I don't neglect business even when I am out on a holiday.   This is exactly what I want for a little picture I am interested in."

"You are interested in everything," said Judith.

"Yes, even with the bores.   Work, act, feel, but never allow yourself time to think—that is my philosophy, and it ought to be the philosophy of every woman who has made an irretrievable mistake in marriage, and who loves the world and the things of the world too well to give them up."

"Is that necessary—to be happy?"

"Yes, and there is a more difficult necessity still—that of inducing the person you want to be happy with, to give them up also—if there be such a person."   Mrs. Borlase drew back to look at her work, pushed her easel further in the recess, and laid down her brushes.   "Life defrauds you," she went on ; "but it is its own compensation. Keep a strong hold on life, and you'll force something pleasant out of it.   I have contrived to get a good deal, though I made a bad commencement.   Why do you look at me so curiously, child, with your great dreamy eyes?"

"I don't think that you like me, Mrs. Borlase, and I am wondering what makes you speak so openly to me."

"Oh ! frankness is a principle of my philosophy," said the artist with a backward toss of her short hair. "I am a latitudinarian, and I don't profess to go in for nice moral distinctions, though I have my own code of right and wrong which I'll be true to at all costs. I keep the broad rules, or appear to do so, and that is enough for the world. I don't pretend to be prudish, or lay claim to the domestic virtues, womanly reticence, and so forth. I don't pretend that I care about my husband, or that I am indifferent to the admiration of other men. I don't tell pretty fibs about the sad necessity for our living apart. I stand fearlessly before the world as I am, and the world believes in me, and allows Christine Borlase, the Bohemian, a longer tether than it gives most unprotected women. I know my world too well and I love my world too dearly to go beyond my tether. That's understood ; and for the rest I 'pay my shot.' I sing and act and make my studio pleasant, and I am a good comrade to women as well as to men. I'll be a good comrade to you if you choose. You are a strange girl. What has put the notion into your head that I dislike you ? "

"Something in your eyes, Christine ; and in your tone when you talk recklessly as you do now. It has only come there since I was left a fortune."

"Jealousy, my dear, jealousy!" Christine patted the girl's hand, and laughed a little discordantly. "You are wrong. I am so fond of you that I am ready to share my popularity, which is *my* fortune, with you. I want *you* to take hold of life, and to be less self-absorbed and indifferent. I want to interest you in my friends, and to interest my friends in you. Your wealth has just so much to do with my estimation of you that it sets off your intrinsic value, and gives me an excuse for calling attention to a very charming and original person. Wasn't I always nice to you and anxious to lighten your bondage? But you are improving without my assistance. I observe that you have taken a new departure. If Major Graysett develops in you a taste for flirtation I shall feel grateful to him, but I don't want him to develop anything more serious."

"Why not?" said Judith calmly. "Am I the prize in a lottery, for which you have all taken tickets? I feel as though I were being exhibited before the drawing takes place. I should like to show that I have a will of my own, though I don't quite know how to do that. Why should you object to Major Graysett? He looks disinterested. He does not jar upon me. I like him—and I think he has an affinity with me."

"Truly you have made great discoveries in a short time," said Mrs. Borlase. "Have you an affinity with Major Graysett?"

"That is quite another matter," answered Judith. "I am an insoluble substance. People don't affect me seriously."

"I think that Major Graysett has affected you; and I give him credit for great cleverness. But don't be too hasty in deciding. What would happen if after marriage you discovered yourself capable of an affinity—with some one else ? "

" I should feel that it was a law of my being, which must be obeyed."

" A dangerous creed, dear, if it were sanctioned. My philosophy would be necessary as a corrective. But I quite believe you. You are capable of anything morbid and dramatic. That man, however, is neither morbid nor dramatic. You had better wait for your affinity. Depend upon it he is not far off. Giants cast long shadows."

She ran lightly down the stairs. Judith followed a little more sedately. The hall, illuminated with rose-shaded lamps and leaping fire gleams, presented an attractive picture. It was alive with the rustle of draperies, the soft laughter of women, and the gruffer tones of a large party of gentlemen. A dash of pink contrasted agreeably with the deep-hued hangings and dark oak panelling. The Master of the Fox Hounds and one or two other hunting men had dropped in on their way homeward, to hear what had been the day's bag and to relate their own experiences.

The muffins were steaming on their brass tripod ; the dachshunds were alert ; servants passed to and fro, bringing in relays of hot coffee and buttered cakes ; while Mrs. Rainshaw, presiding at the tea-table, chattered in her frank, inconsequent manner.

" We are all coming to the Holmborough ball, and to the meet the next day, Sir Roland," said she addressing the Master ; " and I hope you'll find a fox quickly, and not keep us too long waiting by

the side of Dunkley Gorse, for my cobs don't like
standing. If Tom would let me hunt I should
not mind waiting, but he has ideas which I wish
you would try and argue him out of. Don't you
think now, Sir Roland, that marrying is like sign-
ing one's name to a blank schedule, and that the
conditions ought to be specified, especially if you
are going to live in a hunting county ? Won't
you have some nice hot coffee ? Mr. Margrave,
what are you doing over there ? The London post
doesn't go out till eight o'clock."

"I'm earning my living, Mrs. Rainshaw,"
promptly responded Mr. Margrave from a distant
writing-table. "Social articles—smart, caustic,
and inclining to pessimism in the season ; genial,
sporting, and generally muscular in the autumn ;
luxurious in tone, cheerfully philosophic, and
tempered by climatic influences in the late winter.
That is the sort of thing. I don't know that it's
a worse way of getting one's living than any other.
To be sure, one has always the alternative of
giving up living altogether."

"Well, keep your article till after you have
been out with Sir Rowland's pack, or you certainly
won't hit off the tone of this part of the world ;
and in the meantime come and look after Mrs.
Borlase. Since Tom won't let me hunt, Sir
Roland, I am going to revenge myself by dragging
him off to Egypt next month. But travelling is
so cockneyfied now, that you might as well
be in London as at Cairo—at least so they tell
me—I never got beyond Nice. And they say

the management of Eastern hotels is atrocious. Is that so, Major Graysett? You ought to know all about everything thereabouts."

Major Graysett, looking very thoughtful and direct, seemed prepared to enter seriously into the question which Mrs. Rainshaw had not intended to ventilate so thoroughly. But in the midst of his explanation he caught sight of Judith Fountain, and, bringing it to a close, came forward to hand her a chair and otherwise minister to her wants.

Presently the party broke up a little, some betaking themselves to the billiard-room, which opened out of the hall; others lounging in the deep window recesses, and choruses subsiding into duets as people divided into twos. There was a pretty group on the white mat before the fire, where the young hostess and Miss Geneste built toy castles for a golden-haired baby of two, who had been brought down from the nursery. Christine Borlase joined it for a minute. Never had she looked more womanly or more charming than when she caught up the little creature and pressed her lips to its dimpled neck. Her own short hair mingled with the child's yellow curls, and her handsome face, with its finely chiselled mouth, its perfect brows, and clear, frank eyes, which had in their depths an underlying sadness, did not, as she raised it, contrast inharmoniously with the little cherubic countenance that touched her cheek. Christine sighed as she placed the baby again in its mother's arms.

She rose. As she passed Judith's chair she

halted for an instant, and said in her impulsive manner, which imparted to such speeches a naturalness that seemed the outcome of an unsophisticated heart—

" You were talking of affinities. There's none so holy as that between a mother and a child. A woman loses a great deal when she has no children."

She moved on, and seating herself at an old spinet, which was one of Mrs. Rainshaw's triumphs, extracted from it some quavering melodies, abruptly bursting into a child's song about a Tomcat, which was full of quaint humour and spirit.

Judith sat motionless in a high-backed chair, her face turned so that her profile was outlined against the crimson cushion. She was listening to the music and intently watching Mrs. Borlase. She hardly spoke. Once when suddenly addressed she started violently, and replied in so absent a manner that her remark sounded almost silly.

Graysett wondered of what she was thinking. He felt profoundly moved, while recalling her chance revelations of her inner life. He drew a pathetic mental picture of this solitary, neglected girl puzzling over the deepest mysteries of existence with no light but that of her imagination. All sorts of romantic speculations concerning her entered his mind. He wondered whether she had ever loved. Did she possess the capacity for love ? How had she learned the cynical worldly wisdom which her speech sometimes betrayed, and which seemed so out of harmony with the spirituality of her appearance? . . .

He took Mrs. Borlase in to dinner, and found his former impression of that lady confirmed by her conversation, which was very frank, very agreeable, but which undoubtedly suggested an under-current of strong feeling. She questioned him as to his opinion of Judith Fountain, and gave him further particulars of the girl's strange bringing up, and of her female relatives, whom she denounced unreservedly. He was wary in his replies; indeed, it would have been difficult for him to be candid. The artist's candour was, however, almost oppressive.

"I want you to like me," she said, "and to like my studio. You will come and see me in London, will you not? I am painting Miss Fountain's portrait, and you shall tell me what you think of it."

She was very sympathetic; it was impossible not to be charmed by her manner, which was at once brilliant and feminine. He saw that she had exquisite tact, and could imagine that she would be what she had described herself—a good comrade, and also what few women of genius are, able so to adapt herself to the strength and weakness of a man of genius as to become indispensable to him both as a prop and a stimulant. She interested him, though in a very different fashion from her friend; and he could not divest himself of a vague notion that she was destined for a more important part in the drama, the reality of which he now thoroughly believed in, than he might at first have been inclined to assign her.

The party that evening was a small one, and depended for amusement upon poker and a little desultory music. Judith declined to sing, upon the plea of fatigue, and retired to the alcove, where she invited Graysett by a look to join her. It had now become evident to him that each guest at Leesholm was supposed to do as he or she pleased; and that very little notice was taken of flirtations, serious and otherwise, which might have provoked comment in a more starched circle. Not that in Judith's manner there was the least semblance of flirtation; it had lost its little strain of flippancy, and was grave, often childlike in its simplicity. Their talk was less transcendental than it had hitherto been. They talked of books, music, every-day topics, none of which can, however, seem commonplace when touched by the glamour of dawning love. Her remarks showed feeling and taste, a certain amount of cultivation also; but it was apparent that she had only a superficial knowledge of general literature. He asked her if she were fond of reading.

"Some books absorb me," she said; "but very few. I don't care about subjects, or facts."

"Ideas are better than facts," said Graysett, "and it is quite true that the greatest readers are very often the least original thinkers."

"I am not original," said Judith: "I suppose that I am receptive. I take in things without knowing it. I listen unconsciously, and afterwards reproduce some one else's thoughts. I am a sponge." Then she added : "Did Colonel Rainshaw tell you all about me?"

"He told me a great deal," said Graysett, with a sudden pang.

"You see I am to be pitied."

"Indeed," he said, "I think that you are greatly to be pitied."

"I was a very poor girl six months ago. My aunt and cousins barely tolerated me. People were kind to me in a condescending fashion, but no one thought me worth much notice. No one troubled themselves about what I felt or thought. Now I am a very rich girl, and the world has wakened up and troubles itself deeply on my account. I am like the princess whom no one believed to be a princess till they saw her in her royal robes. I wonder if she ever felt as humiliated as I sometimes feel. But at least she was able to test the sincerity of her friends."

"I wish," he exclaimed, "that I had known you before you became a princess."

"Would that have made any difference?" she asked softly. "Don't say it would. I think that I believe in you. You would have been my friend just the same. Perhaps I should not have needed one so much." She rose as she spoke and moved away ; and a little while afterwards when he looked for her she had gone.

Colonel Rainshaw shrugged his shoulders significantly when he bade his friend good-night.

"I see that you must 'dree your own weird,' I

shall say nothing. Most people would think you were a very lucky fellow."

Whatever misgivings Colonel Rainshaw might feel, he was discreet enough to keep them to himself; while his wife, on the other hand, beamed approval and gave Major Graysett every opportunity for enjoying Miss Fountain's society. Under such favourable conditions, to say nothing of the pre-indications of destiny, intimacy naturally ripened rapidly. The following day was spent in much the same manner as this one, and on the return of the sportsmen in the afternoon, a telegram was found from Mr. Colquhoun, accepting the invitation to Leesholm.

CHAPTER VIII.

THE Holmborough ball was always well attended, and was said to be the best hunt ball which took place in the Midlands. When the Leesholm party arrived, the Town Hall was filling fast. It was in an old-fashioned building, and there were curious little recesses, and heavy pillars supporting a gallery which ran along one end. Brilliantly illuminated, draped with bright hangings, and festooned with wreaths of evergreens and flowers, it made a pretty ball-room. Here and there were banks of exotics, and tall palms and feathery ferns filled up the corners. An immense mirror reflected the glassy floor, the airy figures in tulle and lace, the sparkle of jewels, the lustre of satin, and the scarlet coats and various uniforms of the hunting men which gave character to the scene.

A country ball contrasts markedly with one in London. Here were no languid forms blocking up doorways, no bored faces of *blasé* men, no weary, listless girls, no perfunctory performance of duty dances. People came to enjoy themselves, and none did so by sitting still, except perhaps the be-diamonded dowagers ranged on the crimson settees. Sir Roland was there with several brother M. F. H.'s, and many a cheery squire who made a merit of avoiding balls, but always came to this one ; while a good deal of hunting talk went on, and much county business was transacted to the inspiring strains of the " Fox Hunt " galop or the dreamy music of a German waltz.

Every now and then, a well-dressed party from some great house in the neighbourhood would enter, and stand conspicuously by the doorway for a moment before joining the throng. Now an undertoned murmur would announce the presence of a celebrity, or a faint buzz of comment would follow the passing of some country belle unknown to fame. There were the two or three "beauties" about whom every one talked, and the fashionable contingent from the great world, with charms artistically heightened, in perfectly moulded satin bodices and floating cascades of tulle, and a string or two of pearls doing duty for sleeves. Then there were the hunting ladies, the recognized Holmborough set, and there were the ladies on the borderland of county society, and those who, not so clever as Mrs. Borlase, went ever so little beyond their length of tether ; but, as a rule, the Holmborough Town Hall was upon these occasions a very friendly meeting ground, into which ostracized persons did not venture.

There were no dowagers or non-dancing men in the Leesholm party; and before they had been many minutes in the room, all were revolving smoothly to the fantastic air of a Hungarian waltz: Lady Romer and Colonel Rainshaw, Mrs. Borlase in the arms of a striking-looking stranger,

Miss Geneste and Mr. Margrave, and, lastly, Judith Fountain and Major Graysett.

Graysett waltzed well. Judith's reed-like form yielded softly to his embrace, and seemed to sway in harmony with every beat of the melody. It was like floating through space with a spirit of air. The gentle excitement and dreamy delight which he felt resembled the sensations produced by opium. He would willingly have prolonged the minutes for ever.

They paused at last, beneath a projecting portion of the gallery, where two great stone pillars formed a pleasing background to delicate foliage ; and some rich hangings, looped back, disclosed a dimly lighted and fantastically arranged recess. Judith leaned against the pillar, her chest heaving slightly, a faint flush upon her usually pale cheek. At this moment her beauty was undeniable. Her gaze was vaguely fixed upon the moving crowd.

"I like waltz music," she said softly. "It affects me even more than funeral marches, which I love also. If I were dying I should——" she stopped abruptly ; and he felt her hand upon his arm tremble. A man addressed her in a rolling, flexible voice which he had heard before.

"Miss Fountain, you are dancing to-night. May I have the next waltz, if you are free ?"

Judith turned towards the speaker, upon whose arm Mrs. Borlase was leaning. A thrill passed through Graysett's frame. He beheld the man whom he had seen in his vision.

A man considerably above the average height of men, with broad, square shoulders, an expansive chest, a statuesque head, and a throat like a column, its outlines clearly displayed by the somewhat Byronic fashion of his loose collar. The face was clean shaven, oval in contour, and clear skinned ; but there was in it no trace of effeminacy. The lips were of the Greek type, cut in firm, sensuous lines, the eyes prominent and heavy lidded, looking half closed, till suddenly the lids contracted, the pupils dilated, gleaming with extraordinary brilliancy, and a light like that of the sun upon the sea illuminated the whole countenance. A mass of red gold hair was brushed back from the forehead, and fell in thick waves to the coat behind. He had a habit of elevating his chin and throwing back his head when he spoke; then the hairs would separate, quivering, and would stand out like an aureola framing the face. One saw that this mane was curiously crisp, and might fancy that it possessed the magnetic quality attributed to a cat's fur.

A most noticeable person, who, notwithstanding his long hair, his smooth cheeks, and Grecian profile, was a very Samson in physique, and had also the power of combined intellect and will, a man of exuberant vitality, and who only lacked a certain coolness and subtlety to render him absolutely formidable.

Before replying to his request, Judith glanced at Graysett. Her eyes put a question to him, which was answered in the affirmative. Then she said—

"I must congratulate you upon your return to England, Mr. Colquhoun; I hope that you enjoyed America. At all events, the Americans enjoyed you, to judge from the newspaper reports."

"Why did you not tell us that you were going to lecture in London?" exclaimed Mrs. Borlase. "You know that I never read the papers. We should have gathered *en masse.* We would have taken laurel crowns and would have thrown them at your feet."

Again there was the suspicious tremble under her light raillery. Colquhoun's eyes rested upon her steadily as he replied—

"Because, Mrs. Borlase, I was going to address a company of experts. I could deal with them. I knew what to say. Had you been there I should have thought only of how I could make my subject interesting to you. Where the carcase is, there the eagles gather together; and the vultures swooped down upon me and overpowered the doves who had come to hear. Miss Fountain, I may hope for the next waltz?"

Judith bowed her consent.

"You will take one more turn, Miss Fountain?" said Graysett.

He placed his arm around her, and bore her into the moving circle. Lights, music, fragrance of flowers, whirling forms, combined in a sort of phantasmagoria; and he was once more in that world of vague fancies and mysterious possibilities which surely exists not far from the actual life, if —and happily this is not so—the spell which gives

entrance to it were known to all. They glided on,
a fiery hand as it were gripping him, and impelling
him to rapid movement. He could not stop.
He felt as though he were bearing her away from
that weird influence which at this moment he also
realized. Colquhoun had strange eyes. They
were clear like those of Judith, but they were
deeper and brighter. In them was a gleam which ·
hers had not. There was a devil in their depths
which had never lurked in hers. A wild thought
flashed into Graysett's mind. Memory, working
in her fantastic fashion, recalled a chance conversation which years ago he had held with an Indian
mystic. Suggestions contemptuously dismissed
then, unheeded since, returned in this dream-like
whirl, seizing with startling force upon his imagination. Could it be that there were human beings
so constituted that their bodies might become the
tenements of certain elemental forces, which by
magnetic attraction might again act upon other
persons of exceptional organization? Was it
possible that there existed a subtle and unknown
current of communication between minds, dependent for its operation upon exact laws? Was
all life, all human action, merely a question of soul
affinity? . . . And then it seemed to him that he
held the links between the seen and the unseen,
and that he was struggling for them with powers
invisible. He was contending for Judith's safety
—for more than her life, for more than her love.
He pressed her fiercely to him, he uttered wild
passionate words, which in any saner moment

would not have passed his lips—while still they
flew on.

"Stop!" she cried faintly ; "it is over."

They paused, giddy and breathless. To him,
all seemed moving yet—lights, figures, flowers—
and the music was sounding. But presently there
came over him a dazed consciousness that the
band had ceased, and that the dance was done.

They had halted opposite Esmé Colquhoun and
his partner. The man's eyes were fixed upon
Graysett with a curious interest, and then they
turned towards Christine Borlase, who was watching
Judith with an inscrutable look upon her mobile
face. Her look was haunting. Could the artist
have painted herself as she then appeared, her
fortune would have been assured, and no critic
would have dared dispute her genius. Jealousy,
distrust, womanly pity, passionate love, and sublime
renunciation might all have been depicted in the
portrait, and yet have failed to express the emotions struggling in her countenance. Graysett
moved abruptly away, leading Judith to the tent
where they had before stood. She was reflected
in a mirror at the back. Her hands clasped her
bouquet tightly. She was trembling. In her eyes
vague terror mingled with excitement. She interrupted him as he began to speak—

"I know," she said. "You have recognized
him. I knew when you told me your dream the
other night that it was he."

"Yes," replied Graysett, "it is he." Then he
went on in low eager accents, the sentences

bursting from him, and giving him no time to shape them.

"That man will make you love him. He will try to marry you. Will you not be warned? It is I who must warn you—there is no one else—I who must protect you—from myself, perhaps," and Graysett laughed discordantly, "for *I* too love you. But my love is true. There's no self-seeking in it, no motive which will not bear the light of clear eyes. Don't you believe me? It is *you* I love, not your wealth—your happiness is more precious to me than my own. Why? I don't know. Instinct—affinity perhaps. You are right. We are encompassed by mystery. There are unknown spheres above and below us. It is when we touch them that we are called mad. I think that you have turned me mad. Yes, I love you; but it's like nothing I've ever known of or dreamed of. It's not your face or your smile, or your strange talk, which attracts me, or your loneliness, though there's something in that; for I declare to you that you often seem to me like a child set in the midst of dangers which you only dimly suspect; and I want to take you in my arms and bear you away into safety. It's something much more strange and subtle . . . . See! I have known you for less than three days, and I am talking to you in this wild way, and from my very soul. This is how I feel about you. It's fatality. Before I had seen your face you had touched the very springs of my being. I had only to come within the circle of your presence and you developed in me a new sense. It's with this sense I love you—and that's no bodily one. To-night there are only three people in the universe for me—you, him, and myself. A week ago our destinies were absolutely apart. To-night they are mingled by an influence I can't profess to understand. I am between you and him. His power over you is baleful to you. I *know* this. I don't reason about it. There are laws about which we can't reason. We can only obey them. You will obey? You will be warned?"

Judith met his feverish gaze with a calm, rapt look in which there seemed a sort of far-awayness, as though she had not fully realized the import of his appeal; or rather, as if the torrent of his passion had swept by without causing a shock to her sensibilities, and she had seized only upon the abstract idea which underlay his wild declaration.

"Ah!" said she with her peculiar smile, "Birth is a law; Death is a law; and Affinity and Antipathy are laws; but we don't decide when they are to be put into operation. I want to be governed by the strongest force that is in me. I'll not rebel against that. I have never had an impulse which seemed irresistible. When it seizes me I shall obey it. Why do you warn me? Against what? You are stretching out a hand into the darkness. That is all."

"You believe in spiritual potencies," he began.

She shook her head. "I want it explained; I don't know."

"You believe in a sixth sense which brings us

into connection with the occult world. Put it in that way. How do you account for my vision? Does not that give me the right to warn you? I had not seen either you or Esmé Colquhoun. What cause had I for supposing that danger threatened you through him? Yet no reasoning would ever shake my conviction that he will be fatal to you unless I can succeed in counteracting his influence. I have told you that I love you. You may scoff at a feeling which has grown so rapidly. That does not matter. The feeling is there. I can't ignore it. It is myself."

"I could not scoff at you," said Judith gravely. "You interest me too deeply. I cannot help thinking of you, and wondering if indeed you are destined to play an important part in some crisis which is impending. You know that I also have had a presentiment. I had never talked about it till you questioned me. I was sorry afterwards that I spoke so frankly. I used to fancy that I was not impulsive. I see now that I am very impulsive—in little things; I have fallen in with your mood quite naturally from the beginning; and the position, which is very unnatural I suppose, does not seem so to me. It would be an impossible one if you were not true. You may try any experiment you like upon me. I want to feel; and if you become false, I shall be able to tell that you are so."

"You consent to try and love me."

She laughed in her strange way. "How can I consent to that of which I have no knowledge?

I am cold. There is no flame here;" she laid her hand upon her breast as she spoke. "See me," she added, standing erect before him, like a spirit in her white dress, and gazing at him with great eyes as clear and cold as the diamonds on her neck and in her hair, "I am colourless. I am hard. I am like Galatea before she became human. I have never loved. I have never felt. I have never lived. Make me feel. Warm me. Put fire into me. I am willing that it should be so." The musical voice deepened and intensified. "I think that some one with a will strong enough might give me life—that life. But no will has yet been strong enough. No one has come to me with the power. When he comes, I will obey him."

"I have come, Judith," cried Graysett. "And the flame in my heart burns fiercely enough to warm even yours into life."

"I am afraid," she said slowly, almost regretfully, "that you have not the power. It would need great force. Listen. All my life it has been the same. Nothing—no one—has been quite great enough. People were not strong enough—or not quite true. Music might always have been more glorious, poetry might have been more divine, mountains higher, and the sea more vast. There was never enough. Nothing filled me quite. But I always felt that there would come something some day which should drag me imperiously from everything that had gone before, and be a will in me and fill me so that I should be satisfied."

They stood silent for a few moments. Her head was bent over her bouquet. She sighed gently. She looked so plastic, and yet he knew that her words were true, and that marble was not colder. A feeling of helplessness and despair came over him and calmed his excitement. He knew intuitively that her estimate of him was a just one, and that he was not strong enough. He had never willed for more than the desire of the hour. He had never cultivated intensity of purpose. He had drifted through life; and, now that the need for strain had come, there was not the power to sustain it.

They had drawn more into the shadow of the tent. At that moment the curtain between the pillars swayed slightly, but neither of them noticed the movement.

"You may be right," said Graysett, "or you may be wrong. It is too soon yet to be proved. We shall see shortly."

"I have a warning to give you," she said abruptly; then added in a lighter tone, "Let us talk a little less tragically. You show a great deal of skill in making yourself appear dramatic; and," she smiled as if to herself, "you contradict all Mrs. Borlase's theories."

She waited as if expecting him to ask what these were; but he did not do so, and she went on: "You affect my moods. You make me talk in a way that is certainly unusual. I hope you are aware that I can be beautifully conventional upon occasions. I am always so to Colonel

Rainshaw, and to some other people. That is
why I am called stupid."

"What makes you harp upon that fancy? It
seems to me that you are a source of deep interest
to every one."

"That," she answered, with her cynical air, "is
since I have come into my kingdom. For example,
I always used to go to Mrs. Borlase's parties. I
enjoyed them. I liked watching her. But she
never really thought about me till I became worth
studying; and now I puzzle her."

"As a study you are absorbing. I am surprised
that Mrs. Borlase, with her keen insight, did not
find this out sooner."

"She is a very clever woman," said Judith,
thoughtfully, "and a very unhappy one. I am
sorry for her."

"But your warning?" said Graysett. "That
is of importance to me."

"My warning!" she repeated, as though she
had forgotten to what he referred. "Ah! you
might interpret your vision as a portent of danger
to yourself, and a warning to avoid me."

"I have thought of that," he answered, gravely.

"Have you considered that you too are venturing
into the undiscovered country, and that there may
be peril for you as well as for me?"

"No matter. I go hand in hand with you to
explore."

"I wonder," she began thoughtfully, and paused.
"I know that I have a gift; but I know that I
cannot develop it alone. Perhaps, as you say, we

may explore hand in hand—and . . . . But I will be frank with you. I am certain that Esmé Colquhoun has the power, if he choose to exert it, of influencing me in an extraordinary degree. It may not be for my good. I don't know. I only feel that there is the power; and—I'm like a moth, you will say, eager to rush into the flame —I have a curiosity to test it. Our minds have never been brought into direct contact. Perhaps they never may be. Sometimes I think—the thought has several times flashed through me— that *you* may be the link between us."

"*I?*" cried Graysett, excitedly. "Heaven forbid."

"Why not? I had not met Mr. Colquhoun for months. Our grooves lay quite apart. You appear—you have a strange vision in which we are closely connected. Immediately afterwards he is invited to stay in the same house with me. It's all strange, uncanny. Consider whether you had not better leave me alone, and escape from the atmosphere into which I have drawn you."

Graysett laughed bitterly. "Too late. The spell has worked quickly. I am not my own master."

The fiddles began to wail in a sort of sobbing prelude, which was indeed the introduction to Judith's own waltz. To Graysett the sad little air had now a weird significance. Judith listened with head bent as though she also were affected by the music.

"This is Mr. Esmé Colquhoun's waltz," she

said; "the first time he has ever asked me to dance."

"He will hold you in his arms, he will magnetize you with his touch."

"Not at all. He will take me to a seat near Mrs. Borlase; and he will talk to me about the American conception of the beautiful. It is a recognized thing that Esmé Colquhoun never dances."

She glanced at the mirror and started. Graysett followed her eyes. Esmé Colquhoun, leaning in a picturesque attitude against the pillar at the entrance of the tent, was reflected in the glass.

It was impossible to tell from his expression how much he had heard of the conversation. He advanced to Judith.

"There is magic in your music, Miss Fountain. We have never waltzed together. Will you try me now?"

The *tableau* was a curious one. Like a statue with living eyes, Judith stood between the two men. These confronted each other. Colquhoun, massive, erect, commanding, with his aureola of red-gold hair, his fiery glance, his noble, almost inspired face, in which there was, notwithstanding its beauty something sinister and suggestive rather of fallen Lucifer than of an archangel. Graysett, dark, refined, every nerve on the alert, steadily watching his foe. No word had been spoken, but the eyes of the two men had met. They understood each other, and a challenge was mutely given.

The notes of the waltz swelled in mournful crescendo. Colquhoun offered Judith his arm. She looked up at him as though he had awakened her from a dream, and accepted it. As they passed on, she cast a backward, enigmatic glance at Graysett. He watched them glide into the centre of the hall and mingle with the dancers, Colquhoun threading the maze with extreme grace, his fine head towering above all others like that of a young Hercules; while Judith, held in his embrace, seemed to yield herself with languorous delight to his guidance, the two forms floating rhythmically to the passionate harmonies of the violins, the two hearts, as it seemed, pulsing in perfect accord. It was the poetry of movement.

A sound in the tent behind him, resembling that of a suppressed sob, broke upon Graysett's agitated reverie. Looking round, he perceived Christine Borlase, who had entered noiselessly from behind the curtains. A strange fancy struck him, that, like a stricken doe wounded to the heart, she had crept hither from the gaze of hard eyes. She was very pale, and her hand pressed her side as though she were in physical pain. But the collected manner in which she spoke, though it did not remove his suspicion, filled him with admiration of her courage.

"They manage these little retreats very nicely here, don't they, Major Graysett? Do you like that waltz of Miss Fountain's? It makes me melancholy. It's an invocation to ghosts one had hoped were laid long ago. Ghosts have an unpleasant knack of springing up at times—I suppose one never really gets over one's illusions; and we artists are impressionable, you know, we should not be artists if it were otherwise. There's no music so sad as waltz music, none that describes life so well. It always gives me a weird feeling, that the spectres of my dead hopes, dead affections, dead aspirations, are keeping time to my steps— each note a tender thought, a bright fancy, a pure ambition—everything that the heart has given to the being it loved best—and all gone—all gone. . . ." Christine paused. There were tears in her voice. She laughed in a jarring uncertain manner, which betrayed rather than hid how deeply she was moved. "I am the sport of my dreams, Major Graysett. That again comes of being an artist. When I am at work I put all my 'phases' on to canvas. At idle times they are apt to transfer themselves to real life, and one weaves morbid poetry round two such perfect dancers as Esmé Colquhoun and Judith Fountain."

There were faint streaks of light in the east, lying level with the horizon. Out of doors, a milky white vapour was crawling slowly upon the skirts of night. Even within doors, in the long corridor at Leesholm, the grey deathly dawn seemed to creep through closed shutters and heavy curtains.

The silence was profound. The servants were in their deepest sleep, and most of the guests, tired after the ball, were also slumbering. The rooms leading into the corridor were closed and dark—all except one, from which, through the chink of a door ajar, a pale glimmer of light issued.

This was a small sitting-room, adjoining a bed-room, which had been allotted to Christine Borlase for a studio. It looked warm and cheerful. A fire of mingled wood and coal burned on the old-fashioned dogs; and a shaded lamp stood upon the table, shedding light upon the many feminine knick-knacks which lay scattered about. These seemed each to bear some mark of Christine's individuality, and contrasted curiously with indications of more serious employment. Some dainty crewel work, a gold and turquoise thimble, roses in a Venetian bowl, Parma violets half dead and filling the room with perfume, drawing-boards, tubes of colour, an unfinished sketch, a mahl-stick, several photographs of a well-known actress, a Claude glass and books and papers, lying side by side with her fan, her tablets and the ornaments she had just taken off.

She was standing by the table in her ball dress. The feathery cloak had fallen from her shoulders, and her beautiful bare throat and statuesque arms were left exposed.

She was gazing vacantly into a mirror opposite, her eyes full of misery, though her features were not set and hard, but gentle and tremulous. She was thinking, not of herself, nor even of Esmé; but of that poetic love, which seemed to have a being apart from material life, and which she knew neither suffering nor starvation could kill. It is a grand power, that of endowing with a sort of objective existence an ideal love which holds its own against disillusionments. A nature noble enough to love the love for love's sake can never be disillusioned.

This thought passed through Christine's mind, and it excited her to enthusiasm. She threw her arms up suddenly, and tossed back her head against her joined hands. The gesture awoke her to consciousness of her own image, and she beheld herself in a picture which appealed to her artistic sensibilities. The pose, so graceful and unrestrained; the glowing eyes, the half-parted lips, all were admirable, as the embodiment of a phase of passion.

"Dear eyes!" she murmured in a kind of impersonal fervour. "Dear lips! Dear soul of a woman! There's something left to be true to. I'll be true to you."

She moved away from the mirror, and seated herself in a deep arm-chair beside the fire, her elbows upon its arms, and her face bent forward, the forehead resting upon her clasped hands. Thus she remained for a long time. The lamp flickered and expired, and she was alone with the ghostly shadows which dawn had brought. At last she rose slowly, and went towards the inner room. She paused at the door into the corridor, and ere she pushed it close sighed forth a message into the greyness—

"Good-night, my Esmé. Good-morning. Good-bye."

CHAPTER IX.

A HUNTING morning, neither clear nor crisp, but such an one as makes glad the heart of sporting man, just windy enough for the scent to carry, with faint gleams of sunshine striking out from between grey clouds, and playing coldly upon the pools of standing water ; the rime upon the bare trees turned to dew ; the air damp and yet exhilarating ; the ground moist, and the landscape showing that haziness of outline which is often more poetic and suggestive than the hard distinctness of a frosty scene.

A long brown road crossing a stone bridge vandyked, as old bridges hereabouts are.   Beyond, a straggling picturesque village, and entering it, a lengthy string of riders trotting cheerfully to the meet.

Ladies in beautifully fitting habits, with breast-knots of violets accentuating the contours of their perfect figures, and with faces as fresh as though they had not been dancing till three o'clock that very morning ; old stagers got up for convenience; novices in blue habits and much jewellery ; City men with questionable seats and nervous hands ; the regular *habitués* on their splendid mounts, looking thoroughly at home, and as if they pos-

sessed superior information concerning the day's
business ; handsome men admirably appointed,
wearing that slightly bored and languid expression
which may be seen on the faces of the most
daring riders across country ; veterans in weather-
stained scarlet ; grooms and second-horse-men
leading riderless beasts saddled and with stirrups
pulled up ; benevolent farmers jogging heavily
along ; and behind, all the tag-rag and bob-tail,
which was in the habit of collecting by Barsash
Wood on the day after the Holmborough ball ;
while every now and then a smart barouche filled
with fur-wrapped ladies, a dainty victoria or
brougham, containing some more delicate matron,
would dash by, outstripping the ruck of gigs and
pony carts : past a windmill on the outskirts of
the village, and down the irregular street with its
thatched cottages and ancient looking ale-house.
On the wide green the hounds were gathered, the
Huntsman in his black velvet cap and scarlet coat
in their midst, and the whips keeping guard.
Here was assembled a throng of equestrians, and
a motley assemblage of foot people ; while con-
veyances of all sorts, from a baker's cart to a
perambulator, blocked up the approaches.

The arrivals gathered thickly. Some great
personages were expected at the meet, which was
a late one, and a pleasant buzz of anticipation
prevailed. Friendly greetings sounded on all
sides, and cheerful allusions to the entertainment
of the night before. The Huntsman touched his
cap now to one, now to another; and there was

the usul interchange of opinions as to the chances of a successful draw. The Master's keen eye made a rapid inspection of his recruits; grooms adjusted girths' and stirrup-leathers, and quieted restive horses; and as Mrs. Rainshaw's light victoria, drawn by its spirited cobs, dashed up, scattering the fringe of shoemakers and roughs, no scene could have appeared more animated or picturesque. Mrs. Rainshaw had evidently ingratiated herself with all circles, and her fresh voice, which had undoubtedly a charm of its own, rang sweetly above the gurgle of laughter and conversation, as she poured forth a variety of discursive remarks. She had a word for every one, from the Lord Lieutenant to Farmer John Dyke, a local celebrity whom she greatly favoured. He was in the midst of an argument with the Master, and was laying down the law in this fashion: "That 'ere fox never did go to ground here—nothing of the kind; but I'll tell you what. He managed to get to Knipley Wood; and there if you like, he *did* go to ground."

He received Mrs. Rainshaw's salute, and, chivalrously returning it, crossed over to the victoria, observing while he patted the near cob, "Bless you, ma'am, they do look well, they do," and added confidentially, "If you want to see a little of the sport to-day, I'll give your coachman a word or two; for I can guess pretty well that there won't be much done in this draw, and I'm pretty sure of the line the fox will take from Clumping Gorse."

"You can't do better than follow Dyke's advice, Mrs. Rainshaw," said Sir Roland, laughing. "He's generally pretty well informed; I think he has dealings with the foxes, myself; but I don't think people on wheels will see much of the hounds to-day, and Dyke and I don't agree about a certain game old fox in Barsash Wood, that I fancy will give us a real good run to-day, if this ruck will only let us get off fair."

The Leesholm party appeared in full force; and the resources of the stables had been taxed to mount Mrs. Borlase and Miss Geneste, to say nothing of second-horsemen and Mr. Margrave, who could not afford the good things of this life for himself, and therefore expected his friends to provide them for him.

The Romers and Judith Fountain had brought their own horses; and Lady Romer, whose style could be conveniently adapted to her costumes, had exchanged the Rossetti phase for that of the modern sportswoman. Judith's individuality was not adaptable, but she looked less ethereal than usual, and two vivid spots of colour upon her cheeks heightened her beauty in a remarkable degree. Colonel Rainshaw seemed completely at his ease upon a splendid weight-carrier, and Graysett, mounted on a showy but somewhat impetuous thoroughbred, which had been provided by a local horsedealer, felt all the excitement of an enthusiastic sportsman, by whom Leicestershire runs have been for some time only enjoyed in retrospect.

"That's a good looking one," said Sir Frederick

Romer, examining the animal with a critical eye; "but he'll rush his fences, or I'm not mistaken, and will want a little handling. He would not suit my country. You people are all for a stiff quick thing. I like a long slow run. It gives you time to see how much better you are than other people. But you can generally depend upon Stiggins, and I think, Major Graysett, that he has done you very well."

"I am not so sure of Stiggins," said Colonel Rainshaw; and there ensued a short horsey. discussion upon certain transactions in which Mr. Stiggins had not distinguished himself. "I don't agree with you about this country, Fred. Timber is timber, and you know what you are doing ; and, for my part, I prefer timber to a stiff bull-finch with a hairy ditch on the other side."

"Ah !" said Sir Fred reflectively, "they both require mettle."

"And money !" interrupted Mr. Margrave.

"I meant the two things, Margrave—metal—don't you see ?" explained Sir Fred, who was given to heavy jokes of this kind. "A play upon words ; do you see ? How do you do, Esmé ? You haven't forgotten how to ride over in America, have you, for you'll need to do all you know, if you are on one of De Burgh's brutes."

Colquhoun laughed. He seemed to enjoy the exercise of power that was needed to control the fiery animal under him; and his admirers might have thrown in the teeth of his detractors that

their Apostle of the Beautiful was no mean pro-
ficient in manly accomplishments. He sat his
horse as though he were part of it, while his long
hair, and certain peculiarities of his dress, were in
him rather marks of distinction than of affectation.
He attracted a good deal of notice, although
perhaps it was not of a sufficiently dignified kind
to flatter the vanity of a poet presumably sensitive
as to the quality of the homage tendered him.
Unfortunately, Holmborough was the winter head-
quarters of that powerful cabal which had partly
succeeded in affecting Colquhoun's social ostra-
cism; and a certain great lady at its head, whom
he had irreparably offended, was present in the
field to-day. Her "dead cut" was the signal for
others to ignore him, and there was an immediate
stoniness of expression or an averting of eyes on
the part of many, whose caprice he, the idol of the
hour, had once been. Colquhoun winced inwardly.
It was very petty, but susceptibility to ridicule or
feminine affront is an element of the proverbial
" poetic impressionability." A battle with women
is an ignominious sort of warfare, and has about
it a touch of the ludicrous; while the attitude of
the combatant with his hands metaphorically tied,
suggests that of a whipped cur who dare not
retaliate upon his oppressors. A man who is
publicly cut by a lady—a leader of fashion and
her small court—however morally guiltless he may
be, cannot fail to present rather a sorry figure.
Not that there was anything of the whipped cur
about Esmé Colquhoun. On the contrary, his

bearing was somewhat leonine as he tossed back his mane and faced his enemies. It was quite impossible to suppress his vivid personality, and his dauntless composure forced admiration.

Judith Fountain watched him, feeling a thrill of exultation and sympathy. But she held apart. She did not speak to him, only returning his salutation with a grave bow. Nor did she speak to Graysett, who was observing her intently with a passionate foreboding of the effect which the whole position might produce upon her.

Christine Borlase, her blue eyes flashing and her head also erect, rode forward and with the generous partisanship of her Bohemian nature placed herself by Colquhoun's side as if to declare, "We are artists and comrades ; we will stand by each other." Esmé looked down upon her, a curious smile upon his lips, a gleam of deep tenderness in his eyes. The glance which passed between them was full of passionate understanding.

"Always loyal," he murmured. "Why are you angry with Lady Langthwaite and her world ? I am trying to imagine myself into a state of sublime indifference. You disturb the process."

"It is an impossible one," she returned in a very low tone.

"Then rejoice, since I am become more wholly yours."

"No. You are drawn farther from me," she said with melancholy emphasis. "You can never be wholly mine, or wholly the property of any woman. Haven't I often told you that, to you, life without a roar of 'Bravo's' would be stark despondency? You can't act without spectators, and you must be always acting. Ah, my poor Esmé, why did you ever try to be anything but a poet? It was foolish of you to risk losing the world which is so necessary to your happiness."

"Yet for your sake I offered to renounce the world. It is you who found the sacrifice too great."

"Ah," said she cynically, "we artists are obliged to make so many sacrifices to the gods for inspiration, that we cannot waste any upon our fellow-creatures."

"The Empress has come," exclaimed Lady Romer, "and we are moving at last."

The pack streamed up a narrow lane, the procession of riders following, and the carriages as best they could—a long line to the crest of the hill, where there opened out a glorious view of sweeping pastures and low meadows divided by bristling fences. There was a scurry across a piece of furrowed ground, and then some unsatisfactory dawdling, and much wrath expended upon the unruly mob, while the wind on the rise blew sharply, and the sun suddenly shone out, bringing into prominence the knots of red-coated horsemen gathered along the dark line of covert in which the hounds were opening.

The wood rang with music marred by the yells of the foot people. The horn twanged ; there was a shout : "Gone away!" "He's off!" "Tally-ho!"

and a wild scramble through a neighbouring gate and dash across the fields, carriages turning towards the road, excited coachmen holding rapid consultations, and adventurous huntresses on wheels, following as near as they could in the wake of the field. The fox had broken on the other side of the wood, which was long and narrow, so that they who had not followed the Master down the rides were at first in a state of uncertainty as to the direction in which he had gone.

A steep hill led down to the foot of the covert, and here a slight check occurred—a smash, and a halt on the part of the humanely disposed. A pony-cart had come to grief: the pony staked by the shaft, and a girl in a brown ulster lay huddled on the ground, with a gentleman in pink, who probably anathematized his bad luck, pouring brandy down her throat. A pause ensued, long enough to make sure that there was no serious injury, and then the rush onward again, madder than before, for by this time the hounds had gained considerably, and the pursuers who had been fortunate enough to get away with them were happily careering over the open country to the right; while the laggards had before them two or three ploughed fields and some unnegotiable-looking jumps, which might have been avoided by foresight in the first instance.

Major Graysett, one of these unfortunates, presently found himself riding beside Mrs. Borlase, the only other one of the Leesholm set who had not secured a good start. She had candidly confessed to not being in form that day; and her horse having ignominiously baulked one stiff place, she had been prudently availing herself of conveniently placed gates. "We are rather novices in this country, Major Graysett," she said with her charming smile, "and for once Mr. Dyke seems out in his calculations. They've started a good old dog fox, and are likely to have a splendid run. No one expected they would find so quickly in Barsash Wood. To tell the truth, I enjoy the riding, but I don't particularly mind being rather out of it. Don't you mind me, but take a line across those fields. I think he is making a ring, and you may find yourself well in yet."

Graysett's blood was up, and he was not disposed to disregard the advice. It was evident that the fox's movements could not be predicted with any certainty, for now that the stragglers had been left behind, all seemed to be taking different directions, each person apparently animated by the invincible determination to get to the front through the exercise of his individual judgment. Graysett, following the lead of a wiry, well-mounted member of the hunt, the state of whose scarlet coat proclaimed him to be an old hand, gallantly cleared a formidable-looking hedge with an ugly take off, and began to congratulate himself upon having trusted to the honour of Mr. Stiggins. The chestnut flew over the ground, rising like a bird and before long distancing the veteran, upon whose knowledge of the country

Graysett had done well to rely. The hounds were in sight streaming westward, and not far in their rear some twenty or thirty picked men of the field and about half a dozen ladies. He fancied that he could discern Judith's slight figure and Esmé Colquhoun's yellow mane, and grimly recalled Rainshaw's simile, while an intense desire seized him to outdo his rival.

But beyond him there lay a dark line of willows with a white streak flashing between them ; and he was as yet unaware of the fact that the chestnut which could so cleanly fly the fences was absolutely useless at water.

It was in fact one of the most unnegotiable brooks in that part of the country, and might have daunted a rider far more accustomed to following hounds than Graysett. But he was not to be beaten now, and the sight of his late companion pounding along to the right, in the apparent hope of finding a better place, did not deter him from making the attempt here, though the banks were treacherous and the water wide and uninviting. By so doing, if successful, he must gain considerably, and this was at present his first consideration. He shortened his rein, and woke up his mare with a touch of the spur, for the chestnut was flagging, and did not at once respond to his call. Twice she baulked, three times he urged her forward. The third she made a rush, stopped at the very brink, jumped short, and fell heavily against the bank, rolling upon her rider, and striking out wildly with her hoofs, so that he was at once in imminent danger of both drowning and concussion of the brain.

The old sportsman paused, seeing the accident, and turning, galloped to Graysett's assistance. Several others rode up at the moment, and among them they succeeded in extricating Graysett from his perilous position. He lay insensible. It was at first feared that he was dead. There was an evident and dangerous injury to the skull; and no one seemed to know what means to take, while a dozen alarming and unpractical suggestions were made by the onlookers. Mrs. Borlase, who had ridden up and was off her horse in a moment, showed more firmness and knowledge than any of the men present. She succeeded in dispersing the crowd; sent one groom off at once to the nearest village, which was not far away, and where there was happily a doctor, and another to a neighbouring farmhouse for a mattress and conveyance; then, with the assistance of those gentleman who had remained, did what she could towards restoring the injured man to consciousness—apparently a hopeless task.

Meanwhile Judith and Colquhoun, by a lucky start among those in advance, were sweeping over the grass-fields, enjoying what proved to be one of the best runs of the season. There were no very serious obstacles to be encountered, and they took the fences one by one as though it had been a hurdle-race, he turning every now and then to note how she fared, she flying on with a sense of mad delight, her pulses tingling as the wind met her face, while the rapid motion and his proximity filled her with excitement, such as she had never known, and produced in her a strange feeling of irresponsibility. She seemed borne along without exercise of will, attracted, as it were, by a magnet which she must follow even to the ends of the earth. The fantastic thought overpowered every other. Whenever they looked towards her, his eyes commanded. It was like an electric thrill; Judith had never before experienced this sensation. She was caught in a whirl. She could no longer analyze his influence over her. It was beyond analysis; it was simply compelling.

There was room for nothing but the exquisite pleasure of feeling absolutely impressed—dominated. This was what she had felt when waltzing with him the preceding evening. The consciousness of him had been with her through the darkness. It was like a delirium in which his voice, his eyes, his hair, the touch of his hand, seemed living things filling the air around her.

They flew over the brook which was a check to many, and now were striding side by side across a stretch of level country. The hounds had bent towards the left, and far off on the crest of a hill was the low dark line of a covert, for which Reynard was making. There in due course he ran to ground, and escaped with his life. He had earned it gallantly, though the hounds were cheated of their reward.

There was a little uncertainty as to whether another covert would be drawn. The hounds had

run in a semicircle, and the distance was not great
from the place where they had started. As the
council of war was being held stragglers came
riding up, and the rumour spread there had been
a bad accident, though no one seemed to know
much about it. Colquhoun, who had looked
anxious at the news, seemed reassured upon hearing that a gentleman was the sufferer, and rode on
with the Romers, who were in high spirits and
enjoyment. Judith lingered uneasily, and presently
saw Rainshaw hurrying by and looking full of
concern. He had heard that it was Major
Graysett who had been thrown. Later on, in the
road they came upon Mrs. Rainshaw in her
victoria, also bound for the village whither
Graysett had been taken. Before they reached it,
the report met them that he was dead. This
proved to be false. He was still in a state of
semi-consciousness, but the surgeon had made his
examination, and danger to life was not appre-
hended. The inn afforded but poor accommoda-
tion ; and it was decided that he should be taken
at once to Leesholm. A kind of bed was
arranged in the carriage, and Mrs. Rainshaw and
her husband accompanied him to their home.
By the time everything had been settled the
afternoon was waning. Judith rode back sorrow-
ful and agitated. It appeared to her that fatality
had been at work ; and this accident seemed a
strange ending to the first act in the drama
which she also felt was being enacted.

CHAPTER X.

MRS. BORLASE, Colquhoun, and the rest of the
party reached Leesholm before the Rainshaws
returned with their injured friend. Rumours of
the accident had spread—exaggerated at first,
but afterwards toned down by the comforting
assurance that Major Graysett had not lost his
life, and that he would, in all probability, be
incapacitated for only a short time.

There appeared nothing to do under the circumstances except get out of the way of confusion.
Most of the ladies retired to their rooms, and
sipped tea brought them by their maids, while the
men drank something stronger in the smoking-room.

Mrs. Borlase was joined in her temporary studio
by Esmé Colquhoun. She had asked him to
come. Her attitude was one of expectancy.
She stood by the fireplace, her face turned side-
ways to him as he entered, holding a screen of
feathers between her cheeks and the blaze. Her
robe of pale-green plush, confined at the waist
with an old enamelled girdle, and with soft lace
falling away from the neck and arms, suited the
almost girlish lines of her figure, while its colour
harmonized with her golden hair and dead-white
skin. There was a luxuriousness in her dress, in

the subdued light, the rich draperies of the chimney-piece, the faintly scented atmosphere, which was more than pleasing, in contrast with the bleak wintry landscape from which a little while before they had entered.

Upon a small table near her there stood in a blue china bowl the crushed bouquet of hothouse blossoms, still fragrant, which she had carried upon the previous night. Esmé Colquhoun took up the bouquet, which was composed almost entirely of yellow roses, and drew forth one of the flowers with a preoccupied air.

"You were not perfectly successful last night," he said. "The gradations of colour were too distinctly defined. That amber dress is not low enough in tone. It was jarring; and *you* ought never to be inharmonious."

He did not look at her as he spoke, and she stood motionless for some moments apparently not having noticed his remark. Presently she turned towards him, agitating her feather fan with an impulsive gesture, as though she wished to utter some pleading or remonstrative words, but knew not how to phrase her thoughts. She moved a step and stood before him, gazing at and, as it were, through him, with eyes that had that gleaming yet heavy appearance which is produced by unshed tears.

He laid the rose down and sighed. The action seemed significant. His whole manner was full of sadness. Then his eyes turned very slowly upon her, and opened wide suddenly, dilating

with tenderness rather than with passion. The
two looks met and clung to each other.   In them
there was a world of unspoken thought, of lived-
out tragedy—the tragedy of two hearts held aloof
from satisfaction in each other by certain high and
imperious instincts, which are yet strangely blended
with worldly scruples—a drama of the age without the grandeur of renunciation, or the reckless
insistence upon happiness at any cost, which com-
pels some kind of admiration—a pathetic effort at
compromise involving the warring of impulses, the
smart of an equivocal position, the perpetual self-
buckling, and inevitable weariness of contest ; the
strangulation of sensibilities denied outlet ; and at
last the dreary sense that all is bitter-sweet, hopeless, and irreconcilable with the demands of either
God or Mammon : renunciation with a sting, but
through all, the pure love which is the glory of it
and the misery.

They stretched out their hands to each other.
"Esmé!" she said with a faint little cry.

Without a word, he drew her to a couch placed
at an angle with the fireplace, seating himself near
her.   He adjusted a cushion, and she leaned her
head back against it like a tired child, while he
sat silent and brooding, his gaze fixed intently
upon the fire.   Once he lifted her hand and
kissed it, murmuring a word of endearment, but
so low that it could scarcely have reached her
ears.   At last he said aloud, "I have hurt you.
I have dealt you a blow—brave, loyal, faithful
heart!"

She roused herself, and, gazing mournfully at him, said, " It was I who bade you strike."

" I have hurt you," he repeated with remorse in his voice. And then he rose and looked down yearningly upon her. " Christine, are you still so proud? Will you always face the world so with your frank cynicism—your high-spirited independence—artist and woman of the world in one, giving just so much and giving no more? Christine, will you accept no sacrifice? Will you make none—not even now?"

Christine returned his gaze unshrinkingly ; but a tear rose and lay on her lower lashes, held there glittering.

" No, Esmé—not even now. There can never be any question of sacrifice between you and me."

" There should be none. You are right. Love should be a free sacrament, and its own justification."

She seemed to reflect for a moment and asked, as though to gain time, " Why do you say 'not even now?'"

" The situation is changed," he answered.

" That is what I wished. I have thought a great deal about our position towards each other. What happened the night before you went away was a revelation to me. I felt that there *must* be a safeguard—that I was ruining your life. I wish you to marry. It is the only way—for you."

" For me?" he repeated.

" I take into consideration your temperament—

the poetic temperament, which, as you have said complacently, is a problem to itself and to others."

"Is it supposed," he asked, "that the poet delights in going through phase upon phase of emotion? I yearn to arrive at rest—unity. I believed once that I might have done so through you. I believed this—before I loved you. It was a mistaken idea. Restful love must have in it the essence of marriage. It must contain the elements of passion suspended and transformed into the deep, steady attachment, which may be the fruit of years of marriage, or of the love which transcends marriage. That is the psychology of the matter."

"Oh!" she cried. "You would analyze your death-throes, till you ceased to exist."

There was silence for a minute. "Think," said he slowly. "Would you desire that the man who loved you should wish to place you in the arms of another man? If he could so wish, you would know at once, by your unerring woman's instinct, that he had never really loved you.

She started forward. "I felt that you misunderstood me—grossly," she exclaimed in sadness rather than in anger. "I knew it when I read your letter in reply to mine. Did you give me no credit for sincerity, and for clean motive? It was not with us 'soul to soul' then. Didn't we face the position once—fairly and without prudery as we had a right to do? We wouldn't have any flimsy veils. It must be the truth and nothing else. And we decided that we were strong enough to try an experiment in which other men and women have been successful. I'll never think so meanly of human nature as to believe it impossible. At any rate, the experiment was a failure with us. Perhaps it was not meant for poets. Where is the deep tenacious friendship—the intellectual love, of which we dreamed? Where is that larger spiritual insight, gained through annihilation of self, which should claim from our souls a duty to each other? Analyzed to nothingness. You left them behind when you entered the new school. They weren't in keeping with its corruption."

Esmé laughed softly. "I admit that the Age is hysterical; and we artists are children of the Age."

"No," she said; "it is we who make the Age."

"As you will. Do not let us argue about abstractions. At least you know the temperament; and if my frank egotism seems to you brutal, you will approve of its sincerity. Forgetfulness is the tribute which the artist pays to the gods. The man who concentrates the forces of his being upon one sentiment can never give forth a living poem. To long unsatisfied means intellectual stagnation. But the travail of emotion is the birth of innumerable beautiful fancies which enrich the world; and genius owes a duty to the world, and to itself. There must be ebb and flow, crisis and reaction. You condemn me to reaction and its uncertainties. But you will always remember that the choice was in your power, that it is so still."

"No," she exclaimed with some passion. "What

you describe as your 'temperament' places it beyond my power. I know you better than you know yourself. In a month's time—a year's time—I will grant you so long, you would be wearying for the incense which there would be no one to light."

" I am weary now of my life."

She laughed a little joyless laugh. "How much more so if you were confined in a prison ! Applause and adulation are the breath of existence to you. The love and loyalty of one woman would never satisfy your nature, except under conditions which would enable you to take impressions from numerous other sources. You will secure for yourself these conditions. I want you to love your wife. I want you to have the world's incense as well. I want you to touch every point possible in existence. You are the true creature of your own philosophy. You require a thousand sensations in quick succession, and you must analyze each before you can decide whether it is worth experiencing. You profess to worship the ideal; but in reality you are an utter materialist. You have all the weakness, all the inconsistency, all the greatness of a poetic nature. The greatness and the fire kindle in my intellect a spark of the incense you crave. The weakness and the inconsistency touch my woman's heart and make me love you. Being what we both are, sorrow and evil can only come from indulging our love. This I pointed out to you before you went away; and now I am going to place it beyond our power of indulgence."

"That is impossible. You cannot crush down your love for me, nor can I, married or free, prevent myself from loving you. I would not try to do so. You are my inspiration. You are to me the ideal woman."

She was silent for several moments, and her head dropped upon her breast. Presently she looked up with a strange smile upon her lips and a bright light in her eyes.

"I will remain so. An ideal love is a great and glorious possession. An ideal love is divine and actual, and it exists, it *must* exist, apart from material life. Are not love, faith, will, forces more potent than brute strength? Ah, my Esmé! you, a poet and an artist, know as I do that the realities of existence are not the things we see and touch. Human passion is but the stream in which pure, divine passion is reflected. The more muddy the stream the more distorted the image. Drag down the star and it disappears. Oh, teach the world this truth in your books! Let me try to show it dimly forth in my pictures. It is the core of our inner lives. It is the pearl of great price, which has been given to us artists. Let us cherish the ideal. Our outward lives may be false and conventional; but within, there is a sanctuary which should be held sacred. And—ah, Heaven! Every day do we not stumble and fall? Are we not continually yielding ourselves to influences which are debasing? Crisis and reaction! That is true. There is no rest for such natures as ours."

Her voice vibrated with a passionate tremor. She rose and moved away from him, all the time her gaze never forsaking his face. An exceeding softness and beauty crept over her features, and she went on in a more gentle tone. "I will be your ideal, Esmé. When you need sympathy in your work, ask it from me. When you have beautiful dreams, tell them to me. When the fire burns within you, come to me and I will fan it into flame. Give your love to Judith Fountain. She has attracted you already. In time, she will captivate you completely; for she has a subtle charm that must appeal to your artistic perceptions. She can reinstate you in popular favour. She is rich, and can supply the sensuous atmosphere— of dim rooms, Oriental perfumes, soothing music, without which you have often said to me your muse is dumb. But give *me* your soul."

Colquhoun seemed infected by her enthusiasm. His dramatic instinct seized the conception of a sublime *rôle*. The poet is a paradox. In a moment, he may ascend from the depths of earth to the heights of heaven. His mind seems the tenement of some fantastic Protean spirit with a passion for impersonation, to which truth and falsehood are of equal value. His potentialities appear capable of manifesting themselves in either good or evil as the wind blows or the sun shines.

"You are a noble woman," he said slowly. "You are very strong. If we could have been married, we might have conquered the world together. What is it that you are going to do?"

"I am going away in a day or two. I shall leave you here with Judith Fountain."

"And I—what am I to do?"

"What your impulses prompt," she answered with the least touch of bitterness. "It is not for me to guide them."

"I think," he said, after a minute's pause, "that perhaps your enthusiasm gilds merely trite facts and commonplace sentiment. That is the way with us—we artists. Is your star anything higher than the respect of the world?"

"Oh!" she cried. "You can't see. You don't comprehend. It is my own self-respect. It is your love. If you were a god, Esmé—instead of being a poet ; and I an angel, and not a battered, hardened woman of the world, we would fly aloft and seek our star."

As she spoke, she rose from her couch and came to the mantelpiece, where she stood facing him.

"We will be melodramatic no longer," she said with a dreary smile. "There is too much of that sort of thing in your school, and I don't approve of it, you know. You had better leave me now."

He signified his obedience by a gesture. Again he kissed her hand. There was something in her eyes which entreated him not to claim once-granted privileges.

The coldness of the touch startled him, and roused him to passionate solicitude.

"You are cold! You are wretched! What

have I done? I am hurting you! This means nothing, Christine? This—this is not farewell."

"No," she answered with an effort which almost choked her. "There will never be a real farewell between us—while we are both alive. . . . And—and—I mean to be your wife's friend, Esmé. . . . I have a right to that vested interest. I've done nothing to forfeit it. That's something to be glad of, isn't it?" And she gave a little uncertain laugh, which broke short in a sob.

"I am cold," she said—"and tired. I shall lie down on the sofa by the fire for a little while before I dress for dinner."

He arranged the cushions for her head with a tenderness which was almost womanly. "What can I do for you?" he said. "Shall I read you some poetry? Shall I read you to sleep?"

"No no," she cried wildly. "Let me be. I want to be alone."

He left her silently. The blankness that remained was as the darkness when a flame has gone out.

Christine sank upon the sofa and pressed her hands together, biting her lips to keep down the sobs uprising in her throat. It was just that. It seemed to her that the flame had gone out.

CHAPTER XI.

MAJOR GRAYSETT'S injury, though less serious
than had at first been feared, resulted in an
illness that sadly interfered with the somewhat
fantastic schemes he had formed for Judith's
protection against the unknown danger in which
he imagined her to be placed. The blow on his
head, the shock to his system, or something else
unexplainable, brought on a return of the fever
from which he had suffered before and since his
departure from India ; and for several days he
was slightly delirious.

A nurse was sent for from London ; and the
wing which contained his rooms was cut off by
means of heavy curtains, so that no echoes of the
sounds or doings in the other part of the house
could penetrate to his sick chamber. That there
was a great deal doing, he understood vaguely.
Visitors came and went. Mrs. Borlase had gone
to pay another visit in the neighbourhood, but
was expected to return later. Esmé Colquhoun's
invitation had been extended, and Judith Fountain remained indefinitely.

This was all that Graysett could learn when
his senses returned to him. Colonel Rainshaw
visited the invalid frequently ; but his reticence

and apparent dislike to speaking of Miss Fountain convinced Graysett, if in his weak state his brain were capable of entertaining a conviction, that he had betrayed in his wanderings the deep interest he felt in Judith, and the weird fancies which he had woven round her intercourse with Esmé Colquhoun.

He was right.

The revelation of Graysett's state of mind occasioned much dismay to Rainshaw, who, however, notwithstanding his perplexity and annoyance, found comfort in the reflection that the vision, his friend's curious forebodings, and the sudden attraction towards Judith, were entirely due to incipient fever, and would vanish with his restoration to health. In the meantime it was best to avoid the subject.

During his delirium Graysett had never been free from a vivid impression of Judith's peril. He had imagined her about to be devoured in the arena, or bound as a witch to the stake. His fancy had beheld her delivered over to torturers, stretched on the rack, drowning in open sea, or pursued by monsters. He had seen her in every conceivable situation of horror, and he himself always tied down and helpless to succour her. Even when he awoke to reality, his position appeared no less terrible, and his chamber seemed a transparent cell through the walls of which he beheld, in fancy, scenes which heated his blood again to fever pitch.

This condition of things lasted for nearly a

fortnight, by which time, though very weak, he was perfectly clear-headed, longing to leave his room, and eager for such information as he could obtain without showing his anxiety too directly. He was reserved, sensitive, and keenly susceptible to ridicule, and it seemed to him that after his heroic protestations he must cut a sorry figure in the eyes both of Judith and of those who suspected his infatuation.

There was something tragi-comic in the whole situation. He was like a soldier kept from battle by the puerile fact that he had cut his hand or sprained his ankle. Destiny was laughing in her sleeve, and trying to show him how unavailing were his efforts against her. Nothing could, he thought, be more humiliating than his attitude. There was not even the spice of danger to make it interesting. He was simply incapacitated, over-strained, out of order—nerves, brain, and system generally. This was what the doctor told him, and added that the change of climate had been too severe, that he ought to go to the south of France for the spring, and pass his summer among the mountains of Switzerland.

"I think it is the best thing you can do," said Rainshaw cheerily, when the physician had departed. "Let us all go to Monaco as soon as the hunting is over; Molly has a hankering after the gaming tables which I'm in duty bound to gratify. That jungle fever plays the deuce with the constitution. There is nothing like perpetual change of air for rooting it out of one's system. In a few months you'll be as right as possible."

Rainshaw spent a great deal of time with his friend—more than might have been expected considering his duties as host and the claims of his preserves. Graysett was always glad to see him enter the room, for this seemed his only link with the other inhabitants of Leesholm. Not that Rainshaw's conversation gave much insight into affairs. He had not the art of talking pictorially, and had he been inclined to write memoirs of his times, they would have conveyed very little to the unimaginative reader. Moreover, with an elaborate pretence at unconsciousness, he had a way of starting some fresh subject whenever Judith Fountain was touched upon, and seemed to to take it for granted that Graysett could only be interested in topics peculiarly adapted to the masculine tone of mind. He always gave an accurate account of the day's bag, the state of his stud, the after-dinner stories which were told, and most particularly those of a certain Admiral then staying at Leesholm, whose experiences seemed to have been as varied as they were startling, ranging from the abduction of a Mormon bride to the discovery of a new prima donna or professional beauty.

"D—n the Admiral!" Graysett had once exclaimed with savage emphasis; and Rainshaw had looked stolid but had not left off his stories. "I'm sick of the Admiral and of Sir Fred Romer," continued Graysett; "they don't interest me."

"To be sure," said Rainshaw; "Fred Romer's wife is the most entertaining of the two. She is in capital form now that she has Esmé Colquhoun to admire her when she strikes an attitude, or does her hair in a new fashion. She and Miss Geneste between them make the house lively."

"And Miss Fountain?"

"Judith Fountain would never make any house lively, unless she spent her money in hiring professional jesters to do it for her. She is bewitched; she is in a dream."

"How?" asked Graysett, starting up in bed. "Who has bewitched her?"

"My dear fellow, don't excite yourself; it isn't worth it. You know Miss Fountain as well as I do; at all events, you have made better use of your opportunities for studying her. I daresay it is you who have bewitched her. You awakened her out of a dream for a day or two, and now she has gone back to it again. I can't venture an opinion as to the state of her feelings or her mind; I know nothing about her."

"You seemed to know a good deal, judging by all you have told me."

"Oh, those were mere facts which I learned principally through Molly. At present I don't think she would be a source of satisfaction to any one who wanted to make a study of her—unless it were an artist meditating an uncanny subject. She sits in a big chair in the hall pretending to read and never turning a page. She hardly opens her mouth; she stares fixedly into vacancy, and if you came across her in a dark passage, you would take her for a ghost ; and she sings and plays in a weird fashion that gives one the creeps.   She does something else : she inquires regularly how you are, and to-day sent you this."

He produced a little bouquet of Parma violets with a white camellia in the centre, tied together with a knot of ribbon.

"Really," he added, "it is a very pretty attention, and from an heiress extremely significant."

Graysett took the flowers, which were deliciously fragrant.   They gave him more pleasure than he could express.   The little nosegay seemed to him like Judith herself, and the camellia heart to typify her coldness and purity.

"What does Esmé Colquhoun do?" he asked presently.

"He shoots, and uncommonly straight, when he takes the trouble to come out with us; but as a rule he seems to prefer roasting himself before the fire, and dangling after the ladies.   He talks— good Lord! doesn't he talk!—as though he were being interviewed by a dozen newspaper editors. I suppose he got into the way in America, where they seem to have been always interviewing him. I must confess that his conversation is above the heads of a few of his audience ; but some of his anecdotes, when the ladies are out of the way, are really very good, and quite broad enough to suit all comprehensions.   I don't know that I should call his witticisms always refined.   For the most part, however, I am obliged to take it for granted that he is an exceedingly clever young man. To me he appears like a wind-bag containing a few dried peas, which rattle considerably."

"You said once that you suspected Lady Romer and Mrs. Borlase of trying to make up a marriage between him and Miss Fountain. Do you think so still?" asked Graysett.

CHAPTER XII.

RAINSHAW hesitated a moment and eyed the sick man doubtfully, as though it had occurred to him that frankness might be better policy than evasion.

"Look here, old fellow," he said. "If you have ever had any idea of Judith Fountain, you had much better put it all out of your head. I told you so the first night you asked me about her. Molly and I between us, will engage to find you as pretty and as charming a wife as you could desire, and with money into the bargain."

"I don't want a wife, thank you ; and I have money enough of my own. But I've got a particular reason for wishing to know whether there's anything between Mr. Colquhoun and Miss Fountain. If you don't tell me now, you will force me to come downstairs a little sooner than is prudent—that is all."

"It has something to do with that dream of yours ! You know it was all imagination ; the fever was upon you then."

"Very probably," said Graysett ; but you don't answer my question."

"I don't want you to be worried and thrown back," objected Rainshaw. "Of course Lady Romer would like to secure Judith's fortune for

her friend ; and of course Colquhoun would be
only too ready to grab it ; and if he gains an
influence over her, no one has any right to inter-
fere. I don't see why they should. There's
nothing really against him."

"You had a different opinion a little while ago."

"I swam with the tide—that's all. When the
papers say that a man is a knave you believe
them, though, practically speaking, it ought to be
the other way on. I think Colquhoun may be a
fool about business matters, but I won't call him
a knave. He had rascally partners ; and Margrave
was quite right, a poet should stick to his own
line of life, whether it be writing sonnets or making
love to pretty women."

"He has, then, gained an influence over Miss
Fountain ?" said Graysett.

"There's a great deal more going on under the
surface than I care to investigate," replied Rainshaw oracularly. "I have no opinion upon the
subject. I know nothing about it."

"At all events, Miss Fountain, being a connection of your wife's, is entitled to some regard from
you. Her happiness cannot be a matter of complete indifference to you."

"I did not imply that. It is simply that I am
outside the whole affair ; and nothing that I could
say or do would alter the course of events. A
woman cannot do better than marry the man she
loves, unless he be an unmitigated ruffian, and I
am not justified in supposing that Esmé Colquhoun's motives are unworthy of a gentleman. I

don't suppose anything. If Miss Fountain is in love with Colquhoun she will marry him, and I hope she may be happy ; I don't care whether he is so or not. He may run his own risks, and so must she. As a matter of fact, your happiness is of much more importance to me than hers."

"Oh, leave me out of the question," said Graysett with the irritability of weakness. "If there were any risk for her, why did you invite him to stay on ?"

"I didn't do so. It was my wife who asked him. We have got two Australians here whom we are bound to entertain. They want to study the different features of English society. Esmé Colquhoun is decidedly a feature. They were particularly anxious to meet him, and so we have earned their eternal gratitude. That is the history of it. As for Lady Romer's scheme, it is not my business to make or mar it. I am distinctly neutral. I wash my hands of it all. Candidly, I shall not be sorry when Molly is tired of the set, but I can't prevent her knowing whom she likes, provided he or she is respectable. I don't care about the sort of element they have introduced into the house. There's no fun in seeing people make fools of themselves, after a certain point ; at least I don't think so. Thought-reading and mesmerism and hanky-panky generally, are a bore. Mrs. Borlase was wise to take herself off just then. I give her credit for being a sensible woman. However, she is coming back to-morrow."

Graysett moved uneasily, and frowned, as he

uttered an exclamation expressive of resolution.

"What is it?" asked Rainshaw.

"You don't give me any idea of what has been going on. I must judge for myself."

"When?"

"This evening, if possible."

"No, indeed," cried Rainshaw; "who goes softly, goes surely. Here you are for the first time out of bed, and you talk of coming downstairs among a party of strangers! You are looking much better, and we shall have you round in a very short time now; but you must not be impatient. Besides, it would be of no use this evening. We are all going to a county function at Holmborough; some charitable amateur performance, in which Esmé Colquhoun has promised to distinguish himself. Molly sent a message to ask if she might come and see you to-morrow. She is a much better hand at social gossip than I am. But she is apt to colour rather highly; don't take all she says for gospel. There is really nothing to tell, except that Colquhoun seems to find pleasure in devoting himself to Miss Fountain, and that she appears equally pleased to accept his devotion."

"I shall be delighted to see Mrs. Rainshaw," exclaimed Graysett. "Pray beg her to come."

"And bring Judith Fountain with her! I am afraid that would not quite do. Don't worry about it, old fellow; consign the whole business to the limbo of 'might-have-beens' — Judith,

Esmé, the dream, and all your wild fancies. They were the shadows of your illness."

Rainshaw departed——to Graysett's relief; for his tactless sympathy was like the unskilful probing of a painful wound. His vague allusions to mysterious proceedings were sorely disquieting. Graysett determined, contrary to all advice, that he would join the general circle upon the morrow, then groaned and chafed, when, upon testing his strength, he discovered how greatly taxed it had been by the excitement of his late interview. He paced the room for a minute or two with the eagerness of a caged animal, but presently sank back upon his sofa as helpless as a baby.

Judith's little bouquet lay upon the pillow. A thought struck him. He would write to her. He went back to bed, and fortified himself with the restorative food which was brought to him. Propped up by pillows, he began his letter. It was a long one, and in it, he poured out his whole heart, beseeching Judith to send him a word or line which should confirm, or allay, his fears, and thus put an end to the suspense he was enduring. He gave it to the man-servant who attended him, desiring that it might be at once taken to Miss Fountain. He then tried to compose himself and recruit his forces for the morrow. He did not expect an answer that evening. It was now late in the day, and he knew that dinner must be earlier on account of the performance at Holmborough. Faint sounds reached him as he lay nervously listening. He could hear the

muffled beat of the gong, and some time afterwards the indistinct roll of carriages. About nine
o'clock a note was brought him. He had never
before seen Judith's handwriting, which was upright and peculiar, and he found himself stupidly
arguing from it, ere he opened the letter, that a
woman who gave this evidence of strength of
character would not readily yield herself to the
influence of another, and would at least reflect
before committing herself irrevocably.

The letter had neither formal beginning nor
ending.

"I don't know why you should care for me so
strongly and suddenly, but if your affection be as
unselfish as you describe it, you should be glad if
I can find the conditions of life upon which it has
always seemed to me that I must base my hope
of becoming human.

"You may smile at my fantastic notion, that I
am not an ordinary woman with instincts, sympathies, religious beliefs like the girls, wives, and
mothers around me, but an abstraction, a partly
irresponsible creature, a sort of Undine, incomplete
till the force of an irresistible affinity shall draw
my being into that of another who will supply the
element I need for the perfect development of my
faculties. Smile. But my intuition tells me that
this is so. It tells me that when I comply with
the law of affinity, I comply with the highest law
of my being, let the consequences be what they
may."

This letter, with its ambiguously worded phrases, which suggested so much and conveyed so little, intensified Graysett's fever of anxiety. Its indifference to his own feelings seemed to him deliberate cruelty. He was ready to acquiesce in her judgment of herself. She was an abstraction without human sympathies.

He was worse the next day and almost unfit to rise. Circumstances contributed to postpone Mrs. Rainshaw's visit, but he insisted that it should take place; and late in the afternoon he dressed and prepared to receive her in the little sitting-room which adjoined his bedroom.

CHAPTER XIII.

HE was lying on the sofa, looking very pale, and feeling dazed and shaky, when his hostess entered. She, with her fashionable draperies, her exuberant health, her brilliant smiles and frank sympathy, was like a fresh breeze from outside, at first almost overpowering; but the presence of a young, pretty, and kind-hearted woman is seldom too oppressive, even if she be wanting in delicate discrimination. He felt sure that she would, in her impulsive babbling, reveal all that he desired to know without embarrassing questioning upon his part; and, strange to say, felt more at ease with her than with her husband. His welcome was as cordial as could have been desired.

She halted as she approached his couch, and the tears came into her eyes as though she had been a child.

"Good gracious!" she exclaimed. "I am so sorry! What a ghost you look! But you'll soon be better," she added, with a sudden consciousness that the first duty of a visitor to a sick room is to be cheerful. "You *are* better than I expected. Good gracious!" And she sat down in an arm-chair beside the sofa, and looked at him in a very womanly way. "Tell me what I'm to do? Tom said I was to amuse you. But do you like me to talk? Will it tire you? You must let me know exactly what you like, and when I am to go away."

"I want you to tell me all about everything, Mrs. Rainshaw, in your own charming way; and if I shut my eyes and don't speak much, please don't think I am not enjoying it. It's the greatest treat to me to hear the news of the house, and all that you have been doing, without the exertion of asking for it. Tom isn't much of a hand at description."

"How heartless you must have thought us, going on in just the same way as if you hadn't been ill!" said she with compunction. "But we all thought of you more than I can say; and I am furious with Stiggins. He used to be rather a pal of mine; but I told Tom that we'd have nothing more to do with him. It was a great comfort, however, that there was no serious injury —and jungle fever is a thing that will keep coming and going—isn't it? You must not ever go back to India again. I thought you looked very ill the night you arrived, and Tom told me of an odd sort of vision you had which seemed to upset you. That was the beginning of everything. Oh, Major Graysett! and you were getting on so nicely too! I had such hopes. Why did you fall ill?"

The tears started again to Mrs. Rainshaw's eyes. She looked extremely discomposed, and there was an air of suppressed anxiety and importance about her, as though she had some big piece of intelligence weighing upon her mind.

"Why indeed!" he answered. "You can't be more sorry than I am myself, that I have caused so much trouble and worry."

"Oh, that's nothing! It wasn't *that* I meant."

She drew a little table near her and began to arrange some hothouse flowers she had brought.

"You mustn't talk. I am going to sit here and tell you some news; but I won't give you too much at once, lest I should excite you. Now, first all, have you been comfortable?"

"I could not have been more so—that is, under the circumstances."

"I am going to move you at once. You shall have my morning room. At any rate, it is more cheerful than this. Isn't it an odd little room? I think that, in the old days, it must have been a hiding-place, or an oratory, or something mysterious."

"Please don't have me moved," said Graysett. "I like it. And tell me, for nothing reaches me here, has anything important taken place?"

"A great deal that is important—to some people," said Mrs. Rainshaw enigmatically. "I am disappointed. I am perplexed. I don't think that it would have happened if you had been downstairs," she went on incoherently. "I liked you very much, Major Graysett, from the moment I saw you in the hall. I felt sure you were the sort of person a girl might trust. Now one may like some people and yet not have that feeling."

"Indeed I am very much obliged to you for your good opinion. I hope that I deserve it. At all events, I think that you may trust me. But this—is it anything very terrible?" He tried to speak lightly, but his voice trembled.

Mrs. Rainshaw paused in her occupation, and looked at him half questioningly, half sympathetically, from above a cluster of stephanotis.

"Do you know," she said, "that when you were ill and were not conscious of what you said, you talked a great deal of Judith Fountain? Don't be angry with me," she added quickly, seeing that a flush rose to his pale cheek. "Tom told me. I hope you don't think that it was mentioned, or that any one talked. No one thinks anything of what people say in fevers. I don't suppose the nurse noticed it at all. It was of no consequence."

Graysett's eyes met those of Mrs. Rainshaw straightly.

"I supposed that I had been talking nonsense," he said coolly. "As you say, it does not matter. I was only with Miss Fountain for a day or two, but even during that short time I got to know her, and to feel deeply interested in her. I can guess what perplexes you Mr. Esmé Colquhoun has shown himself greatly attracted by her."

"Ah! it is more than that!" exclaimed Mrs. Rainshaw, dropping her flowers. "I don't know why I should beat about the bush. She herself told me to tell you. She is going to marry him."

The blow had been expected, nevertheless it

came upon him like a shock, and for the moment
made him feel dazed and giddy. In spite of his
weakness, however, he had sufficient self-control to
utter no sound of dismay, and presently the beaten-
down feeling passed, and a sort of despairing
excitement took its place. He had an impulse
to rise there and then, and to rush into Judith's
presence and implore her to pause and consider
in what she was involving herself. He did not
think of his own disappointment; his solicitude
was solely for her.

"I must get up," he said. "I must speak to
her. It must be stopped."

"Ah!" said Mrs. Rainshaw, "that will be impossible. She is infatuated. Nothing would
turn her from him. Not that I think we have
any right to try, Major Graysett—if she loves
him. I know that there are people who think
very highly of Esmé Colquhoun. Why should
we suspect him of being a fortune-hunter? He
might have married a rich woman before now, if
he had chosen. I must say that I don't think he
would be a comfortable sort of husband. But
Judith is peculiar; and if she loves him——"

"Do you doubt it?" asked Graysett quietly.

"Judith could not fall in love like any one else.
I think she is bewitched. I have an uncanny
feeling that she is in a dream, and will wake up
by-and-by. She is so quiet. She has no little
ways or airs; and yet you can see that she
neither hears nor heeds any one but Esmé. The
truth is, Major Graysett, I am trying to argue

myself into a comfortable frame of mind—but, somehow, I can't."

"Mrs. Rainshaw," cried Graysett, "you have your cousin's welfare at heart?"

"I like Judith. But she has always been far away from me—I mean in mind. It doesn't seem as though *I* could influence her. She is not my cousin. She is only a distant connection on my mother's side. I feel for her. I wanted to have her staying here a good deal, only Tom doesn't care about her. I feel for every girl who has money, and whom people want to marry, when I think of how they persecuted me! There was an Italian count who followed me everywhere. He always took his seat opposite me at the *table d'hôte*, and when there happened to be an epergne between us, had it removed. He pestered me. He pestered my mother. I am sure we were quite grateful to Tom for delivering me. You see Judith might have done really badly. It might have been an Italian count. There is nothing against Esmé Colquhoun."

"There is everything!" exclaimed Graysett, with emphasis.

"What do you know?" asked Mrs. Rainshaw, looking at him in an alarmed manner. "Has he murdered any one—out of a book? *That's* not a punishable crime. Has he got another wife? What do you mean? If you know anything you ought to tell her plainly. But it would be of no use. Have you any reason for speaking so strongly?"

Graysett hesitated. "He has not murdered any one that I am aware of. I daresay that his moral character is quite as unimpeachable as that of any other man of the world. If I were to tell you the true reason for my prejudice against him, you would laugh at me for being superstitious. I don't mean to tell you—there would be no use in it. I know less of Esmé Colquhoun than you do, but I have the most intense conviction—it amounts to a certainty—that his fascination for this poor girl is evil and unnatural, and that if he marries her, there will be a terrible fatality."

Mrs. Rainshaw uttered a little cry. "I wish you would tell me what you mean. Since you don't *know* anything, there does not seem much sense in jumping to such dreadful conclusions. Are you one of these occult people, Major Graysett? I don't go in for that sort of thing. I don't like it. I think we have had enough of it here. Has your idea anything to do with your dream? Won't you speak to Judith yourself? I think she would listen to you."

"Yes, I will speak to her."

"She is going away to-morrow—she and Mr. Colquhoun, and Mrs. Borlase. I don't know how you will make an opportunity."

"I am coming down to-night," said Graysett, with determination. "You will be kind to me, and will let me sit quietly in a corner of the drawing-room, and you will help me all you can— will you not?"

"Of course I will;" and with the frankness of

a child she stretched out her hand and laid it upon the pillow beside him. "I am so sorry for you. You'll forget about it—won't you? It couldn't have gone so very far—in three days."

"We won't talk about that, Mrs. Rainshaw," he said; "though I am grateful to you for your sympathy. It is of her that I am thinking, not of myself. You'll do me the favour, I am sure, not to allude to that again, as far as I am concerned. Now please be still kind, and tell me how it came about. A fortnight does not seem long for everything to be settled in, though perhaps I ought not to say so."

"Oh, it has been going on much longer—with her at least," replied Mrs. Rainshaw. "She told me, in her odd, mysterious way, that the first time she ever spoke to him she knew he was the only man in the world who could make her feel. I don't think, however, even granting that he is in love with her now, that he ever thought of marrying her till they met at Holmborough. It's a very clever achievement. Judith is not a girl to fall in love readily; and she is quite aware of her value. He is rather played out as a celebrity. People are getting tired of him, and the papers have been writing him down. It was quite necessary that he should take a new departure of some sort—cut his hair, grow a beard, or marry Sarah Bernhardt. Major Graysett, did you ever hear of any one being mesmerized into love?"

"Did he mesmerize her?" asked Graysett faintly.

"Something like it. I will tell you. We were
in the Long Gallery one afternoon. I think it
was the day after your accident. Judith had been
playing to us. We were all in rather low spirits,
and, by way of making us more cheerful, Lady
Romer started a conversation upon occult subjects,
and told us the most ghastly story of a vampire
that you ever heard. I hope you won't hear it—
at any rate till you are stronger—and mind, if you
do, that you don't go to sleep on it. Then Esmé
Colquhoun struck in. His story was in a more
poetic strain, but was quite as creepy. He described a moral vampire ; a human being with the
power of absorbing into his own system all the
vitality and will-force of any one peculiarly susceptible to magnetic influence, till the poor creature
lost all individuality, and became a mere shell,
galvanized into obedience by the will of its de-
stroyer. Isn't it a horrible notion? I dream of
it ; and a weird impression has taken hold of me
that Esmé Colquhoun is just such a monster, and
that he has selected Judith for his victim. Haven't
you ever remarked what strength of will he has?
You can't look at him without feeling it. I have
heard Christine Borlase say that he might do
anything if only he had tenacity of purpose. But
that is the way with poets. They are all flesh
and inspiration, and no bone or muscle—in a
figurative sense, you understand. Esmé went on
to tell us that he had been studying the philosophy
of some queer sect in America, who did all kinds
of wonders, and taught him how to concentrate

and exercise what he calls his 'odic force'—
whatever that may mean. He gave us a lecture
on the subject, using a great many long words
which I can't profess to understand or repeat : but
the gist of it all was, that WILL, when concentrated
and directed, is an actual force—a motive power
—isn't that the expression ? like steam, or electricity, only vastly superior to both, a sort of Vril
—you have read ' The Coming Race,' I suppose—
and that you may remove mountains with it,
animate matter, or perform any other miracle you
might like to imagine. It is simply a question of
having enough of it. . . . . So some one suggested
that the experiment should be tried at once ; and
as there was no professional medium present, and
as we could not, at this elementary stage of
development, expect to make the solid oak cut
capers, it was proposed that Esmé should try and
put some life into the nearest approach to inani-
mate matter among us—Judith in one of her
dreams. Well, Major Graysett, I hope that I shall
never assist at such an uncanny sort of exhibition
again. He made no passes—only looked at her
intently. She did not drop down or go to sleep,
as I have seen people do when mesmerized, but
stood quite still and rigid, with eyes wide open
like a somnambulist, answering all the questions
he asked her quite mechanically. They were
.simple test questions about different things we had
agreed to think of ; and every time her reply was
perfectly correct. Afterwards he bandaged her
eyes ; and she followed him about as though he

had been a magnet, doing everything which he willed. I believe that she would have thrown herself from the window if he had desired it. He made her sit down to a table, put a pencil in her hand, and bade her write. The pencil moved like wildfire, and in a few minutes he showed us a little poem—an Oriental love-song full of imagery and passion, not at all like anything I have read, and certainly not in Judith's style. . . . . But a very curious thing happened. While she was in this state of trance, he led her to Christine Borlase and joined their hands, he holding her left hand and Judith's right, so as to form a circle. Judith awoke with a shriek, and then dropped down right away. It was a long time before we could bring her to her senses."

"What did she say? What explanation did she give?" asked Graysett eagerly. He had been hanging upon every word Mrs. Rainshaw uttered with the most intense interest.

"She was as white as death, and at first did not seem able to speak coherently. She seemed utterly bewildered. Then she looked at Esmé and said rather wildly, 'What have you done to me? I have been in pain. There have been two creatures in me. They hurt each other,' or something to that effect; it sounded great nonsense. She kept looking round with the strangest expression in her eyes. Have you ever taken chloroform?"

"Yes."

"When I asked her afterwards how she had

felt before going off, she said the sensation was like that, and would say no more, except that she had been quite unconscious all the time, till a sharp sudden pain awoke her."

"But Colquhoun?"

"He made a very pretty apology, declaring that he would die rather than injure her, and begging her to remember that she had given him full permission to try his power upon her in any way that he pleased. He said that he had never been so completely successful, and that he had not realized its extent. He said, too, that the experiment had been a revelation to him of natural laws, which he had suspected but had never been able to bring into operation. I can't remember all he told us; it was most extraordinary. He looked intensely excited. I had never seen his eyes quite unclosed before. You don't know what curious eyes they are. There's a little ring of light round the pupil and they glow like fire. I began to feel frightened. I begged him to bottle up his 'odic force,' at all events while he remained in this house, or, if he must exercise it, to do so on chairs and tables. I call it most uncomfortable. It's as bad as dynamite—if at any moment you can be reduced to a state of spiritual nothingness in that way. Tom was very angry with me when I told him all that had happened. He said I should have stopped it. How could *I* stop it? 'Odic force' isn't to be stopped once it's set going. It is too serious a thing to tamper with. I took Judith

away and put her to bed. That seemed the most
sensible thing I could do. She went from one
shivering fit into another: and so I sent for the
doctor. He said that she had had a shock to the
nervous system, and gave her some morphia.
She slept all night and all through the next day.
Esmé Colquhoun was deeply distressed. He
wanted us to telegraph to London for Maudsley
or some other great brain doctor. Tom was still
more angry, and declared that he wouldn't have
his house turned into a lunatic asylum. I had
to remind him that it was my house, and that he
was unreasonable. Then Judith awoke and
seemed all right again. At any rate, she came
downstairs, and everything went on as usual,
except that we did not try any more of those
games, and agreed that, on the whole, it was
better to drop the subject—especially as a new
set of people had just arrived. Oh, Major
Graysett, you must see them! They'll amuse
you ; they are quite out of the common ; they
are Australians. He was something in one of
the governments out there, and used to drive
about with gold nuggets on his harness. Just
think! But she has found out that sort of thing
is not in good taste. She is very pretty, and
would like to be started as a professional beauty,
but doesn't know how to set about it. I think
the Admiral might do it for her. They are looking round to see what they had best take back to
Australia in the shape of European ideas, and
they've come to the conclusion that a little

æstheticism would counteract the utilitarian tendencies out there. Imagine their delight at finding themselves in the same house with Esmé
Colquhoun! In the interests of civilization I had
to ask him to stay on ; and so for the last ten days
they have been drinking in wisdom and art"

The nurse entered with some broth and
medicine, and gently intimated that her patient
might be getting wearied by this brilliant chatter.
Mrs. Rainshaw rose full of self-reproach when
her attention was directed to Graysett's wan
face.

"No, no!" he exclaimed; "your soft voice
doesn't tire me. You babble on like a brook;
it's pleasant to listen to. But it is not these
Australians who interest me, though I daresay
they are very amusing."

"Ah!" she cried naïvely; "another polite
reminder that I am in the habit of making excur-
sions from my subject. I know that I am rather
difficult to follow ; but life is quite as mixed as
my talk. Poor Judith! I don't know why I pity
her, for she assures me that she is happy. She
has been a great deal with Esmé Colquhoun. I
must say that he has behaved beautifully to her
before people——with a kind of chivalrous deference
which one can't help admiring. I don't know
what they talk about when they are alone. If he
finds her as silent and preoccupied as she appears
to be in general company, he has not had a lively
time ; but I don't suppose that is likely. She has
not been living in the world at all. She has

no thoughts except for him. I don't want you to fancy that she has allowed this to be too apparent. Judith could never, under any circumstances, be undignified. I think it is what I have got into my imagination—that he is a kind of vampire, and has absorbed her being into his own."

"When was it finally settled?" inquired Graysett.

"Yesterday, I fancy. She came to me not long ago with the news. She spoke of you, and begged me to tell you the story, if I could do so naturally and without exciting you. They are to be married before the spring—oh! I know what you are going to urge ; but, indeed, it is of no use. If any one has influence it is yourself. She is a strange girl—so cold! It seems impossible to touch her except through her own sensations. I never knew her concerned about any one's illness before? but she really seemed full of consideration for you."

"I have no chance of seeing her unless I go down this evening ?"

"She leaves us early to-morrow. Don't run any risks, Major Graysett, I beseech you. I will bring her to you."

He shook his head. "I want to judge for myself how things are between them. I'll go down this evening, Mrs. Rainshaw. I shall feel stronger after resting a while ; and you'll excuse me from appearing at dinner, and won't coddle me too much afterwards,"

"Everything shall be as you choose. I wish that I could really do something to help you," she said with simple kindliness. "I am grieved that all this should have come upon you under our roof. We have done very badly by you."

CHAPTER XIV.

GRAYSETT was sustained by the strength born of
excitement and resolve.

When the ladies re-entered the drawing-room
after dinner he was there, looking rather like the
ghost of himself, but insisting upon not being
treated as an invalid.

Mrs. Rainshaw displayed considerable tact in
so arranging her guests that he was spared intro-
ductions to new people, and was not bored by the
congratulations and ministrations of those he
knew. She carried off the strangers, among
whom were the pretty Australian and some other
later arrivals, to the end of the long drawing-room,
and left Major Graysett surrounded by the old set
—Lady Romer, Miss Geneste, &c.—which was
presently joined by Judith Fountain and Mrs.
Borlase, who entered together somewhat behind
the rest.

Judith had evidently not expected to see him.
A sudden flush overspread her pale face, mounting
to her brow and dying away as quickly as it had
come. His heart leaped as he beheld this sign of
embarrassment, and he had hardly voice to return
Mrs. Borlase's greeting. The artist was the first
of the two to take his hand and murmur some

words of sympathy. Judith hung back. But in a minute she too approached him, and said in a mechanical voice, as though she were repeating a a lesson she had learned—

"I am very glad that you are better. I have asked for you every day. I hope that you always got my message."

He thanked her, saying that his chief reason for making an appearance that evening was that he might be able to bid her good-bye, as he had heard that she was leaving Leesholm the next day.

" Yes," she answered, with another quick flush, "I am going to London to-morrow. I'm glad you came down this evening."

She moved away. He fancied that she feared he would ask her some difficult question. She turned upon him a pathetic glance, and seated herself at some little distance from him. He determined to bide his time.

He was not sure at first whether she had indeed changed, or whether his imagination, quickened by what he had heard, discerned in her face signs of a new and intense consciousness. He thought of the hackneyed simile of Galatea awakening to life. There was a look in her eyes which he felt might have been in the eyes of Galatea. After he had watched her for a little while, he decided that she had greatly changed.

She seemed more human. Following her own fantastic suggestion, he noted how the influence had worked. She was less cold, less self-absorbed.

Her sudden blushes followed by transparent paleness, the tremor of her lips, a shy hesitation in her manner, a startled expression, neither alarm, wonder, nor dawning passion, yet blending all three, a sort of expectancy in her gaze—all these were to him deeply significant. If she were in a dream, it was not a wholly untroubled one. She did not look happy. She was no longer a fearless investigator of abstract problems, whom no emotion could seize with any strong hold, and who was serene, cynical, or simply apathetic as outward circumstances dictated. Life had become momentous to her. A chord had been struck in her being which must vibrate for evermore.

Such fancies, and many others, grim, bizarre, dreary, passed through his mind while he watched her. Then, as the sound of voices in the hall announced that the gentlemen had left the dining-room, for an instant her face seemed to grow into the likeness of that tragic, despairing face of his vision, and the same sensation of clammy horror overcame him and renewed his superstitious terrors.

She was leaning with her elbow upon a table, one thin little hand shading her brow. He saw the hand drop and clutch the other nervously as the door opened. There came into her eyes a perplexed, rapt look as though she had received an invisible summons. She smiled when Esmé Colquhoun approached her, a smile which had in it more of pathos than of joy. Drawing a deep breath, she sank back in her chair with face upturned, and a gesture, very timid, scarcely observable, but which seemed to imply the most utter self-surrender.

Graysett sighed heavily from the depths of the large arm-chair in which he had placed himself. The sigh was echoed close to him, in a weary, hopeless, despondent sound, rising as it were involuntarily from the heart of her who breathed it. So absorbed had he been in his reflections that he was hardly conscious of the proximity of another person. People had drifted, perhaps with kindly intention, to the farther end of the room, and it had appeared to him that he was alone. Turning slightly, he saw Christine Borlase sitting not far from his chair. Her eyes were fixed upon Judith and Esmé. She was apparently as deeply interested in the two as he himself. He had received an impression at the ball, when he had intercepted her glance in their direction, that there was something tragic in her attitude towards them ; and the impression was strengthened at this moment. He became convinced that she also loved Colquhoun ; and he wondered vaguely that she had given him up so readily. He forgot for a second that she was a married woman. In her case the fact was not self-evident. When he realized the position, suggestions occurred to him not reconcilable with the frank nobility of Christine's countenance. For an instant only her manner might mislead, her face never. She was perhaps an unhappy, a misguided, an embittered woman, but under no circumstances, he felt sure, could she be an actively disloyal one.

Becoming aware of his scrutiny, she moved and was about to address him ; but just then, Mrs. Rainshaw, unquiet till Graysett had found the opportunity he sought, fluttered towards them. In her wake followed the Admiral, a lean, atrabilious, un-sailorlike gentleman, with, nevertheless, a decided air of fashion and distinction, and who had requested an introduction to Mrs. Borlase, and was incidentally made known to Major Graysett also. The four moved towards the fireplace, where had gathered the larger circle, of which Esmé Colquhoun was now the centre.

He stood in front of the mantelpiece, towering above all the others, his head thrown back, his hair gleaming in the shaded light of a lamp placed upon the velvet-draped board, while he stirred his coffee and added his voice to a discussion of the tendencies of modern fiction, and the legitimacy, from the artistic point of view, of turning the story-book into a pathological dissecting-room. The question had arisen *à propos* of a new novel which had grated upon the moral susceptibilities of the critics, and which Mrs. Bearfield, the pretty Australian, was doubtful whether to condemn or admire. She had, so far, compromised matters by elevating and lowering her fan, and exclaiming, "Oh, fie !" at the mention of the book, and was now gazing up at Colquhoun in an attitude that displayed the liberal contours of a remarkably white bust. She was ready to adopt his opinion

as soon as he should be disposed to declare it
explicitly, and was certainly sufficiently handsome
and quite daring enough in her dress to deserve
his attention.

"Oh, she'll never do; she'll never do," murmured the Admiral in the tone of a connoisseur
to whom has been submitted an article of *bric-à-
brac* which is palpably an imitation. "She hasn't
the courage of her ignorance. If she would but
be natural, and perhaps talk a little colonial slang,
she might succeed; but that's where they all make
the mistake. It's only the American who is clever
enough to grasp the situation. This one hadn't
sense enough to come out in the white frock and
straw hat she used to wear in her garden at Gee-
long, and pose as the innocent barbarian. With
that rose-leaf complexion she might have carried
everything before her. But she tries to be modern
and civilized, and European, and is as much out
of place as Mrs. John Wood would be in refined
tragedy. That pink satin dress with the black
tarantulas sprawling over it gives me the creeps.
She over-dresses. It's the way with the Australians; they have not learned yet how to put their
clothes on. . . . . Mrs. Rainshaw, we don't require
Esmé Colquhoun to tell us that the age is corrupt.
Surely we can see that for ourselves."

Colquhoun was rolling forth his sonorous sentences. He had taken up the cudgels on behalf
of the writer in question, and was defending the
school of Gautier and Baudelaire, with which he
identified himself

"What," he was saying, "is our mission—we writers—but to distil the essence of the Age? The critics tells us that we are complex, that we are psychological, that we are corrupt, that we are anatomists of diseased minds. We reply: The Age is complex; the Age is corrupt; and the Society we depict is the outcome of influences which have been gathering through centuries of advancing civilization. The men and women of the world have been refined from field flowers to exotics; the simple conditions of Nature are not for them. The social atmosphere must be adapted to their organizations, as we regulate the air of our hothouses. There is no room for Nature in London. She is too glaring, too crude, and London is essentially the pulse of civilization. Every man and woman I meet is a psychological problem. How has the Spirit of the Time influenced him or her? How will he or she affect me? You are morbid and introspective, say the critics. I grant it. Life is morbid. The reign of healthy melodrama is over : the reign of analysis has commenced. We make dramas of our sensations, not of our actions. Emotion has become a fine art which the artist must practise if he aim at fidelity to his creed. Life is for him a many-sided prism, in every facet of which he sees the reflection of a different phase of his own being. He lives, to feel. He feels, to reproduce; and when he has reproduced, he closes the door upon his experience. The past is shut out, and the world is the richer. He has been dowered by the gods with forgetfulness. He moves on—to receive again, and again to give forth."

Colquhoun poured into his coffee the tiny glass of cognac, which had been standing at his elbow, and sipped it thoughtfully. There was something both fascinating and repellent in his intense egotism and his shallow heartlessness. As he put down the cup, his eyes darting across the room met those of Christine Borlase, who looked at him full.

"You remind me," said she, "of that story of Talma, who when he listened to the death-shriek of the being he had loved best, could only ejaculate, 'Mon Dieu, quel cri pour le théâtre!'"

"Ah!" said Colquhoun, "you underrate the sincerity of the artist. He has two souls, that which feels and that which observes ; consequently two processes are simultaneously at work within him—the emotional and the analytical. He is an egotist—admitted. But if he were not a sublime egotist, he could not be a sublime artist."

Mrs. Bearfield, who looked puzzled and some-what dissatisfied, broke in, in so artless a manner, that the Admiral softly clapped his hands—

"I'm afraid then that we are quite out of it in Australia, Mr. Colquhoun, and that you'll never find the necessary artistic conditions among us. We are all Nature. We are dreadfully glaring. I don't see how we're to help it."

"Ah, do you know," said Colquhoun, smiling upon her with languid magnanimity, "to me there are but two terms, civilization and barbarism?

Conventionalism is the worst form of barbarism. You will strike your own keynote, and evolve harmonies in sympathy with your dazzling noonday. I am a poet of night—the night of city and *salon*—luxuriously illuminated, full of passionate sweetness, suffused with the voluptuous odour of perfumes. But for you, I am mute—an Australian Walt Whitman may perhaps lift you to a higher level than mine. At least you will not have to contend against the debasing influence of the Mediævalists—the influence I am fighting. I confess that Nature is not my inspiration. Only once has simplicity seemed to me a thing beautiful in itself; that was when I went to see the greatest American poet. I mounted to the top of a high house. The room was little more than a garret; the windows were wide open ; the place was bathed in sunlight; the walls were bare ; there was a chair ; there was a great earthen vessel full of clear water ; there was a table, and on the table writing materials, and three great books, Homer, Shakespeare and Dante ; and I said when I beheld the poet, ' I am in the presence of a greater man than myself.' "

" Insufferable conceit !" murmured the Admiral. " At least it would be insufferable, if it were not for its simplicity."

Colquhoun had quitted his position and approached his hostess.

" Are we not to have any music this evening, Mrs. Rainshaw ?"

" I think all that sounded very improper," said she ; " the first part at least—the end was lovely and quite bracing. Yes, Mrs. Borlase will sing for us ;" and the artist was borne off to the piano.

She sang a little French song, tender and sparkling, full of coquetry, yet with an undertone of sadness resembling the tears that laughter hides. The singer urges her undeclared lover to wed a certain rich woman ; setting forth all the cogent reasons for the step, playfully ignoring his affection, yet all the time suggesting the possibility of its return on her part. At the end of each verse the refrain runs with melancholy archness, and the faintest little shrug and raising of the eyebrows :

> Mais—ça ne me fait rien,
> C'est tout pour votre bien ;

while at the last stanza, there is a most pathetic change to the familiar *tu* and *toi*.

> Mais—ça ne me fait rien,
> C'est tout pour *ton* bien.

CHAPTER XV.

In the slight confusion which followed the song Major Graysett found an opportunity to accost Judith unheard.

" Come to the recess yonder," he said, in tones half imploring, half imperative. " I beseech you to let me say a few words to you alone. I may not be able to speak to you again, since you are leaving to-morrow."

She rose without question, and they went together to that alcove where they had conversed upon a former occasion. She seated herself upon one of the divans partly screened from observation by a tall and bushy palm, but started up again when she perceived his extreme paleness. He felt weak and faint from standing, and sank into a chair by her side, leaning back against the cushions, and at first almost unable to speak.

" Oh, you are ill !" she exclaimed. " You ought not to be here. May I not get you something—water—or wine—or call some one to you ? it would be better if you did not try to speak to me to-night."

" I must speak. No, don't leave me. I am quite well—quite well enough. I stood a little too long—that is all."

She sat down again with her hands folded before her.

"You know," he began, "all that has been in my mind since the first evening I met you. I felt that it was my mission to try and save you from an influence which I had been warned would work you evil. Think what torture it has been to me to lie like a log, while you were exposed to the deadliest peril. Oh, don't think that I care about myself! It isn't so— it is all for you. My letter must have told you that."

"I thank you for your letter," she said simply. "I did not know how to answer it. I am afraid I could not feel as you wished or expected. What was it you expected?"

"I need not explain myself," he answered, with a little bitterness. "The letter was too late; it did not touch you."

"You could have done nothing," she said abruptly, after a brief pause.

"Perhaps not. At least, I might have watched you; and indirectly might have tried to shield you. Had I been present, that scene in the Long Gallery would not have taken place."

"Ah!" She drew a long breath. "You know about that. I did not know how much Mrs. Rainshaw had told you. I wanted her to tell you everything, but I did not like to ask her outright. It was very strange. Other people have made passes over me, and have failed. He did nothing; he only looked at me."

"It was what you had imagined?—the experience?"

"No. I used to think that if I could be put into a mesmeric trance a new world would be opened to me, and that I should become clairvoyant. This was so I presume; but I seemed to see nothing. I was not conscious of any revelation." She stopped and asked, "Did Mrs. Rainshaw tell you about the writing? Do you suppose that his brain was working through me?"

"I suppose that would be the scientific explanation, if the term can be used in connection with such phenomena."

"It was not the least in his style; it was like nothing I could have imagined. It was very curious. Spiritualists would declare that it was inspired by some dead person : but that theory is to me absolutely abhorrent. It is vulgar; it is degrading. I can believe in unknown forces ; I can believe in occult laws ; but I can't believe that wandering souls are at our beck and call, or we at theirs. . . . I knew nothing," she went on rather brokenly. "There was at first a dreamy feeling of far-awayness, and lightness—a sort of ecstasy. I can't describe it ; and then the shock and intense pain of becoming myself again. I have never felt any pain like it. Do they not say in the Bible that a certain man was rent sore when the dumb spirit departed out of him ?"

"It was an evil spirit, and this man's influence over you is evil. Has not such an experience been sufficient to make you shrink with horror from submitting yourself to it ?"

"I don't know," she replied dreamily. "It is not a matter of choice."

"Do you mean that you are in a state of bondage," cried Graysett, "and that you cannot free yourself?"

"I might struggle—but I don't think that it would be of any use," said Judith. "I don't know why I should struggle!"

"Because," he said sternly, "it is degrading to a pure woman to be in the power of a bad man."

"You must not speak against him," she said simply. "I love him. I am going to marry him."

"And I," he exclaimed, "do *I* not love you?"

"Ah!" she cried, and her accent smote him like a knife, it was so nearly joyous. "It is too late for that : it was always too late. You were not magnetic enough. You remember what I told you? It needed some one not like you. He has what you wanted. He has made me feel."

"He has done more," said Graysett bitterly; "he has made you cruel."

"I am very sorry for you," she said after a moment's pause, speaking slowly. "I did not mean to hurt you. I was ready to yield myself to the power if you had possessed it, but that was not so. You know what I said—that some day there would come one who should fill me with life. He has come. I could not wish for more than to fulfil the law of my being."

"Are you not afraid?"

She shook her head.

"It is stronger than fear. Do not think that I have not thought of your warning. At first it found an echo here"—she touched her breast; "but that's gone. And the faculty I had of seeing what is false and artificial in him is gone too. He has absorbed me into himself."

"That can hardly be an enviable fate, if the nature with which you identify your own be base."

"Then I am base. I do not say that my fate is enviable. I do not think of it in that light. My tendencies and my affinities are my fate. Flame will to flame, and water to water. If his soul be bad and impure ; then mine is so also, or it would not be attracted towards him. Why do you speak ill of him, and insinuate bad things?" she added almost fiercely. "You know nothing to his discredit."

"I know nothing. But you believe in intuition. I have the most terrible forebodings. "Are you certain that he loves you ?"

"Oh, if he does not," she exclaimed, "I don't wish to know it. It would kill me."

"Judith," said Graysett gravely, "shall I tell you what it is that I fear for you ?"

She bowed her head and listened without speaking, though every now and then he waited, as if expecting some comment upon his words.

"I have been thinking deeply about you and him—about all these things—during my illness, more especially the last day or two. I can't reason about my intuitions, which may or may not be flashes from a higher intelligence. . . . .I don't believe that there are spirits which can, at the instigation of a human being, enter in and take possession of our souls. But I think, as you do, that a magnetic atmosphere emanates from all of us, and that some have a stronger power of attraction or repulsion than others. Is it not so?"

"Yes. I can tell when I enter a room whether the magnetism of the people who live in it is congenial to me, or the reverse."

"It is this force which heals many diseases, and may give health and vigour to the weak. But there are persons whose magnetism might be noxious to subjects of a peculiar mental bias: while their fascination would be as that of the serpent over the helpless bird."

She uttered a little cry and started to her feet.

"If there were such a thing as moral poison, it might, by frequent contact with the infected person, be conveyed to one who was pure. There is this terrible possibility, but I do not fear it for you."

"This is wrong! This is wicked!" she cried; "you have no right to say such things—no reason."

"I have no reason, I admit; and I have no

right, none—I know that—except my deep, pure love for you. And do you know how deep, how pure it is? Do you know how strong is my conviction? I would save you from Esmé Colquhoun at the price of never seeing you more."

She sat down again, and gazed at him with wide, startled eyes.

"If you do not fear that of which you speak, what is it that you fear?"

"You have a most sensitive and delicate organization. You are, I am certain, peculiarly susceptible to magnetic influences. Your body is frail. Your nerves are highly strung. Our mental and physical systems are so closely united, that a shock to the one may completely disturb the balance of the other. I think that you received such a shock when you placed yourself under the power of Mr. Colquhoun's magnetism; and that if he continues to exercise it, your vital force may be slowly sapped, your reason perhaps impaired."

"My reason impaired!" she repeated in so startled a tone, that he, remembering suddenly what Rainshaw had told him of her family history, regretted bitterly the words he had used, and felt a pang, so keen, that for a moment he was unnerved. She leaned forward and put her hand to her forehead, with her brows puckered, as though he had aroused some painful, slumbering consciousness. She seemed to be thinking deeply. At last she sighed in the half-resigned, half-relieved manner of one who recognizes the inevitable. Then she rose again as if wishing to terminate the interview, and laughed, in that gentle light way which was a fashion with her, and which seemed at once to hide and to reveal so much.

"Indeed, Major Graysett, you set a pleasant prospect before me—death or madness, with the alternative of separating myself from the man I love. You have been very eloquent. Ah, you have developed your belief in the occult very much since the first night we talked. You have advanced even further than I. All these terrible predictions are founded upon—an intuition! Intuition is a great and wonderful faculty; it was I who laid stress upon that; but, to avoid argument and to spare us both needless agitation, I am begging the question and taking refuge in the materialist camp—in this case, I prefer reason."

Her words seemed a dismissal. Standing close to her, he poured forth a torrent of passionate, incoherent entreaty. She listened in silence. When he paused, she said, with a break in her voice—

"Thank you; thank you; you are good and sincere. I feel sure of that; I would trust you above all men. I wish that it could have been otherwise, and that I had not hurt you so much. Forgive me. I must obey what is so strong in me. You cannot hold me back; nothing can do that. Do not, I beg of you, try to see me again till after my marriage—till I bid you come to me. Your magnetism," and she smiled softly, "has for

me the colder, purer attraction of friendship. I
may need it some day, and I promise you that, if
that day comes, I will send for you. Till then—
good-bye!"

She stretched out her hand to him, and let it
linger in his clasp.

"What is your name?" she asked suddenly.

"Edward," he replied mechanically.

"Good-bye, Edward—my friend! I will bid
you come when I need you. If you wish to do
me good, will that I may have peaceful nights,
and that my soul may be once more bathed and
warmed in that heavenly sea I told you of. I
cannot reach it now."

There was something inexpressibly mournful in
her manner of pronouncing the last words ; her
eyes were large and wet with tears. A sort of
triumph thrilled him. He also had made her
feel. Oh, for the " might have been! " She turned
away. He watched her glide across the room,
and saw Colquhoun advance and place himself by
her side.

A strange dizziness overpowered him. The
sound of voices and music, the lights, the fashion-
ably dressed figures, the room in its homely
luxuriousness, struck upon his senses with mocking
unreality. He could scarcely determine whether
the scene, the conversation with Judith, the striking form of Colquhoun, the torture of his mystic
previsions, were not all a dream. Was there,
then, side by side with the objective world, one of
spirit and idea—the causes there, becoming the

effects here?   Had he stepped upon the threshold and from thence caught shadowy glimpses of the operations of these causes? His very love for Judith—so spiritual, so swift and mysterious— seemed to have had its origin in those unknown regions.   The common things of life appeared to him, at such a moment as this, but empty shells, and those things which were hidden and tran- scendental seemed to him the actualities of exist- ence.   In this confusion of his being, due perhaps to sickness or to latent delirium, to reason was an impossibility.   He was like a man possessed by a monomania, and with no guiding light but the lurid flashes of a disordered imagination.

CHAPTER XVI.

As soon as he had sufficiently recovered from his illness to travel, Graysett left Leesholm, and by the advice of a London physician spent the spring months on the Riviera.

The fever and his mental suffering, disproportionate though this seemed to the short-lived hopes of which the disappointment had caused it, left traces which could never be obliterated. A great change had come over him. He was not the same man who had landed in England a few weeks before. His whole organization had received a shock. His nerves were shattered ; his views of life utterly depressed. A crowd of morbid symptoms beset him, and they in their turn reacted upon his physical frame. He shunned society, and shrank from sport and the pursuits in which he had once delighted. His thoughts glided in fantastic circles, and, forsaking rational subjects, dwelt upon the mysterious, the horrible ; while all the while he was conscious of a certain disturbance of his intellectual balance, and would try to turn his mind into a healthy channel, only to wander back into the former groove. At these times, he would begin to entertain vague fears as to his sanity, and to speculate upon the possible result

to an excitable brain of a long residence in a
tropical climate, and of the blood-poisoning inci-
dent to malarious fevers. A celebrated nerve
doctor whom he consulted took this view of his
case, and glibly mapped out his summer, pre-
scribing Gastein and the Engadine, cheerful
companionship, a dietary regimen, and wholesome
concrete interests.

But while hinting at abnormal fancies and at
his bondage to one persistently recurring idea,
Graysett had found it impossible to confide to a
physician the curious psychological experience he
had undergone, or to describe accurately his mental
condition and the terrible fears which preyed upon
him. During night and day he was perpetually
haunted by his mystic vision of Judith and Colquhoun which, more vivid than the most realistic
painting, thrust itself between him and the objects
towards which his eyes were bent. The possession was at one time so complete that, with a
reactionary impulse, he tried to account for it
materially and to combat it by the force of will.
In a measure he succeeded. Change of scene and
the gradual restoration of his strength lightened
the burden ; yet though reason might compel the
phantom to retreat into the background, he knew
that it was always close to him, and that in hours
of darkness or depression it invariably returned to
his side.

The Rainshaws did not join him on the Riviera,
as had been at one time suggested, but they kept
him posted in all English news which they

imagined would be of interest to him. Mrs. Rainshaw gave him an elaborate description of the wedding of Judith and Colquhoun, which took place two months after the announcement of the engagement, hurried on with diplomatic though hardly seemly haste. It would, however, have been difficult for him, even had he wished, to escape the buzz of comment which preceded and followed the event. The newspapers aired it freely, and the British and American communities of Cannes and Nice seemed to regard it as a sort of apotheosis of the poet, who, whatever his claims to substantial fame, had certainly succeeded as an unmarried Apostle of the Beautiful in creating a sensation. His admirers prophesied that under purer and more favourable conditions of development his genius would soar to heights it had never yet attained. His detractors considered it advisable to commend the policy of a man who at the critical time of his career had been clever enough to secure the affection of a beautiful woman and the command of half a million of money. Exaggerated reports were circulated about Judith's infatuation—if indeed it could be exaggerated— and of the magnificent humility with which Esmé announced his determination of living up to the ideal standard she had framed for him, and in accordance with his own sublimest conceptions of moral beauty. An article of his in one of the magazines, in which he exhaustively analyzed concentrated love as opposed to diffused love, was credited with a personal application ; and a tiny volume of sonnets published at this time, glorifying spiritual passion and allegorizing wedlock in the most pure and elevated phrases, was supposed to have been inspired by his rapturous yearnings after sweet domestic life. It was a peculiarity of Esmé's chameleon-like nature that, given a dramatic situation, he could regulate at will the quality and the intensity of his emotions. Judith's ethereal beauty and absolute dependence upon his will, as well as a certain scientific pleasure which he found in awakening in her new sensations and in watching their effect, were sufficient to create a fervid impulse which exhausted itself in song. He threw off the bundle of leaflets at white heat, in the first days of their engagement ; it was dedicated to her, beautifully bound in white vellum, and might be seen in most fashionable drawing-rooms, where it did much towards creating for him new sympathies. It was a fresh departure. It seemed that he had carried his philosophy of the Beautiful from the objective to the subjective field, and was demonstrating the soul of æstheticism, as distinguished from its material manifestation in the shape of furniture and hangings, peculiar modes of hairdressing, velvet suits, knee-breeches, yellow brocade and peacock's feathers.

This was the season of private views in studios, artistic parties, and social excitements of the minor kind. The great world was out of London and politicians were resting. The journals, from mere dearth of matter, revived an old theme with a new blare of trumpets. People were interested in reading of the wonderful and artistic fabrics, out of which the poet was designing costumes for his bride's trousseau ; and the suggestions that Judith was "occult," that Esmé, by the exercise of will-force, was possessed of a mysterious power of fascination, set the imaginations of a great many emotional wonder-seekers at work. These were delighted to scent a vague connection between the school of æstheticism and that of a tiny community of esoteric philosophers, just then the centre of one sphere of spiritual activity in London, and who in their turn professed to reconcile all existing schools, and to bridge over the gulf between protoplasm and disembodied spirit.

Esmé encouraged the impression by mysterious references to hidden agencies. So also did Lady Romer and her fellow-disciples in supernatural investigation, whose *répertoire* of facts, theories and phrases was vast enough to embrace, impartially, the Esoteric Doctrine of Christianity, the revelations of the Mahatmas of Thibet, the disintegration and reintegration of matter, the phenomena of spiritualism, the flight of astral bodies, psychological telegraphy, the miracles of Lourdes, the feats of Mr. Irving Bishop, Platonic affinities, "occult diet ;" and so on indefinitely. A new dispensation, in short, heralded, as of old, by prophets who dreamed dreams and saw visions.

The critics sneered, the wits made epigrams, the scientists reflected caustically upon the gullibility of mankind, the social moralists emptied phials of dignified contempt, but the sensationalists were in the ascendant, and Esmé Colquhoun gathering all currents, as it were, into himself, and gaining strength from each, was, by force of an irrepressible individuality, more than ever—Esmé Colquhoun.

Immediately after the marriage, he sailed with his bride for America. Reports of their brilliant reception dribbled through the papers, and paragraphs dilating upon Judith's beauty and ethereality, upon her wealth, and upon the devotion of the young pair to each other, with details of their dress, their personal habits and private life generally, were now and then copied into " Galignani," or some English society journal. Mrs. Rainshaw when at the end of the summer she met Major Graysett in the Engadine, called his attention to one of these paragraphs.

" I am afraid that one ought not to place much reliance upon such reports," she said ; " but I can't help feeling some satisfaction when I read them. It looks, at all events, as though Judith had got what she wanted ; or that, if he can't give it to her, she has not yet found out the fact."

Another event, which occurred about the time of Judith's marriage to Colquhoun, made an impression upon Graysett, and caused him often to wonder whether, if it had happened two months sooner, the union would have taken place. This was the sudden death of Mr. Borlase. Christine

was telegraphed for the very day before that fixed
for the wedding. She set off at once for the
foreign town where her husband was consul, and
arrived in time to see him expire.

She was now free. Too frank and too completely a Bohemian to affect a grief she did not
feel, the fact made no radical difference in her
mode of life. She devoted herself with even
greater ardour to her work, and after the first six
months of her widowhood resumed, in part, her
former habits, enjoying the company of a few
intimate friends, and mixing again with the fellow-
artists who sought her studio.

She passed the winter in Rome, studying assiduously. There, she painted a picture, which
afterwards, when it was exhibited in the Academy
brought her much renown. She was cheerful, and
her excellent health increased her capacity for
physical enjoyment. She gave her energies wide
scope, and allowed herself no time for sorrow or
regret. She was a brave woman, and, young
though she was, had become hardened to the
realities of life, while she possessed a singular
independence of character. She had never loved
any man but Esmé Colquhoun, and she loved
her art perhaps even more than she cared for him.
She, too, possessed in a measure the artist's power
of rebound. The part she had taken in bringing
about Esmé's marriage had been passive rather
than active, and she would not let herself consider whether what had been done was well or
ill. The woman who stands alone, fenced in by

an enthusiasm for some abstract pursuit, has a vantage ground denied to her weak and idle sisters. To such an one, life can never seem utterly barren. A sustaining interest must spring up from the grave of a dead passion, and the buried heart may send forth a rose to be the wonder and admiration of the world.

CHAPTER XVII.

IT was June. Every one was in London. The Rainshaws had taken a house in Eaton Place. Esmé Colquhoun and his wife had come back from America. The Romers were in town. Mrs. Borlase had returned from Rome, and her Thursday evening receptions were in full swing.

Little more than a year had passed since she had lost her husband. She made, however, no pretence of mourning, and went out as before. She wore black, but her velvets and brocades, cut as was her style, after an old picture and trimmed with deep Flemish or Italian lace, did not suggest the idea of widowhood. By this time most people, except those who had peculiar and personal reasons for remembering the fact, had forgotten that poor old Stephen Borlase, British Consul at ———, who had not been "artistic," was dead and that Christine was free.

She lived in one of those quaint detached houses in West Kensington, that are to be found, surrounded by meaner dwellings, in streets of which the name is hardly known, and which seem particularly affected by members of the literary and artistic professions.

It was a long way for the votaries of fashion

to drive; but they came nevertheless in flocks; and on one especial Thursday evening the string of carriages, longer and wider than usual, almost blocked up the narrow thoroughfare.

Mrs. Borlase's "At Homes," were called "small and early." As a matter of fact, they were only early in the sense that people came as soon as they liked, and that cigarettes were permitted after twelve; and they were never small.

One by one, guests descended and entered at the open door; then, delivering their wraps into the hands of a smiling little French maid who waited in the ante-room, found their own way through the conservatory, and down the flight of wooden steps leading to the studio.

This was a large room painted in dull Venetian red, with a high-pitched roof and gallery which afforded a vantage-ground for studying the amusing scene below; and it was as picturesque as it could be rendered by Indian stuffs harmonious hangings, Japanese screens and umbrellas, quaint pottery, carved cabinets, paintings on easels in all stages of development, and "properties" generally, professional and bizarre.

But it was too crowded to-night for such accessories to be of much consequence. The human element held itself supreme; and the buzz of talk was almost deafening. All sorts of people were present. There were tired-looking Belgravian dowagers, fashionable beauties, and eccentrically dressed æsthetes. There were a celebrated tragic actress, the queen of refined comedy, and a bevy of minor theatrical stars, representatives from the musical world, amateur and professional artists, and ordinary humdrum people.   There were men with decorations, Society men, and men who never went anywhere but here ; *littérateurs*, scientists, art patrons, Academicians and long-haired composers ; commonplace men with pretty wives, and commonplace wives with distinguished husbands : here and there, a bright-eyed foreigner or dreamy German enthusiast, while every now and then, a word or two of French or Italian rose above a low roar of sound.   Mrs. Borlase reconciled all nationalities and all diversities of interest.

Now there was a sudden lull as a composer, whose music every one loved to hear, seated himself at the piano, and his small frame, bent almost double over the keyboard, sent forth the most sweet and thrilling harmonies.   Then presently a charming foreign singer, whom he had accompanied a little while before, and who was standing close to him, would ask, "Do you know this ?" humming a snatch of some unfamiliar air ; and he would take up the melody and improvise variations upon it—grotesque, fantastic, melancholy and jocund, glancing eagerly round every now and then, as if seeking sympathy, and almost forgetting where he was till murmurs of "Bravo, bravo !" would remind him of his audience.

There was singing after this, and the very best ; none but professionals performed at Mrs. Borlase's Thursdays, and they did for her what they never did except among their own set. When it was over, the flutter of drapery and murmur of talk recommenced.

Little scraps of conversation reached Graysett's ear, as the crowd in the gallery hemmed him in more closely—banal and frivolous enough, yet amusing to one not in the swing of such gossip—and he listened as he might have done to the by-play on the boards of a theatre.

" . . . . Do you care for De Rivaz's singing? You should hear Miss Geneste take him off—eyes, and languishing airs—it's delicious. Mrs. ———," naming an actress noted for her unflattering candour, "said to him the other night, 'I admire your voice, De Rivaz; but I don't like the way you roll your brandy balls about.' He was so angry."

"Will she do for the Fancy Fair?" indicating Miss Geneste.

"No," decidedly. "She is not famous enough; she is only going to be. She does the most perfect imitation of Sarah Bernhardt you ever saw. But budding celebrities won't suit your purpose. Wait a year or two till they have blossomed."

Graysett leaned over the railings and tried to follow with his eyes the movements of the people he knew. He saw but few of his acquaintances. The Rainshaws were there, but too far off to be approachable. Several others of the Leesholm set were present: the Australian belle very *décolletée*, talking to a used-up-looking gentleman with an eyeglass; the Admiral, making sinister observations to himself; Sir Frederick Romer, apparently in the last stage of boredom, blocking up a doorway. Seeking for Lady Romer, Graysett perceived her, posing now after the statuesque model, with classically braided tresses and flowing draperies, seated upon a couch at the upper end of the room beside one of the strangest and most striking-looking women he had ever seen.

This lady was certainly not English. A good many guesses might have been made before her nationality could have been arrived at. The thickness of jaw, the massive conformation of the face, and something fixed, cold and tragic in her full gaze, suggested the Egyptian Sphinx; other peculiarities pointed to a Kalmuck origin. At any rate there was a wide margin for possibilities.

She might have been sixty, but looked younger. Her skin had once been fair but was browned by exposure to weather. She had light brown hair, very thick, and with a curious natural wave which made it crinkle all over her head close down to the roots. It was arranged in one big coil above her forehead. Her chin was square and heavy, the lips firmly cut, set, and resolute, the nose short with dilating nostrils which gave to the face a character of alertness and sensibility, again con-tradicted by the prominent, clear, steady eyes. These eyes, light in colour, were extraordinarily deep and luminous. They seemed to draw the light into themselves like a jewel of which the depths appear unfathomable, and exercised on the beholder a fascination akin to that of the serpent. They were too remarkable to be beautiful. They compelled awe rather than admiration or, indeed, any strictly human feeling. The whole countenance, if wanting in feminine sweetness, was noble and mysteriously attractive. She wore a loose garment of some clinging black stuff. It was fashioned like the robe of some ancient priestess, and had loose sleeves which left bare a white and shapely arm. She was short and stout, and in ordinary dress her figure would have been quite devoid of dignity, but her straight draperies seemed to impart to it something of classic ease and uprightness.

This, Graysett had an opportunity of remarking fully as she stood up for a minute or two, apparently that she might view through the high studio window the effect of some Japanese illuminations in the garden. Presently she sat down again. She had evidently attracted notice, for a number of people pushed their way towards her ; and two or three, gathering round her, drew her into animated conversation. Her manner and gesticulations were distinctly foreign, and partly contradicted the Sphinx-like impression which her face gave when in repose. Her form swayed. She waved about her flexible hands, upon the forefingers of which there gleamed some magnificent Eastern jewels, and her eyes seemed to grow larger and to dart forth lightning as she talked, apparently with great rapidity, and, to judge by the play of her own features and the aspect of her listeners, upon a subject more than commonly interesting. Graysett, absorbed in speculating as to its nature, started at the sound of his name, pronounced in the neutral tones of Mr. Margrave, one of his fellow-guests at Leesholm.

"How are you? Mrs. Rainshaw spied you and gave me a roving commission to bring you to her at a convenient opportunity. But it is impossible to move in such a crush; there are more people than usual here to-night."

"Mrs. Borlase appears very popular," said Graysett.

"Oh, that is of course. But there are two attractions this evening; the Esmé Colquhouns and the New Hypatia."

"Are the Colquhouns here?" asked Graysett abruptly.

"They are expected. I don't think they have arrived yet; Esmé is always late. Have you read his new book?"

"No."

"People are making a great fuss over it. I think that I prefer his more carnal style. Air-drawn abstractions are incomprehensible to my material nature. I am trying to cultivate spirituality to keep in pace with the times; but it is beyond me. I have not seen the Colquhouns since they came back from America. I hear that she is greatly altered."

"How?" exclaimed Graysett eagerly. "For the better or the worse?"

"The worse, I fear. She was always a little odd, you know. I fancy all this occult business has been too much for her; it generally affects people's heads in the long run, as I tell Lady Romer, if they take it seriously. Don't you think so?"

"I don't know anything about it," replied Graysett.

"Nor I, for the matter of that; but I am a bit of a social philosopher; so, I imagine, are you. Has it ever struck you what a queer process of fermentation must be going on under the surface in an assemblage like this? One can't help wondering what fresh sort of spiritual gas is being generated. I see that you are interested in the New Hypatia?"

"Do you mean the woman in a black bedgown, beside Lady Romer? Yes, I have been watching her for some time. Who is she? Where does she come from; and what makes her get herself up in that extraordinary fashion. She looks like a cross between the Sphinx and the Cumæan Sibyl."

"Oh! the black gown is the dress of female sages in Thibet. I refer you to the Abbé Huc and Mr. Laurence Oliphant. Madame Tamvaco—that's her name—has dwelt in Lamaseries and Cave temples, has kissed the shadow of Buddha, and assisted at the re-incarnation of the Dalai Lama, so I am assured. What country she hails from in the first instance, and how long she has lived, are mysteries. The profane declare her to be a Russian spy. The faithful will swear that she has been traced back to the Magians, and that she has found the Philosopher' Stone and quaffed the Elixir of Life. There are, at any rate, some credulous individuals who solemnly believe that she is in the habit of getting out of her body, and of making aërial journeys to Asia, where, though in what particular locality it is not stated, she holds grave council with Eastern sages. That these conclaves affect the destinies of the human race goes without saying. I should be grateful if Madame Tamvaco would instruct me how to get out of my body when I am bored or have a fit of the gout. I don't know that I should go to Asia, though it's a wide place and might offer an agreeable variety to English life."

"So Madame Tamvaco is a spiritualist?" said Graysett.

"A spiritualist!" repeated Mr. Margrave. "If I introduce you to the Sibyl, don't insult her by telling her that she is a spiritualist. The New Pythagoreans—that is what they call themselves —hold the vulgar phenomena of spiritualism in supreme contempt. They have phenomena of their own by the way—a species of Indian jugglery which bases itself upon strictly scientific principles. The word 'supernatural' is not in their dictionary. They produce what we call miracles by manipulating the secret forces of Nature, and their high priestess claims to be initiated in the esoteric knowledge of the old philosophers, which has always mocked us like a will-o'-the-wisp, and which, granting that it exists does not promise us any practical result."

"I have read something of the doctrine of these

people," said Graysett, "and was deeply interested. It has often seemed strange to me that we have not more seriously investigated the profound truths which manifestly lie at the root of the Esoteric philosophies—those of Pythagoras and Plato for instance, which are built upon the old systems of the East."

"Oh!" said Margrave. "It all comes to the same thing. That which is, was from the beginning, and there is no new thing under the sun. I suppose that we are all of us—all, that is, who think—searching after a religion, and happy should we be if we could find one that would satisfy alike our reason and our aspirations. I will say for this new, or old, scheme of cosmogony, that it is extensive enough to embrace all the geological and astronomical facts which puzzle the theologians—so vast that even the Creator of our universe is lost in it and becomes a mere secondary cause."

Graysett smiled. "You begin as a scoffer, you end as a sage."

"It's the question of soul apart from the digestive apparatus which interests me," said Mr. Margrave in his serio-comic manner. "I have never been able to dissociate the two in my own case, and when I heard that these New Pythagoreans professed to do so, I thought that I should like to hear how they managed it. So I went to a conversazione they gave really in the spirit of an earnest inquirer, and prepared to listen with great attention to all that Madame Tamvaco

had to tell me. All London crowded there likewise—a few seriously inclined like myself—the
most part in search of a sensation. They expected to hear astral bells ringing, and to see
flowers raining down from the ceiling. I must
frankly admit that I also had a lurking hope that
something miraculous would happen. Nothing
did happen. There were no phenomena. There
was not even any startling denunciation of existing creeds. The 'Brotherhood of Humanity;'
the 'Evolution of the Race;' the 'Higher Life.'
These are stock phrases. Self-sacrifice, purity,
truth. We have heard of such things before;
and when the noble example of the Prophet of
Nazareth was set before us, and He was incidentally described as an Initiate in those ancient
mysteries of which Madame Tamvaco and Co.
claim the key, I felt inclined to cry out, 'Jesus I
know, and Paul I know, but who are ye?'"

Graysett laughed thoughtfully.

"It's a strange world!" he said. "I should
have liked to hear that lecture."

"I daresay that you would have remarked, as
did an advanced young woman in my hearing,
'Why, it's nothing but Christianity, after all: and
this is the nineteeth century! We did not come
here in evening dress for this!' The whole produced a moral effect upon me. I sought out
Madame Tamvaco the next day, and asked her
why she had not warned me that she was a
Christian. There was plenty of denunciation
then; but it was of ecclesiasticism, not of Christ's

teaching. I came away impressed and inclined to agree with her, that since not one of us in ten millions can hope to become a perfectly developed being short of a long series of incarnations, we had better disestablish the Church, go straight to the Bible, and start another Reformation for ourselves. Come with me on Saturday, I'll introduce you to the Sibyl. She will give you an uncanny feeling, at first, that her eyes and ears are seeing and hearing what you cannot see or hear, but that will wear off after a bit."

They made their way down from the gallery. Mrs. Borlase, at the foot of the steps, was playfully coaxing a French tenor to sing. She was leading him off in triumph to the piano, when she saw Mr. Margrave and stopped to offer him a cigarette from a silver casket she carried.

"See the perfect hostess!" he said. "But your crowd hasn't begun to thin yet, it's waiting for the lions. I went out into the garden, as you desired, and saw lots of lanterns but no love."

"I did not guarantee the love: I said that there was a garden and that there were lamps. You were to find the love."

"Failing that, I am going to find wisdom. Major Graysett wished to be introduced to Madame Tamvaco."

"After this song," said she. "Wait a minute. Major Graysett, this is the first time you have been inside my studio. Do you remember my asking you to give an opinion on Miss Fountain's portrait. There it is, still unfinished. . . . . And here," she added after a moment's pause, "is the original."

"Good heavens!" ejaculated Mr. Margrave. "How ill she looks!"

CHAPTER XVIII.

THE picture to which Christine had called Graysett's attention stood back in a recess close to
where they were standing. Some Oriental hangings, falling low, framed the nook ; and the easel
itself was draped with a quantity of creamy Indian
muslin which added to the somewhat vaporous
effect of the unfinished portrait. A cunningly
shaded lamp concentrated its rays upon the
features and more particularly upon the eyes,
which gazed out of the canvas with that startled,
unearthly expression which was at times Judith's
most striking peculiarity.

Only the head had been worked in, and this
with touches so delicate and yet so telling, that
the face seemed that of some unique being hardly
to be bound by material laws, rather than the
countenance of a woman of flesh and blood,
leading the life of society, and subject to the petty
interests and desires of ordinary womanhood.

Christine had approached her subject with that
rare sympathy, that power of discerning the ideal
man or woman through his or her grosser covering,
which in the portrait-painter is inspiration. She
had caught that ineffable something in Judith's personality—not coldness, not purity, not ignorance

of evil, but something even more negative than
these, which seemed to place the girl upon a
different level from warm, passionate, frail, yet
strong humanity.   For in Judith this unlikeness
did not seem owing to the spirituality of a more
highly developed and refined nature.   It appeared,
rather, the conscious want of an embryo spirit,
prematurely evolved, who had somehow missed
the intermediary experience by which human
sympathies might have been gained, and to whom
all experience must be more or less bewildering
and abnormal.

At Mr. Margrave's exclamation, Graysett turned
from the face of the girl he had known to the
woman he longed yet dreaded to see.

She was descending the steps, leaning upon her
husband's arm, and for a moment they halted and
surveyed the scene.   Esmé sublimely self-conscious, vigorous, beautiful as of old.   Judith
clinging to him, as though from his magnificent
vitality she derived all the life force that animated
her own feebler frame.   Involuntarily, there
occurred to Graysett Mrs. Rainshaw's simile of the
Vampire, and a shudder of horror turned him
cold.

So altered was she, and in a manner so subtle
and strange, that at first his fancy could only grasp
the suggestion of contamination and slowly working morbid poison.   He seemed to see looking
out from her eyes no longer the untainted, if
partly irresponsible, soul, which he had loved and
yearned to guard from contact with anything that

could defile, but a vexed spirit struggling wildly to escape from maleficent influences which held it in thrall.

This was the allegory he read. To the gay crowd watching her entrance she was a very beautiful woman, in a fantastic costume that illustrated Esmé Colquhoun's noted perception of the harmonious—a woman who had married and enriched the man she loved, and who was probably now making the painful discovery that her infatuation had been a mistake, and that poets must ever be the property not of one but of many. For it was evident to the most casual observation that her body was being worn by some wasting disease or mental care, and there was a wildness in her eyes which roused the unspoken comment in the minds of those acquainted in any degree with her family history, "There was always something strange about her ; and don't people say that her mother was mad ?"

She was dressed after a fashion very unlike the conventional simplicity of her attire before her marriage. The rich velvet brocade falling in heavy folds about her figure, its sheen displaying gleams of dark red and flame colour, was made somewhat in the Italian style of the fifteenth century, with full sleeves and stiff jewelled bodice cut low in front, its gorgeously sombre and tawny hues contrasting agreeably with the old lace covering the bosom, upon which lay a quaintly set pendant of opals and rose diamonds.

Her hair was now curled more elaborately

above her forehead, and lay coiled upon her head in a mode that lent majesty to the graceful poise of her throat. A bodkin encrusted with opals apparently held the luxuriant masses in place, and gave forth a shifting light. A slight touch of rouge upon her cheeks seemed to make the pallor and emaciation of her face more noticeable, and to intensify the distraught look in her eyes. Except, however, for their unnatural gleam, she was quite composed, and her bearing showed no hesitation or sign of embarrassment at the attention which she excited. Her mind appeared far away; and though her gaze rested blankly upon Graysett for a second, it was evident that she did not at the instant identify him. Her husband stooped and said something to her in a low tone. She started as though collecting herself, and greeted a lady standing near her, while there was a dressing up of her face with mechanical smiles.

Christine Borlase advanced with outstretched hand. It was the first time since the marriage of the one, and the widowhood of the other, that Judith and she had met. To those who guessed at the emotions lying below the surface, there was food for curiosity and conjecture in the demeanour of these two women and that of the man whom they had both loved. With the deepest interest Graysett watched the faces of the three.

Esmé stood with lashes drooped, and features set, as though he were aware of the necessity for composure, and prepared to mask any sign of agitation. Christine had turned very pale, and there was a look of pain and perplexity in her eyes, which she kept steadily averted from Esmé and fixed upon his wife. In spite of her self-command, her lips trembled and her voice vibrated with a womanly sympathy, that, had she not already possessed it, would have won her Graysett's friendship.

"My dear," she said, "I am glad to see you again. It was good of you to come, though you are late, and good of you to bring Esmé so soon to see an old friend. He will find many more here—for his reward—and you also. But I am very sorry that you are not looking stronger."

"My wife is a hopeless sailor," said Esmé, in his rolling tones which travelled far. "I owe her a debt of gratitude for having crossed the Atlantic to please me. The American climate did not suit her. We are glad to breathe the atmosphere of London once more. There is none more congenial to us than that of your studio, Mrs. Borlase. You have altered it—a little, I see. It is always artistic and charming."

Christine replied constrainedly, and Esmé, accosted by a lively American who piqued herself upon saying smart things, and who now began to question him as to the success of his mission, entered into a serious dissertation upon the susceptibility of the New Yorkers to impressions of the Beautiful, and disarmed sarcasm by the declaration, "I am charmed with the loveliness of

American women, they are my mission realized. And I am charmed with the American openness to truth. There I have not to contend against the hydra-headed monster, Conventionalism, which I cannot crush in England. I am also charmed with the American sense of humour. They bur-. lesqued me sometimes, but, do you know, I really enjoyed it very much."

Judith had not spoken. She was gazing intently at Mrs. Borlase, her lips parted in that terrible smile with which one wounded to the death might try to conceal an almost unendurable pain. There was no reproach, no resentment, no repressed passion in her face, only the look of dumb agony, physical rather than mental, which the sufferer knows cannot be cured.

Christine relinquished her hand. A spasm as of relief seemed to pass through Judith's frame. Christine watched her in troubled wonder, and tried affectionately to draw her into conversation receiving only mechanical and dreamy answers. Graysett came forward and joined the group. Perceiving him, Esmé turned and shook hands with him in a manner remarkably cordial, pressing him to visit them at an early opportunity, and giving their address, which, with a start, Graysett recognized as that of the house which had been left to Judith, and which she had identified with the scene of his vision.

"We are there only temporarily, of course," said the poet carelessly; "till we can furnish another abode to our taste. It was ready, and

its incongruities, if bizarre, are not vulgar. And
at least it is less glaring than an hotel."

He turned away and sauntered through the
room, smiling and bowing now to one and now
to another with the serene self-complacency of a
monarch dispensing favours. Judith suffered her
hand to remain for a moment in that of Graysett. She smiled with much sweetness, and her
features lighted up, as he remembered so well
had been their wont when the conversation.
had touched upon the subjects which interested
her.

"You are better?" she exclaimed earnestly.
"You are quite well now! Oh, I have hoped so
that you would get quite better! I have often
thought of you—and wondered———"

She paused abruptly, and withdrew her hand.
His heart swelled with pleasure, and then was
pierced by a pang of sorrow. It struck him
vividly that this was the first time in his knowledge of her—which was so small in measure and
yet so rich—that she had seemed drawn out of
herself by natural and healthy solicitude for
another. In the old days, even when his whole
being had been wrung with passionate yearning
towards her, no corresponding sympathy had been
awakened in her. She had never appeared
capable of entering into his feeling. She had
never regarded him by any other light than that
of her own egotism. Her attitude towards him
and towards herself had always been analytical ;
and his pain, his anxiety, had moved her only in

so far as they affected her strange theory of self-development.

The same thought seemed to occur to Christine Borlase.

"You and Major Graysett were always great allies at Leesholm, I remember," said she, "and I will place you in his care, for you are not strong enough to stand; but St. André is gazing at me reproachfully, for I promised to persuade Signor Torriano to play his accompaniment. You have never heard St. André? He is quite new. You will be charmed. Major Graysett, I see a seat vacant beside Madame Tamvaco. Take Mrs. Colquhoun to it. Mr. Margrave is waiting there to introduce you, and is seizing the opportunity to imbibe a little wisdom on his own account. I have been accusing him of flirting with the Sibyl, and I begin to think that his soul is not so dependent on his digestion as he would have us believe. Judith, I leave you in confidence—unless, indeed, Esmé has weaned you from Occultism to Art. You used to be very much interested in Madame Tamvaco."

Graysett offered Judith his arm.

"I remember," he said, "this is the lady of whom you spoke to me at Leesholm."

He felt that she shuddered slightly. "Yes," she replied. "It was she who warned me against crossing the Threshold. . . . . How strange that evening was!" she went on dreamily. "It was the beginning. You interested me; and I only made you unhappy. I am glad that I did not

do you lasting harm.   You have not gone back
to India ?"

"I am never going back again," he answered.
"I am here, ready to help you, if at any time
you need me."

"I need help now," she murmured.   "I need
it sorely.   I need the help which would turn me
into a little child again, and make me think of
good things instead of what is wicked and horrible.
That is what you cannot do for me—neither you
nor any one else.   Hush, don't speak.   I will try
to tell you—some day when we are alone—not
now."

The sweet notes of the French tenor rang
through the room, and every one listened   They
had reached the sofa on which Madame Tamvaco
was seated.   Mr. Margrave rose and retired into
the background pending the conclusion of the song.
Two or three eager-looking men pressed round
the Sibyl, but she was not talking.   She had
been following Judith's movements ; and now
that the latter approached her, silently bowed her
head, and motioned her to her side.   When Monsieur St. André rose from the piano, there was a
little confusion and dispersion.   Madame Tamvaco
turned to Judith, and looked her through with her
great witch-like eyes.

"I have not forgotten you," she said at length,
in a deep, rather harsh voice, with a very un-
English intonation.   "You used always to wear
white, and now you do not dress in white, but in
red and flame colour.   It would be better if you

were in black, as I am—I whom they call a witch. You are in witches' garments! Why do you not keep to your white? Why did you marry Esmé Colquhoun?"

"Madame," said Judith calmly, though she was trembling with suppressd excitement, "I married my husband because I loved him."

"Hear!" exclaimed Madame Tamvaco in an accent which had in it more of pity than of irony. "This fever which wastes the flesh and burns the soul is Love! You would not listen to me. You did once come to this ugly wise woman for knowledge, and I said, 'Wait. Grope in the darkness till your eyes can bear the light. Never yield your will to another. Fly any influence which threatens to overpower it. Cling to your intuition as you would cling to your Saviour. They were golden rules, but you would not heed them. You would be another Eve. And see— you come to me again and I can do nothing for you."

"Madame Tamvaco," said Judith, with a dignity of which at that moment Graysett could not have imagined her capable, "when I need your help, I will not ask for it in a place like this."

Her reply seemed partly to amuse, partly to please, the strange woman. She put out her thin, bird-like claw, upon its forefinger a ring engraved in Oriental characters, and patted Judith's arm.

"That is good. I forget that I am in the world where masks are always necessary, and where the nakedness of your minds must needs be covered. For me, there are no masks. It is strange to see you all as you are, and to see the thoughts which project themselves from you. I will tell you," she added, looking round the group, "something which you perhaps do not know, but which is true—as true as that you have each an astral body ; though that is a fact these scientific gentlemen deny."

A smile crossed the faces of one or two who were listening.

"Ah !" cried Madame Tamvaco, "I am not scientific ?   Herr Klein will not admit me into his brotherhood of physiologists !   Is that so ?   Well, listen to me.   There are a great many mysteries which puzzle you scientists but which are no mysteries to me. I know them. They are facts, and I have been shown the natural laws which govern them. For example, can you physiologists tell me anything about the spleen ?"

"Its functions have not been clearly defined," said a heavy-looking man, who spoke with a German accent.

"Then, when you have learned to define the functions of the spleen, which we consider the storehouse of vital energy, you shall tell me why the laws of Nature will not permit me to have an astral body. And now, I will inform you that around each of you there is an aura—an emanation, in which your thoughts, the likeness of those upon whom your imagination dwells, and the influences which prompt your words and actions, take shape and are visible to the eyes of those who see. And I can assure you that if you believed what I said you would be sorry that I should see through the foul and mephitic atmosphere which encompasses some of you to whom I am speaking—the noxious things you have attracted to yourselves."

"You are frank, Madame," said the German who had spoken before. "But will you submit to a test of your powers of thought-reading ?"

"I am true," rejoined she ; "and truth has ever been stoned and crucified. You crucify me in your papers. You stone me with your ridicule. You like to call me a charlatan and a fraud, because I will not ring astral bells and perform juggling tricks to please you. If you desire it, Herr Klein, I will tell you what I see."

She bent towards him, and for a few moments talked rapidly in an undertone. She spoke in German, but so fast and so low that only a word here and there was intelligible.

Herr Klein looked visibly discomposed. "Cease, Madame. That is sufficient."

"Well?" she asked with triumphant irony. "Do I not tell you truth? Am I a clever thought-reader? Will you have me on a platform in competition with your Mr. Irving Bishop? Say, and let me light my cigarette. Mr. Margrave, where is my fan? It is sandal-wood and I cannot lose it."

Mr. Margrave opined gravely that the fan had

taken to itself an astral body, and that it would be impossible to account for its vagaries.

Madame Tamvaco puffed reflectively for a few moments, then threw the cigarette away. "*Dame!* Why did I not bring my own *tabac?*" she cried. "Say," she repeated imperatively, fixing Herr Klein, "did I tell you truly?"

"I do not recommend these gentleman to test your powers, Madame," drily replied the German.

"Ah, my good Klein! it is possible to have an aura which will bear the scrutiny of clear eyes. But now you shall leave me. I will talk to you no more. I am going home, and before I go I wish to speak to Mrs. Colquhoun."

The knot dispersed. Graysett would have withdrawn also, but Madame Tamvaco detained him by a gesture. "Stay. I do not know your name, but you interest me."

"Madame Tamvaco," said Mr. Margrave, who hovering near had caught her abrupt address, "I had already charged myself with the pleasure of making you acquainted with Major Graysett. He is good material—a convert worth making."

"I am not a propagandist, Mr. Margrave," said the Seeress coldly, "or *you* would have been converted, as you term it, ere this. Take care. No one ever yet escaped me who rashly plunged into the maelstrom of my psychic influence. However, for the present, I am not concerned with you. Come and see me on Saturday when I receive. And if you would do me a favour, go and look for my fan. . . . . I am charmed to know

you, Major Graysett," she added with a very win-
ning smile. "You will see that I have both my
exoteric and esoteric sides. You may safely hear
what I have to say to this sadly unfortunate
woman, for in your aura I behold only one pre-
dominating thought; and that shapes itself into
her image."

Judith looked up at him with a strange smile,
in which there was mingled joy and reproach.

The blood rose to Graysett's brow. "Madame
Tamvaco," he said gravely, "there is in my mind
no thought of Mrs. Colquhoun which may not be
read by a true-hearted woman."

Madame Tamvaco did not reply. She appeared
to be studying him closely.

Judith, no longer composed, touched her hand.
"Tell me," she whispered with a sort of passionate
eagerness, "what is it that you see in me? What
is it that has changed me? Is it a crime to love?
What have I done to be so tortured?"

An expression of the tenderest compassion
swept over the face of the Seeress, humanizing
its hard grandeur, while her voice softened as she
replied in a dreamy tone, unlike the brusqueness
of her former mode of speech—

"Do you not know that each life we live is but
one step of the Infinite Ladder which we must
all mount to reach Eternity—but one day in the
ages through which each spirit must pass to gain
the Perfect Rest! You Christians preach that
whatsoever a man soweth that shall he also reap,
and never was more sublime truth conveyed in

simple words. But you fall into the error of taking an infinitesimal part as the Great Whole—of regarding one day as all Time, one night as Eternity. For in Nature there are no contradictions. The night of dreaming which follows day is not the harvest. That which we reap is sown in the previous life, and the seedtime of the one is the harvest of the other."

"Tell me," said Judith again, still more earnestly, "how can I learn from you? I have no faith. I have no hope. I am haunted by terrors. I am in chains. Can you not break them? While I am with you, a light seems to come to me; but I know not at what moment the darkness may fall again. Save me from becoming wicked. You refused to teach me once. Will you refuse again?"

"My poor woman!" said the Seeress. "I can teach you, but I cannot deliver you. If compassion and love could work deliverance, would not the whole earth have been freed by One who said, 'Let me be cursed, but let Humanity be happy'? Salvation is within yourself, in the immortal spirit over which neither man nor elementary thing can gain the complete mastery. It may be driven from your body, but while there is in your heart the faintest aspiration after good, the faintest shrinking of evil, it will never forsake you. You came to me once, and I warned you. I could do no more. I knew that the peculiarity of your organization exposed you to perils which you were not capable of comprehending. To rise to the spiritual plane, meant for you an ordeal for which in this life you could never be prepared. Safety lay for you on the physical plane, and in the development of your human sympathies, and heart love—a different thing to the mere magnetic attraction which could only re-awaken in you a dormant sense, and which is the medium of approach to your worst enemies."

"And now?" interrupted Judith with agonized eagerness.

"How can I here, in a few words, expound the most subtle of philosophical problems? What is Evil, and by what means does it gain influence over the soul? The theologists would do away with the Devil; but while matter exists they can never do away with evil. Evil and good are the two opposing forces, which, acting and reacting upon each other, result in the life of the universe. Listen. The atmosphere around us is crowded with forces, currents, influences, intelligences—call them what you will—to which we are more or less sensitive, according to individual temperament and moral and physical conditions. In some the barrier which divides our souls from these invisibles needs but the lightest touch to be thrown down. This may be done by the force of our own purified aspirations, or by the will of a strongly magnetic person dissimilarly electrified to ourselves, who has within himself the power of controlling these forces, and, who in proportion as he is pure or impure, attracts the malignant or the beneficent, not only to himself, but to the subject whom he has infected with his own magnetism.

"You are one of those unfortunate beings unprotected by a physical barrier, or by the strength and inherent purity of your own soul. Had you listened to the voice of your intuition, you would have fled from the man who is your husband as you would flee from a foul vapour. To you he is deadly. He has the potentialities of a god or a demon. Ages to come will determine which. It is more than probable that knowledge will direct his will : and his aspirations —for he has the capacity to aspire—becoming gradually purified, may force him to choose the good. But with this, *you* have nothing to do. Your love for him has been mere physical attraction. You have never inspired him with one holy impulse. In marrying you, he did violence to his better self. You have never stimulated his yearning after the ideal even in its lower forms. Therein lies *his* hope of salvation. It is not *you* who have any power to influence his highest destinies."

She ceased. All this had been poured forth very rapidly and in a low, penetrating voice which seemed to come from far away, and yet pierced the very souls of her listeners. Her eyes were strangely large and luminous, with a shadow of trouble in their depths ; and they were bent neither upon Judith nor Graysett, but gazed into space, as though there, this mystic drama of conflicts and affinities was unfolding itself before her inner vision. By some strange spell she seemed to have abstracted herself and these two from the noisy throng, so that the incongruity between her transcendental utterances and the frivolous scene of which they made part, did not seem apparent. A few people passed to and fro, but none halted to address them.

The crowd had now somewhat thinned, drawn into the illuminated garden by a miniature display of fireworks planned by one of Christine's aides-de-camp. The success of Mrs. Borlase's receptions was certainly due to their absolute informality, and to the fact that no one appeared to see anything remarkable in the doings of any one else. The studio and garden were the Paradise of lovers and the initiatory scene of many a flirtation. Now, cigarette smoke clouded the atmosphere, and the corks of soda and seltzer water bottles flew as the guests helped themselves at the little refreshment tables placed at convenient angles within and without. The large window rising from the ground was thrown wide open, and the soft night air sent a fresh current through the heated room.

At that moment Colquhoun entered with Mrs. Borlase on his arm. The latter detached herself from him, and, accepting the escort of Herr Klein, returned to the garden.

Judith rose as though obeying an inaudible summons. That strange, rapt, yet wild, look returned to her face. She was ghastly save for the artificial colouring on her cheeks, and her hands trembled violently. She made a few steps forward, and then tottered blindly, and would have fallen, but that her husband had reached her side, and received her unconscious form in his arms.

CHAPTER XIX.

JUDITH'S attack seemed rather a vertigo than a
fainting fit.   In a few moments she recovered,
and, gazing bewilderedly around, uttered some
incoherent words, then quietly suffered her husband to lead her away from the studio.   Shortly
after they had gone, Mrs. Borlase re-entered from
the garden.   She looked anxious and alarmed,
and went straight to Major Graysett.

"What was the matter with Mrs. Colquhoun?"
she inquired abruptly.   "I am told that she
fainted."

"That is true," he replied ; "but she recovered
almost directly, and has gone away with her husband.   She does not appear to be at all strong."

"Do you think that she is happy?" asked
Christine pointedly.

"No," he answered bitterly.   "Did you expect
to find her so?   I never imagined that the marriage—whatever its advantages to him—would
bring her happiness."

"Oh, Major Graysett, do not speak in that
tone!" exclaimed Christine earnestly.   "Have
you not always been a little unjust to Esmé?   No
one could doubt her devotion to him ; and even
his worst enemies acknowledge that he appears

deeply attached to her. You do not understand his nature. We all need a little sympathetic allowance—we artists. It is our spontaneity which misleads."

She waited for a moment, but he said nothing. It occurred to him that she would hardly expect sympathy or spontaneity from one so apparently self-contained as himself. In truth, there seemed to him something exquisitely pathetic in this identification of her own weakness with the faults of the man she loved.

"You don't answer," she exclaimed.

"What can I say? You plead eloquently; but I make no accusation. I am not an artist. It needs a wide range of sympathies to embrace all motives."

"Few people are capable of understanding Esmé," continued Christine. "He is judged too leniently or too harshly. In spite of his affectations, his egotism—I admit these—there is in his nature a simplicity—a clinging affectionateness— an intense admiration for what is beautiful, tender, and lovable, which cannot fail to make the happiness of his wife. Then think of the gratitude which a man in his position must feel towards the woman who has given him everything, and who has freed his genius from sordid shackles. And Esmé has more than a spark of nobility: he has the capacity for greatness—greatness of soul. You will not believe so?"

"Indeed, Mrs. Borlase," said Graysett, "you are right. I am not a fit person to gauge Esmé

Colquhoun's moral capabilities. But if there were needed any impetus to elevate a man's character, it would surely be found in the trustful love of an innocent girl, and in the faith of a woman like yourself."

He had spoken absently, hardly realizing the personal application of his words. They produced a marked effect upon the artist. Her frank eyes drooped; she coloured deeply, and turned away, saying no more.

Madame Tamvaco had come forward to bid her hostess good-night. The strange figure, in its loose, black robe, surmounted by that majestic head and the coronal of crisp, magnetic-looking hair, struck Graysett anew with admiration mingled with a sense of the grotesque. The feeling was intensified, perhaps, by the contrast which the Seeress presented to an extremely tall, unpliable-looking lady, much younger than herself, who stood evidently waiting to accompany her.

This lady—an American, to judge by her accent, which, to use a vulgar phrase, might have been cut with a knife—wore a high-necked cashmere gown that draped her slim, angular, but not ungraceful, form in straight folds from the waist, and suggested the divided skirt, and theories concerning the dress of rational woman. She did not, however, despise ornaments, for diamonds twinkled in her ears and round her throat, and the frizz of fair hair above her forehead was decidedly after the prevailing mode. It was certain that she had a very distinct personality, and the sort of gaze which seemed to indicate that she knew what she wanted, and that her aims were somewhat higher than those of the herd. She was undoubtedly interesting; and, notwithstanding her lankness, her unpleasing voice, and the peculiarity of her attire, was feminine and even spiritual in appearance.

Madame Tamvaco accepted, or, more correctly, demanded, Major Graysett's escort to her carriage; and on their way through the suite of rooms, while they were waiting for their wraps, introduced her friend as Mrs. Edye.

"Well," said the latter with a quick little nod, "I shouldn't wonder if we get to know each other pretty well; for I suspect that Madame has found out you have got capabilities; and if that is so, you won't be too anxious to escape from her."

"At this moment," said Madame Tamvaco, "he is angry with me. He thinks that I have been cruel."

"Oh, you mustn't mind that!" said Mrs. Edye quietly, taking Madame Tamvaco's hand with an affectionate gesture. "The old lady has her faults. Isn't it so? She is a little ill-balanced; she is impatient. But she is a great woman. She is so great, that if she were the horned devil himself, I couldn't be induced to leave her. You'll come to feeling like that. She is great enough to see through your faults and weaknesses and to take you up beyond them, for the sake of your capabilities. Come to our reception on

Saturday, Major Graysett. Come with Mr. Margrave — 98 Barlow Crescent, St. John's Wood, that's the address—from three-thirty to six."

"Thank you," said Graysett, "I will certainly come. In the meantime I had better see whether there's any chance of your getting off."

The brougham which a fashionable devotee had placed at Madame Tamvaco's disposal could not be found; and it was with difficulty that the footman was discovered, and sent in search of it to the nearest public-house. Graysett informed Madame Tamvaco of the delay, and put a chair for her in the window recess, from which position she could watch the people passing to and fro. She immediately asked him for a cigarette, and philosophically proceeded to smoke, though she gave vent to a forcible and unphilosophical ejaculation as she again lamented not having brought her *tabac.* This contrast between her unfeminine speech and habits, and the music of her voice and eloquence of her manner, when her deepest feelings were stirred, was extraordinary and bewildering. Graysett marvelled at the opposing characteristics she presented, and the idea struck him that her exoteric demeanour, not assisted by "phenomena," was hardly calculated to create, in the minds of the uninitiated, a lofty conception of her esoteric doctrine—whatever that might be.

But a gesture on her part arrested the thought, and claimed his attention.

"Major Graysett, listen to me. I know that you have a deep and pure interest in the welfare of this miserable woman, whose heartstrings have been strained almost to breaking this evening. She will send for you shortly. Go to her. Encourage her to open to you the secrets of her struggling soul. Do not let any personal consciousness, any doubt of your own motives, deter you from facing the ordeal which is before you. I warn you that it may be a severe one. She is shadowed by a diabolical influence, which is urging her to her destruction. Gain her confidence. You can do for her now what I cannot. Then come to me. Hereafter, I may be of the greatest service to her and to you; but she must first be released from her bondage. That is your task. . . . . No, not a word more at present. Go and talk to Mrs. Edye, and come and tell me when I must move. I am in no hurry. I want to finish my cigarette; and I have a word to say to my American Professor whom I see yonder."

She beckoned to a light-whiskered, disjointed-looking individual, with an enthusiastic eye, and general air of inward preoccupation, who was in the act of struggling into his overcoat, and who obeyed her summons with alacrity.

Graysett approached Mrs. Edye, to whom the knots of prettily cloaked women waiting for their carriages, the snatches of frivolous chatter, and the prevailing characteristics of a scene in which she stood a comparative stranger, seemed to afford food for interest and amusement, for she was smiling seriously.

"Where's Madame Tamvaco?" she asked. "Sitting down! Oh, I guess she is exhausted by the mixed magnetism. It's very trying to a sensitive."

"May I inquire," said Graysett, "whether you divide the world into the persons who are 'sensitives' and those who are not?"

"That's very much how it appears to us," said Mrs. Edye frankly, "if you are just taking humanity into consideration. It's the people with the psychic powers who interest me—the men and women of the future. I was watching a lady this evening. You know her. She was talking to Madame; and she is married to that poet they make such a fuss over. I couldn't quite place her. I was a long way off her. But I'd like to diagnose her. I think she is an opportunity for me. There's something queer about her any way."

"That lady is a friend of mine," said Graysett abruptly. He felt an involuntary repugnance to hearing Judith discussed by Mrs. Edye.

"I didn't mean to be irreverent," said Mrs. Edye, with her clear straight look. "I shall place her next time, I daresay. That's my way of diagnosing a case. I look and look, then gradually all that I want to know unfolds itself, and I see what people's lives and characters are, and what they are suffering from. I often think it isn't exactly fair; but I do it for practice; and it is purely a scientific interest that I take. I wasn't very successful this evening. If I had been close to the Old Lady, I should have got strength from her."

"Is that possible?"

"Why, certainly. Just as another person gives you a light for your cigarette. Impetus of the will, you know. But you mustn't take me for an authority, I only came over to learn; I want to find truth; I want to be true to my highest capabilities—that's the only thing worth living for; all the rest is froth. I just *will* a thing, and I go on."

"Go on—to what?" asked Graysett gravely.

"Why, to the higher development," said Mrs. Edye. "Your scientists allow us to evolve up to humanity, and there they build a blank wall, as though because we had got so far, it wasn't possible to get any farther. I don't call that logical—do you? We've been developing our bodily and intellectual senses, and now we are beginning to develop our spiritual ones. I don't see why we are to jump straight from men and women to angels, any more than we jumped from molluscs to men. That's reasonable, isn't it?"

Graysett assented.

"We who are a step or two in advance," went on Mrs. Edye, "should be ready to help the struggling children forward—to teach them to exercise their growing powers, and how to avoid dangers. That is what I want to do, Major Graysett: I want to be a doctor on the higher

system. I don't care two straws about phenomena ; but I want to see the laws of spiritual
chemistry applied to the Evolution of the Race.
In marriage, for instance, the affinities ought to be
regulated. You know, the influence of a grossly
material person must retard spiritual progress.
Just think of the positive injury which may be
received from impure magnetism! Why, it's
terrible! There's a great deal written about the
sacredness of marriage and the union after death ;
but it's all a question of affinities. If you have
been in contact with a person only upon the
physical plane, you cannot be together upon the
spiritual one."

"That's a bit of Swedenborg's doctrine," said
Graysett.

"Perhaps it is," said Mrs. Edye. "Anyhow,
it's the doctrine of the New Pythagoreans."

At that moment the servant made his appear-
ance, and Graysett went back to Madame
Tamvaco, and offered her his arm to the carriage.
Mrs. Edye accepted that of the American
Professor, with whom she appeared to be on terms
of good understanding.

CHAPTER XX.

UPON the following morning a note from Judith was delivered by hand to Graysett, requesting that he would call upon her at half-past four that afternoon. He had not expected so prompt a summons. Remembering Esmé's cordiality the evening before, which at the time had surprised him, he felt a sudden and inexplicable conviction that the poet, rather than his wife, was the originator of the invitation.

He could not account for the feeling, and yet it haunted him all day, and more persistently than ever during his drive to the Colquhouns' house.

The villa, which Judith had once called her monstrosity, was situated in a suburb not usually resorted to by fashionable people. It stood within narrow grounds, and had the conventional lawn, fountain, and shrubbery, with stucco figures surmounting the important gateway. The building itself was a chaos of gables, miniature turrets, Gothic arches, and excrescences generally, which seemed to represent the architectural nightmare of a City alderman.

Graysett was taken into a magnificently furnished drawing-room, with a conservatory leading out of it, which, nevertheless, gave the impression

of an uninhabited desert, it was so evident that no
one lived in it.   The servant retired, but presently
re-appeared with the announcement that Mrs.
Colquhoun would be glad to see Major Graysett ;
and led the way through a long corridor into
what was evidently another wing of the house.
Graysett shuddered, as he entered the oblong
Japanese ante-chamber, through which he had
passed in his vision ; and recognized the bronzes,
the Florentine cabinets, the mixture of Oriental
and European *bric-à-brac*—the double door. . . . .
A second time he halted upon the threshold of
the boudoir, again overpowered by that feeling of
clammy horror and indescribable dread. . . . . It
seemed to wear off after a moment or two ; and he
became conscious that Judith was alone, and that
she was advancing to greet him.

She was dressed on this occasion, also, after a
somewhat fantastic fashion—in a robe of a peculiar
yellow tint, profusely trimmed with old lace, and
embroided in a sort of arabesque pattern, glittering
here and there with threads of gold and silver.
The clinging folds falling from her shoulders had
a gleaming, scaly appearance, and seemed to impart
a serpentine grace to her movements.

The change in her—to be felt rather than
defined—afflicted him now with even keener pain
than when he had first beheld her upon the previous
evening.   Had he been a dispassionate observer
he might have fancied it the sort of transformation
which may take place in an actress, whose genius
identifies her with a revolting character, when

so ghastly is the reality of the impersonation, the spectator is tempted to believe in witchcraft, and in the possibility of her body being possessed by the spirit of the being she represents.

But the suggestions which rose in his mind were even more tragic.

Judith's cheeks were flushed, and her eyes glowed with the unnatural lustre which had struck him as so unlike their former dreamy expression. At the same time, they had a rapt, fearful look, as though she were preyed upon by some terrifying inward consciousness. A smile lighted her features ; but was it his fancy which discerned in it a seductiveness that jarred against his finer instinct ? In her whole demeanour there was something false—something meretricious, something dangerous—he knew not how to characterize it, which thrilled him with a vague uneasiness. He saw no reflection of the sweet, impersonal enthusiasm which had in old time lent such charm to her too thoughtful countenance.

She was agitated ; her gestures were nervous. A tremulous movement fluttered the lace which lay over her bosom. Frail and attenuated as was her frame, it seemed more pliant ; the pose of her head less statuesque ; and the loose fall of her ruffle back from her throat, where the robe was but carelessly closed, revealed dimples and delicate curves and depressions, as captivating as the soft contours of a child.

The room was suffused by a dim, rose-coloured light, and breathed a subtle perfume : Oriental odours, blending with the scent of tea roses and hothouse flowers, which lay in profusion upon the table, and crowed the fireplace. In spite of incongruities of taste, a fastidious, almost enervating, luxury pervaded the apartment. At first, Graysett longed to throw open the shutters, and to admit fresh air and unblenching sunshine, so that he might counteract, as it were, the spell which in his imagination was woven round them both. For this Judith——strange, languid, alluring, full of tender *abandon*, was not the ethereal being who had once seemed to him too pure for coarser worship than that of the soul.

For an instant or two, his heart swelled with passionate revolt. . . . . And then the enchantment stole over his senses, and he was in a new dream from which horror and tragedy had faded away.

It did not occur to him as strange that she should not refer to the identity of the room in which they were, with the scene of his vision at Leesholm. He hardly knew what words were first spoken between them, or whence had arisen the mutual consciousness, at once delicious and embarrassing, which put explanation out of the question. He only knew that he was holding her little hot hand, and that its touch was like that of no other hand he had ever pressed ; it was trembling ; and the feeling of it lingered even after it had been withdrawn. He was overcome by the charm of her appearance, and by the gentle emotion that seemed to exhale from her, and to float caressingly around him. It was with a start that he suddenly recalled Madame Tamvaco's warning, and Judith's fainting fit at Mrs. Borlase's reception. He felt a sensation of shock, of horror at his temporary aberration. His mental attitude changed. It was as though some one invisible had touched him and brought him back to himself. The spell was partially broken. He inquired in a conventional manner after her health, and hoped that she had recovered from her indisposition of last night.

A little pucker of pain or perplexity knit Judith's brow.

"Last night!" she repeated. "Was I ill? I don't remember. I am quite well. Don't let us talk of those things. I don't want to think of last night now."

"Of what things shall we talk?" he asked, gently. "Of old days at Leesholm?"

"No, no; I was not kind to you then. I did not understand. I was in a dream, and I only knew the things which came to me in my dream."

"The dream was sweeter than the reality," said Graysett sadly.

"No," she repeated doubtfully. "It may have been to you, but it was not to me. Life is all dreams," she went on. "Some are cold and formless, full of shadows; and some are terrible, like nightmares; and in others the shadows seem real things—delights of sense and sight and sound. Then beauty thrills one, and love speaks. Why may we not always dream such dreams? Why should we strain up towards the stars when the earth is full of flowers? Why should we not live and enjoy?"

She sank upon a pile of cushions heaped upon the hearthrug, and put out her hand to a great china bowl filled with blossoms. She drew forth a cluster of tea roses and some sprays of delicate heliotrope. She held the flowers before her, touching the rose petals tenderly, and brushing the heliotrope with her lips.

"Why should we not live and enjoy?" she repeated. "There's nothing else in the world that's real. The spirit, which seemed so beautiful vanishes away. But the form remains; and that is beautiful too. And if the flowers fade, there are fresh ones to be gathered."

"Oh, Judith!" he cried. "Is this the highest philosophy which your marriage has taught you?"

She gazed at him for a moment in an absent way, as though something in his voice more than in his words had arrested and turned the train of her thoughts.

"You have never called me Judith before!" she said meditatively. "It is not a pretty name. It is harsh and unsympathetic—as I was. I don't want to be that—any more. . . . . Do you recollect when I asked you your name? Edward! Are you going to be my friend?"

"You know," he answered, "that my life is consecrated to you."

"Is that true? You give me a great deal. How can I repay you?"

"I want no payment, except to help in making you happy—and good."

"Happy!" she echoed. "Yes. You make me less unhappy. I have been better since I saw you last night. Good! That's something positive—it is a different matter. I don't think that I know what is good, and what is bad."

She rose abruptly, and hovered restlessly about for a minute or two, while he watched her in wretched wondering and excitement. She paused before an inlaid table, upon which stood a tea equipage in old silver. The pedestal of the table was twined with curiously wrought brazen serpents, the tails of which formed its support. The hissing of the kettle seemed to proceed from their distended jaws. The blue flame of the spirit lamp leaped up. He watched her put it out with a quaint sort of extinguisher, which attracted his attention from its singularity. Everything was strange, but nothing so strange as Judith herself. There even seemed a curious aroma about the tea which she poured out, and handed to him.

"It is not made in the English way," she said; "but you will like it."

He drank, and put down the cup.

"Do you like it?" she asked; "if you do, I will teach you how to make it."

"Yes," he replied almost angrily. "But what do I care?" and added passionately, "It's you I want to hear of. Tell me of yourself."

She sat down again upon her pile of cushions. "I am so tired," she murmured plaintively. "If I were to tell you about myself, I should never end. Last night—I was ill, you know. . . . . I very often turn giddy suddenly, and afterwards I am tired and stupid for a little while."

"If this be the case you ought to consult a doctor," said Graysett decidedly. "Why does not your husband call in a physician? No one could look at you and not feel sure you were in bad health."

"I will not see a doctor," she exclaimed with excitement. "I am my own mistress, and no one can force me to speak against myself. I will tell *you*, but I will not tell a doctor. I have thought for a long time that I would tell you everything. And if you hated me and turned from me, I should know that it was true, and that I was a wicked woman—without hope."

"I *could* not hate you," said Graysett in a deep shaken voice. "I could never turn from you. Even if you were really bad, and that is impossible, it would only be the stronger reason why I should hold fast to you, and save you from your worst self. This is what I want you to fix firmly in your mind. If you could realize it, you would open your whole heart to me. And then you could never question my sympathy—my devotion."

For several minutes Judith sat silent. There was a look of effort and of struggling conscious-ness upon her face. She put her hand to her forehead in a helpless manner.

"You don't know how difficult it is to explain it in cold blood. You don't know the strangeness of it. It is like living two lives—the one his life; and the other—how can I describe it? When I am not living it, I could fancy it the memory of a nightmare. And when the horror grows and becomes real, I feel that I am possessed by a devil. . . . . And then, I have gone down upon my knees to him and have prayed that he would kill me. I cannot tell him what it is— the horror—I have tried—for I have thought that in his knowledge there might be safety. But the words are stifled in my throat, and I cannot. If he knew, he would strike me dead."

She spoke quite quietly, giving utterance to the gruesome hints as though she were alluding to the experience of another person, which her intellect comprehended, but which her imagination failed to realize. He longed to question her; but dared not, recognizing the necessity for allowing her broken revelations to come forth in their own way.

"Do not tell me anything more now," he said soothingly. "Wait till your mind is clear. I only want to feel sure that you will give me your confidence—and you will, in your own time. Then I can try and comfort you. Now, it is difficult, when I know so little. I can only feel for you to the depths of my heart. If you think it would be better, I will go away and come again. You have only to send for me, and I will come."

She seemed to shrink from his suggestion.

"No, no ; I could not bear you to leave me. Be patient for a little while. You must let me talk to you as the thoughts come. You said that you wished to make me good. Don't try that ;" and by a curious but brief transition to her first mood, she resumed for a few moments her former tone. "That would mean some sort of conflict, and it's rest I want. . . . . And, then, I don't believe in goodness. It's like the spirit which vanishes. It's the shadow which eludes you, and yet is always before you mocking your soul, and blackening the pleasures which might satisfy the bodily part of you. Only try to keep me at peace. Don't let me fall back upon myself. You might be a defence against——" She paused and shuddered. Her voice broke, and became a whisper that froze his heart. "You might keep the glamour always round me, so that the horrible things which swarm in the darkness could not come near me, and——" Again she shrank, and looked up at him with wild eyes, like a frightened child. "You would have kept me from this once, if you had been stronger. You know I said that it would need some one very strong. . . . . But now—now, if you were to will with your whole strength that I should not suffer——"

She half stretched forth her hands with an imploring gesture ; but they fell nervelessly, and she sat quite still, with her eyes downcast, and only the muscles of her mouth working.

"As God is above me," he said with an intensity that almost robbed him of voice, "I would give my life that you might be spared suffering."

He had started up at her appeal, and was standing over her. It had seemed to annihilate strangeness, conventional remoteness—even personal feeling. All the bewildering emotions she had roused in him since he had entered her presence—the sense of spell, the confusion of his motives, the need he had felt of some definite word or action on her part, which should give him full realization of the position—all were merged in the fierce desire to save her at any cost to himself, which welled up within him like a fountain of spiritual strength answering to her call.

His old fantastic belief, that in the power of his will lay her protection against evil, took shape in a passionate fervour of resistance, so that it appeared to him that he was beating back invisible foes, and, by the might of inward prayer, creating round himself and her a rampart against the assaults of malignant influences.

So vivid was the impression, so fiery and intense his resolve, that the only natural result seemed a corresponding effect upon her; and he waited, in unswerving faith, for the change to come.

She, too, had risen, and stood before him with limbs relaxed and dazed eyes. But the consciousness which crept slowly over her countenance—

heartrending to witness—was yet like the alteration in one from whom an evil spirit had been
expelled. Her lips quivered ; and her paleness
was as the pallor of a corpse. Her gaze sought
his with the most pitiful earnestness and questioning. He took her two hands and clasped them
within his own. As he held them, a quiver
passed through her frame. Tears gushed forth.
Some broken words fell. "It is going from me.
. . . . I said . . . . Do you remember ? . . . .
The spirit rent him sore—Don't leave me. Don't
forsake me."

She tottered, and would have fallen, had he not
supported her. He placed her gently in the
chair where he had been seated, and kneeled by
her, still holding her hands.

She trembled violently. Sobs shook her whole
body, till it seemed that she could have no more
strength to sustain the deep gasps which were
wrung from her bosom's core. Though his heart
was strained in an agony of compassion, he had
no words to soothe her. He could only dumbly
caress her hands, and stanch her tears, as if she
had been a child whose passion must from its
very vehemence ere long exhaust itself.

Gradually the shuddering convulsions ceased,
and she lay back stricken but calm. He waited
for her to speak. After a little while she said—

"I want to tell you everything. I can tell
you now. Come and sit by me. Don't kneel, so."

He obeyed ; and still waited in silence. He
could not urge her to speech. He had released

her hands ; but her fingers now groped helplessly, seeking his ; and he took them again, and, impelled by an involuntary impulse, reverently kissed them.

She opened her eyes. The strange light had left them. They were soft and clear.

"Let me hold your hand. It makes me feel that I am not alone. You could have no power if he were near me. You *can* only help me when his purpose relaxes, and his will ceases to be a force in me."

"You are speaking of your husband ?" said Graysett with determined quietude.

"It began that day—at Leesholm—you know ; in the Long Gallery, when I told him that he might do what he liked with me. I gave him leave. . . . . I can feel it all now. I had a reckless idea that it was Fate's doing ; and that the time I had been always looking forward to had come—the time against which Madame Tamvaco had warned me. Yes. She knew. She warned me. I did not tell you all. If you had been there, and if you had made me resist, the evil in me might always have remained dormant; or I should have married some one good, who would have kept bad things from getting power over me." . . . . She paused, and the dread returned to her eyes, as she took up her retrospect brokenly. "It was always there—from the first time I spoke to him in Christine's studio—you remember—that strange fascination which was half terror, but which seemed always drawing me. I could not help thinking of it, and wondering always, and longing to test his power. . . . . And then, that day, came the opportunity. Something within me told me to resist; but I could not. It was stronger than I. Everything went through my mind like a flash. . . . . I thought that this perhaps was the love I had dreamed of, but had never really known—for I had had vague feelings. I can't describe them. I was afraid of them, and yet I liked to feel them. I liked to think that that was perhaps how other women felt when they loved, and were married—and if it were so, it must be right and human. I wanted to be human, and like other women. I was so frightened—of myself. For I always knew, even when I was a child—I used to hear people say that I was strange—that I had no heart—no soul. . . . . ."

Again she halted. He pressed her hand sympathetically; but dared not speak, lest by some untoward word he might retard her confession. Presently she went on, her brow puckered, her eyes fixed on vacancy, as though she were trying to gather together the fragments of her inward experience.

"I did not know then that there could be a different kind of love—pure and spiritual, like God's love—like the light which warms and strengthens but does not burn—the light I told you of—I have only felt sometimes—since then—that it *might be* . . . . sometimes, when I have thought of you, and how little I used to care what I made you suffer. . . . . And that day, when he seemed to be drawing me to him . . . . it was like the desire to throw oneself down from a high place—like dying, to be made alive again in a new world. For, you know—the fancy I had—that I was supernaturally gifted—and that he could open to me the door of the Unseen and make plain to me the hidden things my mind was always striving after. I had read—I fancied—that to the clairvoyant there are no limits—no mysteries. I believed that if a will—strong enough—could unseal my inner eyes, many other unknown senses would be developed in me, and I should be a perfect woman—and far greater than a woman. . . . . But it was all false: it was a lie." The compressed passion in her low-toned utterance blazed up, and her voice rose. " I was deceived. I deceived myself. In that unseen world there was for me—*nothing*—nothing but the wicked thoughts, the foul imaginations, which were born of me, and which took shape there and became devils to torment me. . . . . *They* were our children—his and mine ; the offspring of our minds—mine diseased, and uniting itself with the evil in him. . . . . For you don't know—the bad things which had lain as it were, germinating —the books I had read—there was no one to mind what I read. They were there, though I hadn't understood them quite, working in me, poisoning all my thoughts and making me wicked. . . . . It was true—what Madame Tamvaco said —*I* have never appealed to his nobler aspirations. *I* have never influenced his better nature. It is

with his worst self that *I* have to do. . . . . And
so with me, while I am under his influence, I am
what his thought makes me.   I see with his eyes.
I feel with his heart.   If he wills what is bad,
then I am bad.   If he hates, I hate.   The evil
that is in him is in me—and more-—more."

"But you struggle against the influence?" cried
Graysett, his slowly gathering horror finding vent.
"You do not yield yourself to a power which your
soul tells you is your destruction!"

Judith smiled in the melancholy yet acutely
intelligent manner of one afflicted by a monomania which tinges every phase of thought.

"Do you not know, that when the soul is
driven from the body during a trance, its place is
liable to be usurped; and as the bonds between
spirit and flesh grow weaker, return becomes more
and more difficult.   Don't you believe this? Don't
you believe the story of the unclean spirit which
went forth and took to himself seven other more
wicked spirits? . . . . Oh, there are things in the
Bible which no one heeds now; but which are
true—just as they were true then—and thousands
of years before.   There are Mary Magdalenes
still, possessed by many devils; but in these days
there is no healer to cast them out.   Death is the
only healer; and he will not come when he his
besought."

"Judith," said Graysett, almost stern in his
passionate earnestness, "no power, human or
superhuman, can separate us from our immortal

spirit, which comes from God and will return to Him."

"Yes! through death," she answered with the same unnatural calmness. "I know that. I know that my body is a shell which will crumble into dust; and that when I am dead, my spirit, which is indestructible, will be once more the real *I*, working on through endless ages to its destiny. In the long night between this and the future day, I shall rest and dream. But it is with this body that I feel, and suffer, and love. It is with this body that I sin; and the longer I live the more awful will be its doom."

"Do not talk of sin or of doom," he urged with gentle insistence, feeling the hopelessness of reasoning with this wayward, stricken mind. "You have done no evil. I do not know yet what it is that you fear; but I know that it lies in your imagination only, and that when your fancy ceases to dwell upon it, the terror will vanish. You have been very unhappy. Your mind is unhinged. Try to believe that help is near you, and that a way will be opened by which you may escape from your trouble."

"Yes," she answered slowly, "I have been very unhappy. You said that it would be so," she added, another thought appearing to strike her. "You said that you feared for me death or madness. Do you remember?"

"Oh, don't recall wild words that I had no right to speak!" he cried, shocked by the suggestion that his own prevision of the terrible reality might have preyed upon her imagination. "That's all past. It's the present we must think of. When I know your position more definitely, I shall be better able to help you. Try to take back your memory to when it first began—I mean the horror you spoke of."

CHAPTER XXI.

"IT was after our marriage," she almost whispered —"very soon—when we were in America. I can't describe the beginning. . . . . I think I must have been ill," she went on after a little pause, piecing her recollections together in the manner of one following lost clues of fact through a labyrinth of confused sensation. "I can't remember distinctly. Often everything got dark. It was all glamour. The happiness—I *was* happy at first—was like an opium dream. . . . . Oh! I have taken many drugs. I have tried everything. Nothing is of any use. . . . . Sometimes I felt only excitement and joy, and everything was bright. Sometimes I was morbidly miserable; and sometimes dazed. I don't think other people noticed. . . . . I don't know. . . . . It was a sort of restlessness. I used to want to walk—any-where—to be always moving. . . . . Then, to soothe me, Esmé used to put me into a magnetic trance. . . . . He was very kind to me at that time. He is not cruel. It vexed him to see me disturbed. He was interested in the magnetic experiments. . . . . At first, I could not remember what happened to me, when I was in the clair-voyant state; but afterwards I had dim impressions

—always of Christine Borlase—always in her studio. . . . . Sometimes he showed me poetry that I had written—you remember that day at Leesholm. . . . . That was the first thing which frightened me—for often the poems were not good. There were thoughts in them, passionate, bad thoughts, which should not have come into my mind. He published them; the papers praised them; but I begged him, I implored him not to make me write more. . . . . After a little while I began to feel a curious sympathy with him—to know of what he was thinking—to see his mind all naked and horrible—to feel as he felt—not fiercely, or so that it hurt me; but as you feel pain when chloroform is given you; as though it were a long way off. And that was how it came to me—the agony of knowing that he did not love me. He had never loved me. His whole being was bound up in another woman. It had all been false, false from the very first. He had married me for my money. And now he had got my money; and his heart was beating and struggling like a mad thing, to escape and be with that other woman whom he loved. . . . . The knowledge crept into me—gradually. I felt it in that numb way; then with lightning-like flashes of pain— knives stabbing me as it were, in a dream; and confused memories when I awoke. The two lives were like two dreams, distinct from each other, yet blending in after-recollection. But there was a third state, when I was myself; and then, I suffered—oh God, how I suffered! . . . . And then, I think it was, that the horror commenced. I was always thinking of what I could do, at those times : of hate and revenge. I hated him and yet I loved him. I wanted him to be all mine. I couldn't kill him, for my life was in his. . . . . But the impulse to kill was so strong—like thirst —it got to take shape. It became like a live thing. It used to whisper 'When you go back to England, then you can do what you wish.' And because it was impossible there, I was always seeing it in a picture, at night ; and in the day, it was before me painted in blood. . . . . And I would kneel down and pray—and pray. But that was of no use."

She fell to shuddering again, and into a long silence. Graysett clasped his hands together, and involuntarily moved, changing his position slightly. The strain of following her wanderings, through which ran a thread of such ghastly tragedy, was almost unendurable.

"If thought could cross the ocean, and strike like a thunderbolt "—she exclaimed suddenly, her voice breaking under its weight of passion. Then it sank to a whisper :—

"All yesterday it was in my mind. I dreaded to go last night. I prayed him not to take me ; but he forced me. He said I was mad. . . . . And I dressed—you know. And in the glass, it seemed to me like the face and the dress of a murderess. . . . . After I was dressed, I took out the dagger—I had kept it hidden away ever since we landed in England— for I was afraid of it. He gave it to me, one day in America. It has a jewelled handle ; and it is sharp and deadly —it is like a live thing. I shudder at it. I've tried to lose it—to fling it into the water, or out of the windows of railway carriages ; but it clung to my hand ; it seemed alive. . . . . And when I was looking at it and thinking—he came in ; and I thrust it away. But it was before me all the time—all the time, in the carriage. And when we were going down the steps, with all those people looking, I kept seeing the picture between my eyes and theirs—that picture of her and me. . . . . She at her easel painting and singing—don't you know how she sings in snatches —and tossing back her hair while she looked at her work : and I, creeping into the studio by the garden door, and under the gallery, where the tapestry makes a dark passage—creeping so softly that she could not hear a sound ; and coming close—close—with the dagger raised——"

"Good God !" ejaculated Graysett, rising to his feet shaken out of self-control by the fearful vividness with which she pictured the scene. "This is too horrible!"

The words escaped him unawares. He stood gazing at her in anguish, his eyes big and smarting with tears. The rush of thoughts which crowded into his mind seemed thrust back again by grim despair, leaving him helpless. What could he do ? Of what avail were his feeble efforts at consolation to still a convulsion such as this ? Every suggestion that rose to his lips died there, stifled

by the overwhelming difficulties which pressed
upon him.   To rescue this poor distraught creature seemed the work of the physician rather than
of the lover.   He felt like a man standing power-
less on high ground watching a storm-beaten
vessel founder on the rocks.   How could he urge
her to confess her murderous impulse to her husband, or condemn her to any course which would
obviously lead to her being placed under restraint.
Again, at such a crisis, action was imperatively
necessary.   Instantaneously, he remembered a
case he had heard of, in which the avowal of
homicidal impulse, unheeded, had preluded the
commission of crime.   A black gulf of horrible
possibilities yawned before him.   He staggered
and grew dizzy. . . . . And then, as by a lightning flash, he saw himself bearing her away in his
arms to an unknown but hopeful future ; devoting
every energy, every emotion of which he was
capable, to the task of preserving her from danger,
and restoring her to health and sanity.   He saw
himself battling with the phantoms which tortured
her, and shedding peace and purity upon her
vexed soul : his love her shield against the powers
of evil, and an antidote to the baleful influence
which had blighted her body and mind.

This, he thought, was the meaning of his
prophetic vision ; this, the mission he was charged
to fulfil.   He might save her, at a cost terrible
to contemplate, but which he must not pause to
count.   If higher law demanded that conventional law should be violated, let them await

judgment at that loftier tribunal, and defy the anathemas hurled at them by the world. Here lay the prospect of her release; it was for him to break her chains.

Swiftly, schemes shaped themselves; and dim outlines became clear; but, in the tumult of his being, it was impossible to commit himself in words. He walked a few paces from her, and his impulse translating itself into gesture, he flung open the jalousies, letting in a flood of soft evening light, and a gush of the balmy summer air. She had been sitting motionless since his outbreak of horror: it had subdued her, or her strength was spent. Now, his movement roused her. She looked towards him with wild but timid entreaty, and spoke in piteous accents.

"You see," she said, "I have told you what is true. How should I make you understand if I did not tell you the truth? And you cannot bear it—you are afraid!"

Still he did not answer. His mind, straining onward in far-reaching vision, was hardly pierced by her reproach. In his fervour of devotion there was not room for the idea that she might believe herself forsaken by him. He let her go on quaveringly.

"Do not be afraid. It has passed by me now; I could not have told you, if it were not over. It will not come again—for days, perhaps. But then," and again her tones sank to tragic intensity, "what shall I do when it comes? What *can* I do? Who will help me and hold me back?

There's no one—I am quite alone. I can trust no one but you. And if you leave me—if it becomes stronger than I—and I am led on. . . . . And if you turn from me——"

He had come back to her, and stood beside her chair, realizing with a pang that she had misunderstood his silence.

"I will never leave you," he said. "I love you, and my love cannot fail you. If I seemed to turn from you now, it was not because I was afraid of any burden you might lay upon me. I want to take up all your burdens, if you will trust me. It was because all natural ways of escape seemed so beset with obstacles ; and might bring you to perhaps even worse suffering, if that could be possible——"

"I understand," she interrupted ; "I know. I have gone over it all in my mind at times when I have been able to reason. There have been such times ; but always, in the background, there was the horror. I knew it would come back. I wanted to prevent myself from yielding to it. I have read about people who have had feelings like mine—mad people. And I knew they would say I was mad, and lock me up. That is what you meant ?"

He hesitated for a moment, while he sat down again beside her. "It is a danger to be feared," he answered slowly.

"I am not mad," she said quietly. "I was mad when I thought Esmé loved me, but I am not mad now."

There was a brief, painful pause, then he said falteringly, "You have considered? Other courses have suggested themselves to you?"

"I have thought of ways. I have thought of how I would go away from him. I would leave him my money. That is what he married me for, and he should have it—all—all. I would take my hatred with me, and lock it in my heart, and try to live another life. But that would be of no use. It would get outside of me, and drag me back. That's what my feeling is. I hate him; and yet I'm a part of him. I loathe him as I loathe my bad self; and yet I love him as I love my own flesh. Do you understand? Last night, when I saw Madame Tamvaco sitting there, and reading me through and through, I knew that she heard the evil thing whispering, 'The time is coming'; and that she saw the picture which was before my eyes—between them and everything else. It came to me like a flash then, that she who is so strong might be strong enough to deliver me. I had a wild fancy that she might, if she would, seize me and drag me away—away from everything, and cleanse and heal me. But you heard her words. . . . . And then, when he came into the room I knew that there was no hope. I was forced to rise and go to him."

Her voice failed; and she leaned back in her chair with wan face and eyelids closed. So white and still was she that he feared for a moment she had fainted. But she opened her eyes again and looked at him with her wide gaze, which questioned him so despairingly.

"Judith," he said, meeting her eyes full, and speaking incisively, and with the deliberate intonation which subtly conveys both doubt and conviction, "I have something strange to say to you. There is a means of escape. I think it is the only one. When I tell you what it is, you may be shocked and repelled. But when you understand me aright, your reason will convince you that it is the only sure way in which you can be delivered from your husband's influence, and from all those terrible desires."

He paused. Her eyes still sought his, but less despairingly. "I—don't know—What way?"

"You spoke of being dragged by force—from yourself—from everything which makes your present unhappiness—of being cleansed and healed. I do not think that this can be done by Madame Tamvaco; though, I believe, I feel sure, she may be of service to you. I believe the instinct which causes you to turn to her is to be trusted. She is a strange, impressive woman. She may have wonderful gifts. I don't know. I have no means of estimating her will or her power to help you. But it does not seem to me that she, unaided, can wrench you from your present life. There is only one way of doing that. It would be like death. It would be an ordeal, the worst almost for a woman. Do you comprehend me? The prisoner who escapes from his prison places himself under a ban. That is the price he pays for his freedom.

You are a married woman; and you are a prisoner, bound by the law. There's no appeal for you. Society does not recognize such a case as yours. You must free yourself from the jurisdiction of the law. You must do, or seem to do, that which will divorce you from your husband. Do you understand? No one can help you but a man who loves you so purely and devotedly that, while he asks nothing from you but your trust, he takes the right to be your champion, your defender, against the world, against your husband, against your worse foes, which are in yourself. Judith, do you know what I mean? Do you trust me?"

There was a slight quivering of her eyelids; and a faint blush rising to her cheeks—a little while ago so like marble—told him that she understood him. But her eyes were still wide and piteous as she answered brokenly—

" I have no one but you. Whom else should I trust? I said long ago that if you were strong enough——"

" I *will* be strong enough. I *am* strong enough. I might have taken you from him then—if I had been near you—if Fate had not been against me. I loved you then. I love you now. The love is the same, though all the circumstances are changed. You are the same; for you love me at this moment no more than you loved me then. I'm glad. It makes the—the ordeal easier. I only want you to trust me. . . . . There's no holier affinity in life or after death than the pure love of two hearts. That can't be for us. And

I will have nothing less. So, do you understand? There should be nothing, and yet everything. For is not such love as mine, such faith as you'd give me—everything ?"

She uttered a little cry, and rose to her feet, stretching forth her hands to him with a gesture of complete self-surrender, a gesture which said unmistakably, " Do with me what you will."

So he interpreted it, though no word was spoken. He took her hands in his ; then, bend-ing forward, kissed her gravely on the forehead. It was the seal of a solemn obligation. It was the outward dedication of his life to a task which he knew might be humanly almost impossible. He did not shrink from it ; but he foresaw, with prophetic distinctness, difficulties well-nigh insur-mountable. He drew a deep sigh of pain. His inward gaze towards the troubled future was clear and steadfast ; no passion obscured it. His mind was able to grasp practical exigencies ; and there was a certain relief, after the strain upon his emotions, in unravelling perplexities, and in rapidly sketching a vague plan of operations. The burden of his responsibility was greater than could be borne without the stimulus of action. His position seemed so unnatural that he longed to assure himself of its reality by grappling with definite detail.

Judith uttered no protest, asked no question. Her dumb acceptance of his momentous proposal brought home to him, as no words could have done, her utter helplessness, the bewilderment of her faculties, and her incapability of resistance to the influence which was at the moment dominant.

And yet, while this very helplessness strengthened his resolve, and spurred him to more intense self-devotion, the doubt quivered through him, whether he was justified in committing her irrevocably to a course of action of which she hardly comprehended the full import.

"Judith," he said, "you know to what you are consenting. You are separating yourself for ever from your husband. You are going to leave England. You are giving your life up to me."

She made an acquiescent movement but did not speak. He was smitten with compassion. She looked so worn and weak.

"I will leave you now. You are weary and need rest. Can you rest? Are you safe? Shall you be afraid to be alone now that you know that my whole heart is with you, and that your life is my care ?"

"I am not afraid," she murmured. "I am very tired. I think that I could sleep ; and then I should be ready to do what you wished."

"You will think of all that I have said ; and I will come again to-morrow at five. Then you will tell me your decision."

"It is for you to do what you will—what you can," she replied submissively.

Her voice sent a chill through him ; and the unnaturalness of the situation, the mockery of his position, struck him with new force.

He led her to the couch beneath the window, and, arranging the pillows for her head, laid her there with the utmost tenderness. Her eyes closed, and she sank to slumber like a tired child. As she lay there, with her strange hued, gleaming draperies massed round her she reminded him of a gorgeous tropical lily felled by a storm. The breeze entered, ruffling her hair, and stirring the lace on her breast. Her thin hands were folded one above the other, the rings falling loosely. Her poor wan face looked peaceful and sweet, though in its quietude the signs of alteration appeared more marked ; and the dark hollows round her eyes, the transparent temples, the sharpened outlines and depressions in the cheeks, told too plainly of the havoc which mental and bodily suffering had wrought.

CHAPTER XXII.

ON leaving Judith, late as it was, Graysett drove straight to the address of Madame Tamvaco.

The Sibyl's abode seemed singularly out of harmony with herself and her reputation. There was nothing sinister or suggestive of mystery in the semi-suburban terrace, with its air of middle-class respectability, its mean portico, its conventional bay windows, framed by hangings of dull moreen, where one naturally expected to see the usual flowerpot of crude design and colouring, enfolding an etiolated india-rubber plant, or mangy fern.

The blinds of the lower windows were drawn, and Graysett was thus partially prepared for the announcement, made by the Hindoo servant who answered his summons, that Madame Tamvaco was out of town, and would not return till the following afternoon. Graysett inquired for Mrs. Edye; but she also was absent. "The Sahib Balàji might however be visible," added the Hindoo; and at that moment an inner door opened, and an Oriental gentleman, slender, supple, and comparatively youthful, with long, black, curling hair, clear olive skin, finely cut features, and full, luminous eyes, appeared in the passage.

He wore a sort of tunic of dark velvet reaching below his knees, which seemed to aim at the combination of an admirable distinctiveness with that unobtrusiveness so desirable to the stranger in London. From his appearance, his scholarly air, and the remarkably good English in which he inquired whether he could be of any service in delivering a message to Madame Tamvaco, Graysett judged him to be a Hindoo of high caste, probably a Brahmin, educated in one of the Universities and an aspirant to the honours of punditship.

He confirmed the servant's information. Madame Tamvaco would not be in London till three o'clock on the morrow, when she would hold her weekly reception, previous to which she had promised an interview to some members of an association for the purpose of psychical research. The Oriental gentleman suggested that if Graysett wished for any private conversation with Madame Tamvaco, he should present himself punctually at three, and take advantage of a possible opportunity of finding her disengaged. Such opportunities, he added, were rare ; and upon a leading question from Graysett, remarked that Madame Tamvaco was deeply occupied in directing the operations of the Society, on the astral plane. He went on to say that the Western mind had displayed an unexpected attitude of receptivity, and that the development already clearly traceable among

Europeans, gave great hopes of spiritual advancement. Now, German metaphysics had made a stand against materialism, and the opportunity must not be lost.

At any other time, so mysterious an announcement would have excited Graysett's curiosity; and he might have found an interest in interrogating this occult personage upon the stupendous cosmogonical operations in which Madame Tamvaco appeared concerned; also in gleaning particulars as to the tenets of the sect she represented in London. But his inward preoccupation allowed play to but one round of thoughts. He was in no mood to take an outsider's humorous view of a situation in which he himself was so deeply involved; but which indeed seemed to have gathered, as it were, and focussed the contrasting elements of pathos and farce, mystery and vulgar sensationalism, enthusiasm and flippant intrigue, passion and frivolity, refined comedy and grim, stark tragedy —these and many more, which seethe beneath the waves, and rise like foam upon the surface of modern society.

He courteously acquiesced with the Hindoo's suggestion, and withdrew, rattling home to his chambers in his hansom, his brain in a tumult, minutes swelling in his imagination to hours, scenes flitting before him, and facts and fancies grotesquely blending as in the confused sensations of a man under the influence of hashisch.

He spent the evening in writing business letters,

studying railway routes, arranging plans, and providing against possible emergencies.

In the morning he drove to the temporary residence of a French physician, celebrated for his treatment of mental disorders, who was now seeing patients for a few weeks in London. Graysett had consulted him upon the subject of his own health sometime previously, and, a few evenings before, had unprofessionally renewed the acquaintanceship at the house of a friend.

He had to wait a long time for an audience. When at last he was shown into the great man's study, he found himself confronted, for the first time, by the real difficulties of his paradoxical position.

He had come to consult this man as to the sanity of an absent woman, whose name he could not give, with whom he was unconnected by any tie of relationship, the details of whose case he knew only from his own intuition and her fragmentary revelations—a case involving complications of so delicate a nature that to place it in any way clearly before the physician seemed an impossibility. A moment's reflection, a look into the depths of those keen-sighted eyes made him decide to trust their owner. He determined to be absolutely explicit and to suppress only two facts—the identity of Judith, and his own relations towards her as her lover and would-be abductor.

Graysett told Judith's story in full detail, prefacing it with a guarded apology for his own unconventional course of proceeding, which the physician received, forming his conclusions in silence. Dr. Dupas was at once a man of the world and an enthusiast in his profession, possessing an extraordinary insight into human character and motive, but priding himself upon a superiority to prejudice, both social and scientific. He listened attentively, every now and then interrupting the narrator with a request for more detailed information upon some particular point which struck him, asking many questions—some apparently irrelevant, others with a direct medical bearing, and carefully noting down the replies.

From his own knowledge and all that the Rainshaws had told him, Graysett was able to give a fairly accurate *résumé* of Judith's history—her hereditary predisposition, her uncared-for girlhood, her tendency towards the mystical, her curious idiosyncrasies, the little traits of temperament which he had observed during the first days of his intimacy with her, her extraordinary attraction towards Esmé Colquhoun, and the circumstances attending their first meeting—her susceptibility to his magnetism, and the shock which her nervous system had sustained upon the occasion which Mrs. Rainshaw had described, when Esmé had first exerted his influence, the subsequent change in her, and her marriage—all these facts he related as they had unfolded themselves to him, and finally recounted minutely the events which had taken place at Mrs. Borlase's reception, and the awful revelation as to her mental state, which Judith had made the day before. He then briefly asked Dr. Dupas' opinion.

The physician did not make an immediate reply. "It is clear to me," he said at last, "that there are complications of a private nature into which you are unwilling or unable to enter. It is impossible for me to speak with authority unless I see the lady in question."

"That is not practicable at present—in London. I wish that it were so," replied Graysett. "But if, as I understand, you are returning to Paris in the course of a few days, a formal consultation might take place there. Frankly, your voice cannot affect the immediate line of action which has been determined upon. I ask your opinion for my own satisfaction—upon what you may consider a hypothetical case. By giving it, you can be in no way prejudiced professionally."

Dr. Dupas smiled in an enigmatic manner. "I will give it," he said, "on that understanding. Major Graysett, I think that I comprehend your position and that of this hypothetical lady more clearly than you perhaps imagine. Such a case is unfortunately not unique in my experience. To judge it from a conventional standpoint would be an absurdity. I have nothing to do with ethical considerations, or with your private affairs. If you ask me whether a man is justified in breaking a social law in order that he may save one dear to him from certain misery, I reply that a man is justified in doing anything he pleases, provided that his action is calculated to produce . more happiness than pain, and that his individual obligations are not violated. There is no such thing as abstract morality; and I would paraphrase the precept, 'The Sabbath was made for man and not man for the Sabbath.' But that is beside the mark. I am a physician, not a priest. You ask my opinion upon certain facts and symptoms. Briefly: All that you relate makes me fear the existence of epileptic mania, of that degree of intensity which we describe as the *petit mal*, complicated by hereditary tendency. You look startled; but I need not remind you that the terrible seizures with which epilepsy is usually associated, constitute but one form of the malady. It may manifest itself in numberless subtle phases, and may attack the moral and mental faculties, producing a train of most interesting psychical phenomena unaccompanied by any distressing physical symptoms. It may indeed, in the first stages, be allied with an extraordinary vividness of imagination and intellectual capacity of a high order. I note all the morbid traits you mention in the early period—variableness of mood, concentration of the thoughts upon abnormal subjects, extreme nervous susceptibility, semi-religious exaltation, and slight attacks of vertigo, taking place at night, or of such brief duration as to cause no uneasiness.

"For example—the partial ecstasy and dual consciousness experienced by your friend at her first interview with the man who had already disturbed her emotional balance ; and again at the mesmeric *séance*—the acute pain at the heart, the apparent fainting fits, the subsequent dreaminess and confusion of ideas—are all significant.   Marriage and its consequent physical and emotive agitation would have accelerated the disease of which I now trace the process distinctly.   The indications are clear, vague as must necessarily be the patient's own account of her state—the sort of divided existence of which she is conscious, her confused impressions resembling the recollection of a terrible dream, the lapses of memory and occasional hebetude, the aimless desire for movement, the increasing powerlessness of the will, before the pressure of an imaginary fatality ; the belief in demoniacal possession, and the alternating fits of sensuous satisfaction with life, and of unspeakable gloom—the impulse towards, and terror of, some criminal act, recurring at stated intervals—these are marked characteristics of this form of mania.   They are warnings which demand the gravest consideration. . . . .

"Is the disease curable ?   You beg me to be absolutely frank, but without more than my present knowledge, I can commit myself to no statement.   Cases of complete restoration are rare.   It is possible to modify the disease, and to procure such long intervals between the attacks that a truce may be accepted as peace.

"In such a case as you have described, the only hope of radical improvement lies, according to my judgment, in complete and immediate change of scene ; in the entire breaking up of the existing conditions of life ; in the removal of all exciting causes ; and in soothing moral influence, combined with medical treatment and high, bracing air. It is impossible to estimate the effect of such measures. I have known instances in which they have speedily produced a beneficial result."

Graysett's anxious questioning elicited no more definite or detailed expression of opinion. The interview had been a long one ; and Dr. Dupas politely drew it to a close.

K

THE clock had hardly struck three when Graysett drew up at Madame Tamvaco's door. To his disappointment he saw a brougham standing there, and a hansom just driving away. The Seeress had evidently other impatient devotees.

The Indian servant admitted him ; and he was ushered through a second door further along the passage into a double sitting-room on the ground floor, where several people had already assembled.

Madame Tamvaco was seated in a large cane arm-chair placed in the draught of two windows. She was reading a newspaper, and fanning herself in an agitated manner, every now and then glancing up, as she delivered a volley of ejaculations in a language unknown to Graysett. She suspended the rapid swaying of her fan, to nod to him, and motion him to a chair.

The Sibyl was attired as at Mrs. Borlase's party in classically falling black draperies with her arms bare to the elbow. There was, however, a suggestion of frowsiness about her apparel and about her odd crisp hair carelessly arranged and partly covered by some folds of black lace.

She looked tired, ill, and much older than when he had viewed her in the rosy light of Mrs.

Borlase's studio. He thought now that she might be any age from fifty upwards. It was evident that she was in a state of nervous exasperation. She tapped her foot with a kind of repressed impatience. Her features changed their expression every instant, and were certainly not now distinguished by the serene dignity they had worn when in repose. Her voice was harsh and its foreign accent more noticeable. Graysett decided that her moods were as variable as her physiognomy.

She was the centre of a little knot of scientific-looking gentlemen. These she began to introduce with a comprehensive wave of her fan. " Professor Dowsett, Professor Woakes, Professor Borrodaile." Then one or two others were shown in, and, in the confusion of greetings, no notice was taken of Graysett by the Professors who seemed much intent upon their own business. Professor Dowsett, small, alert, with a note-book open in his hand, rushed up to the American Professor whom Graysett had seen at Mrs. Borlase's party, and inquired in an eager aside, " Have you had any phenomena ?" proceeding to make a note of the reply, which appeared to involve some explanation. Madame Tamvaco called to the Hindoo whom Graysett had seen the day before, and who stood in a dreamy attitude against the mantelpiece.

"Balàji, why do you stand there like a kangaroo ? Speak. Tell these gentlemen the difference between *Linga Sharira* and *Mayavi Rupa*."

Balàji started, and folding his thin brown hands

upon his velvet tunic and leaning a little forward so that his long black hair fell over his shoulders in front, began in a foreign melodious voice to expound Eastern wisdom. He did not appear however to make things quite plain to the Professors, who faintly questioned.

Balàji gazed round with the air of one in an *impasse*. "You have not the intuition. I cannot make you understand," said he in a compassionate tone. "You must lead the life, you must not eat meat or drink wine. I would like to tell you all these mysteries, but I cannot. You must lead the higher life."

"*Dame!*" cried Madame Tamvaco much incensed. "We do not want the higher life—you can speak facts? No, you are a fool. You are a sloth. Your head is in the clouds. Go and commit suicide. Tell Ram Dow to bring my coffee."

The Hindoo turning patiently away spoke to the black servant. Graysett followed him and held out his hand in his greeting. The Hindoo drew back, folded his hands together again, and made a deep bow.

"Madame Tamvaco seems to be an imperious taskmistress," said Graysett.

"Oh!" cried the Hindoo enthusiastically, "there is not one of us Chelas who would not cut off his hand for Madame Tamvaco, though she has made all our lives miserable in the beginning. Her temper is so strange," he went on plaintively. "She has led a wild life—in the desert with the Bedouins—on the Russian steppes talking wild languages. Would you have her a Parisian lady? But she is a great Upasika. She is high in occultism. She has a motive for her sharp words. She does not wish us to depend on her, but to walk the Higher Path alone."

"And you have found that path a hard one?"

"I would go to sleep saying, 'How shall I live to-morrow?' I would wake and sit thinking, 'How shall I bear the burden of my faults to-day?' It is always so when one begins to live by conscience and not by conventional shams. Every action is momentous. By some occult means she would learn my thoughts and call me to her. And then she would abuse me as if I had been caught red-handed in a murder. 'Balàji, you must have been a profligate in your last life. There is no good in you. You are a sloth. Why do you not give up trying after the higher life? You had better resign occultism.' 'But, Madame,' I would ask, 'what have I done?' 'No matter, you are vile.' If Ram Dow brought her coffee five minutes too late, I was vile. If two men fought in the street, it was my fault. I had no peace. I was thinking seriously if I should not die. I had no time to eat. I would feed myself with one hand and wipe my tears with the other. At last I could bear it no longer—a Brahmin dare not commit suicide—I ran away. At the risk of my life I passed the frontier—I passed into Thibet—and blessed are these eyes," continued the Hindoo, with a strange, reverent gesture—"for they have seen the Master."

"Who is the Master?" asked Graysett deeply interested.

"He is one of the mighty hierarchy, one of the Thibetan Brothers," replied the Hindoo gravely. He moved away. The rooms were now filling rapidly.

A lecture seemed to be going on in the front drawing-room, which was screened from the other by a partially drawn curtain.

Hither Graysett turned. Some ten or twelve persons, men and women, were gathered round a foreigner—not another Hindoo student, but a Persian, Greek, or Italian—it would have been difficult to decide his nationality—in plain English dress, with an agreeable bearing, and a singularly vivid, intelligent face. Graysett caught the words uttered in a low, finely modulated voice, "The astral body thus projected, transcends the limitations of sense. It is not trammelled by the ordinary conditions of existence. It assimilates knowledge without effort. It can pass through material obstacles "—when Margrave, who was standing in the circle perceiving his friend, moved out of it, and said in his dry, neutral tone—

"You will not imbibe any wisdom from the fountain head to-day, if that is what you have come for. Here is your Gamaliel. The ladies prefer his eloquence to that of Madame Tamvaco."

"Who is he?" asked Graysett.

"A Chela—as they term it, or student of occultism. This one is a native of the Ionian Isles, I believe, but hails immediately from Northern

India, where he has been under the tutelage of an adept. He has been explaining the scientific process by which Apollonius of Tyana separated his astral body from his physical one, and was enabled to be in two places at once. Have you come from the inner circle? The Sibyl was in good form the other day, and rang some astral bells greatly to the edification of Professor Dowsett, who has brought his brother professors of the "Psychological Investigation" department to make a report. But the old lady is in a singularly impracticable mood to-day. She will neither work wonders, nor expound doctrine. She has an indigestion, and the papers have been making fun of her."

"Surely a Sibyl should be above these weaknesses," said Graysett, with a strained attempt to enter into his companion's mood.

"Sibyls are women," drily remarked Margrave. "And then the theory of incarnations accounts for all inconsistencies. Accidents will happen, you know, even in so serious a business; and as it is to be seen that our Prophetess labours under disabilities—shall we say of temperament?—the suppositions are, either that the spiritual monad made a bad shot, so to speak, or that the ethereal and material affinities haven't kept pace with each other in the round of incarnations. Don't you see? A philosophy which provides satisfactorily for all contingencies commends itself to the latitudinarian mind; and I am travelling back to my old first principle that the soul and the digestion are one."

"Why do you come here?" asked Graysett.

"For instruction and amusement," promptly replied Margrave. "History informs us that once certain persons had the power of getting out of their bodies; and I should be glad to assist in reviving a lost art. Moreover, it appears to me that astral travelling must be an agreeable and convenient mode of locomotion. I am told that there is a Psychical College in America, where the process may be learned upon the payment of twenty guineas. Here I am taught for nothing. 'Embrace opportunities,' is one of my ruling maxims. But I candidly own that I am puzzled by the small practical use which these people seem to make of their astral bodies. Why, for instance, doesn't Madame Tamvaco take an immediate flight to the moon, where one presumes that there are no Society journals?"

Some fashionable friends of Mr. Margrave's entered and diverted his attention—a Belgravian dowager, with an eyeglass, and two æsthetically dressed daughters. They were followed by others, mostly ladies, and of all types, from smartly dressed London beauties, to spectacled advocates of woman's rights, emancipated spinsters, and ecstatic-looking spiritualists. To all of these the handsome Greek Chela appeared an object of deep interest.

Graysett looked about for Mrs. Edye, but could not discover if she were present. The buzz of conversation increased; and above it rose the exquisitely modulated tones of the Chela, who was guardedly replying to a pointed question from Margrave's friend, the dowager. "The Western mind, Madame, must be gradually prepared for the reception of the highest truth. There are many secrets which the Great Masters do not permit us to divulge to the superficial inquirer, or to those who are still in bondage to superstition."

The dowager dropped her eyeglass, through which she had been scrutinizing the Chela, and turning to Margrave, said in a *sotto voce*, audible to Graysett, "Really, Mr. Margrave, it is too bad to bring us to this distant suburb and put us off in that way. I thought we were to see the genuine article in a turban, straight from Thibet;" while an elderly lady of massive proportions and inflexible aspect, broke in—

"Oh, I have got beyond Christianity, if that is what you mean. I'm ready for a new revelation ; and all that about cyclic evolution and the planetary chain, seems to me very scientific. But what I can't understand is, how the Life Impulse is to be conveyed from one planet to another. If you will explain that to me I am ready to believe all the rest."

The Greek put his flexible hands together, turning the points of his fingers backwards, and directed a seacrhing glance into space.

"How does thought travel?" he asked dreamily. "How does knowledge travel? How is it that a seer in London can in his trance witness a scene which is at that moment taking place in Birmingham ? Knowledge comes, not by reason but by inspiration. How is it that Goethe, the most unscientific of thinkers as regards method, divined the truth concerning the structure of plants ? You Westerns have stifled inspiration by your process of induction. The Aristotelian method has been the curse of Western Thought."

"Yes, yes," twittered a thin, bird-like young woman, with her head upon one side, and a bunch of grass nodding on her bonnet. " That terrible Aristotelian method."

Graysett moved back to the inner room where Madame Tamvaco still sat, the centre of her little knot of scientists, but on its threshold he was accosted by the American Professor, who inquired in the tone of one yearning to discover a kindred soul—-

" You are going in for this ? You are a student —a Chela ?"

" Oh, no !" said Graysett ; " nothing so advanced."

" A spiritualist, perhaps ?"

" No," said Graysett again, quoting Margrave with a bewildered feeling that he was dreaming vividly ; " I come here for instruction and amusement."

" And I," said the Professor, sitting down, while he motioned Graysett to a chair by his side, " I come here in search of a faith. Well, now !" he went on, leaning forward with that queer mixture of earnestness and dryness—an

American characteristic, " I've tried everything ; and if these New Pythagoreans give me what I want, I'm a happy being. The doctrine promises well, I will say that. It appeals to the intellect. Now, I'm a scientific man. I may say that I'm one of the leaders of the scientific school over with us. I used to be the associate of Tyndall and Huxley, mentally you understand. Protoplasm, and uncreated and unvivified matter, that was my theory, till I began to investigate the phenomena of spiritualism. Protoplasm and ghosts don't pull together. I believe in ghosts. I've seen thousands of 'em. I have talked to them. I may say that I've kissed them. They upset my creed. What was I to do? Protoplasm on one side, modern Christianity on the other. I can't swallow that holus bolus with a gulp and a wry face. I'm tossed on the horns of these two dilemmas. Materialism won't do. Modern Christianity won't do. The first denies that I have got a soul at all ; the second gives me a soul but denies me the management of it. These New Pythagoreans let me have the bringing up of my soul ; and that's something gained. As for their scheme of cosmogony, they tell me it is based on exact science—occult science you know. I'm all science myself, and I shall pretty soon see how far that assertion is to be depended upon."

The American once set going was not to be lightly arrested. Graysett listened and looked on, forcing phrases and details upon his attention, after the manner in which a drunken man tries to convince himself that he is sober.

His faculties and emotions had been so strained during the last twenty-four hours, that they were incapable, for the moment, of sustaining any further burden. His deeper consciousness seemed stunned ; and his mind was a chaos of grotesque and ghastly fancies. He laughed to himself with a grim appreciation of that jumble of the tragic and the ridiculous which the situation presented, and which indeed is apparent to the humorist in all phases of life. He had come with quickened pulses, and an exciting if unreasonable hope, that some spiritual light might be thrown upon his own and Judith's destiny. But now, inspiration seemed bathos, and Madame Tamvaco a very ineffective link with the supra-mundane sphere.

She had thrown herself back in her chair, and was rolling up cigarettes with nervous energy. The three professors maintained their position near her, notwithstanding the pressure of new comers. Professor Borrodaile, a stolid-loooking person with a heavy beard, a massive brow and distinctly contemptuous air, sat at one side of her chair, silent and sceptical, but with eyes and ears alert. Professor Woakes, lean, Carlylesque in counten-ance, cavernous about the eyes, and hollow of voice, seemed aiming at an attitude of judicial im-partiality. Professor Dowsett, the showman as it seemed, looked uneasy and conscious of responsi-bility. He cast deprecatory glances at his colleagues, while in persuasive accents he urged his request. "Madame, will you not do something for Dr. Borrodaile? It would be so very satisfactory if you would give him a proof of the reality of occult phenomena."

"What do you take me for?" cried Madame Tamvaco. "Am I a juggler? Did you expect that I would make cups and saucers, and give a manifestation of electric bells in all your pockets? I cannot do it. I am ill. I am worn-out and ill-used. It's time that I disintegrated. I can tell you the world is not a pleasant place to live in when people write lies about you. . . . . Now listen ; I have devoted my life to a search for Truth. I, weak woman, weighted by bodily infirmities, less worthy than many of you here to be an instrument for the service of Humanity, I frankly tell you that I have clamoured till the door has been opened to me. I come forth to do my people good. What then? What do they call me? The Champion Impostor of Christendom. Oh, you Christendom! you are worse than the wolves. They only eat one of themselves when he has been killed by others. But you—you kill a man first and then you devour him."

A faint smile played over the impassive features of Professor Borrodaile, and Professor Dowsett burst forth in eager protest.

"Upon my word, I am very good to you gentlemen," continued Madame Tamvaco fiercely. "You come here to question me ; and I answer your questions, while all the time you call me to yourselves a cheat and an impostor. I am not angry at that. But when you say my Masters are a fraud, my blood boils. I cannot bear it. Attack me if you will; but do not blaspheme against that which is sacred. Respect the faith of millions. Respect those mighty ones who tread in the fourth path of holiness; for *they* are holy."

As her enthusiasm intensified, her voice became sweet and bell-like, and the changes which took place in the countenance of this remarkable woman were astonishing in their rapidity and variety. They resembled the play of lightning upon a landscape which alternates between sullen gloom and dazzling splendour. She took a cigarette from the heap which she had been accumulating, lighted it, and after a few whiffs, began to question Professor Woakes in a composed, candid manner, about certain experiments he had been conducting, on the effect of the electro-magnet upon the human body.

A card was brought to her by the Indian servant. She glanced at it, and her face grew dark. "Esmé Colquhoun!" she exclaimed. "What does he want with me? I am not æsthetic, I will not see him;" and resumed her conversation.

Presently another carriage rolled up; and a contralto, foreign voice, sounded in the hall. Madame Tamvaco started up radiant as a child, and crying, "It is Princess Golovine; she must come in;" called out a greeting in Italian through the half-open door.

The group of scientists dispersed a little, and an interested glance was directed by even stolid Professor Borrodaile, towards the lady who entered —evidently no insignificant personage.

Princess Golovine had the reputation of being able to influence the destinies of Europe. She was in the confidence of statesmen, and her movements were supposed to shadow forth an Imperial policy. Graysett had often heard of her as one of the most remarkable of female diplomatists. She was tall and striking in appearance. Her features were slightly irregular but suggested volumes of interpretation. She had dark hair and velvety black eyes which glowed as she talked. Her complexion was rich in tint—that of a brunette; and she seemed possessed of an almost superabundant vitality. She was one of those women who may be credited with every attribute, and a single one—that of "charm" always remaining uncontested. Princess Golovine was full of charm. Her manner had a delightful frankness and spontaneity. It was calculated to put politicians off their guard. She had a host of pretty alluring ways. It was said of her that she was wily as the serpent, innocent as the dove. It was known of her that she was a generous friend and a bitter enemy. Her appearance at Madame Tamvaco's reception was significant. Had it not been hinted that the doctrine of the New Pythagoreans cloaked a scheme of deep political import?

Princess Golovine advanced, and embraced the

Seeress with that mingled grace and impetuosity of which no Englishwoman becomes the mistress. This lady was absolutely without self-consciousness, or so supremely self-conscious that her abundant gesticulation was perfectly natural and effective.

The two spoke together for a few moments in the same language as before. Then Madame Tamvaco took up from a table near her, the paper she had been reading, and pointed out a paragraph to her friend. The Princess sat down and read, smiling serenely.

"But it is not true," said she in English, with her sweet foreign pronunciation. "There were no revelations. I did not give any letters, and I did write to the *Neue Freie Presse*, to say that. I cannot say more."

"You should bring a lawsuit, Princess," grimly remarked Professor Woakes.

"Oh!" said she, looking up and smiling in her peculiarly engaging manner, "it is so little matter. I am so indifferent."

"Why do you not join us, and devote your talents to the highest science?" cried Madame Tamvaco. "Your politics are beneath you. Do you know, gentlemen, the secret of Princess Golovine's influence? She has the most lovely voice in all the world. It is for her voice that the statesmen listen to her."

"Ah, you do speak to humiliate me," said the Princess with her liquid laugh. "They do listen to me, because I say what is worth listening to."

"Princess Golovine is a stateswoman herself,"

gallantly murmured Professor Dowsett; while the American Professor broke in with repressed impatience—

"And now, Madame Tamvaco, are we to have no phenomena? not even a precipitation—a portrait produced without contact with the pencil? It is a promise."

"No," exclaimed Madame Tamvaco. "I have said before, I am not a conjuror. My Professor, I will keep my promise; but another time; not for these gentlemen who have brought their note-books, and who will go from me to Errington the medium, and say which is the greatest cheat. Errington is not a cheat;" and she tightened her lips and shook her head. "That I will tell you, though I do not like mediums. I have shown Professor Dowsett some phenomena; and that is not enough. Here is Professor—what is your name? Boro—Borrodaile. He is a sceptic. He is a disciple of your Huxley. He will not give to any one but himself and his Huxley the right to think. Come nearer," she added, turning abruptly to Princess Golovine, "you have more brains than them all. Come and talk."

"Mais j'aime tant écouter," pleaded Princess Golovine.

"Well, what can I do to convince you?" exclaimed Madame Tamvaco, fiercely addressing Professor Borrodaile. "Would you believe if you had phenomena?"

"I can't say," replied Professor Borrodaile, still stolid, but with the slightest movement of his

eyelid; "it would depend upon the conditions."

"Would you believe if you saw me in my astral
body?"

"I cannot say. I must be quite satisfied first
about what I had eaten for supper?"

Madame Tamvaco glared at him tragically.

"Oh, Protoplasm! Protoplasm!" she cried;
"Huxley's Protoplasm! Why, you are the most
sceptical sceptic I ever beheld. You are a worse
doubter than Thomas Didymus. I do assure you
that you will go to the other extreme. That will
be your fate. You will become credulous. You
will turn spiritualist when you are a little older."

There was a general laugh, in which the Professor in question softly joined, but he said nothing.

"Why do you not speak?" cried Madame
Tamvaco.

"J'aime tant écouter," replied the Professor,
parodying the Princess; "I know that I am very
barbarous."

"Well," said she again, leaning forward, "do
you believe in Errington's slate writing?"

"I cannot say."

"Do you believe he is a charlatan?"

"I cannot say."

"What do you believe?"

"In nothing as yet," replied the Professor. "I
am reserving my judgment."

There was a pause. Professor Dowsett rose,
preparatory to taking leave, and observed that
doubt was the scientific attitude. Professor Borro-

daile did not move, but stroked his beard contemplatively. It was hoped that he was about to
make a concession, but it was a long time coming.
The American Professor was impatient for the
Psychical Investigators to be gone, and whispered
to Professor Dowsett, who was reluctantly putting
up his note-book, "I guess you'll get no phenomena to-day."

"I admit," said Professor Borrodaile, at last,
"that I am surprised. It is my impression—so
far—that Errington is not a fraud. If I could be
sure that the pencil wrote when the sound was
produced, I should be disposed to accept other
phenomena—as possible. At present there is no
evidence to convince me that the dead have the
power of communicating with the living, or that
the spirit, if it exist, is capable of operating upon
material bodies."

"It does not follow that because there are
phenomena they are caused by dead people,"
said Madame Tamvaco. "There is an astral
body, or there is not. If you admit the astral
body which is invisible, you must admit that it
can produce phenomena."

The Professor again stroked his beard, and
shook his head.

"You are sure that you have got a body?" sarcastically demanded Madame Tamvaco. "I can make
you invisible to Professor Dowsett if you please;
for I will magnetize him so that he cannot see
you. Well, you will admit that you have a body,
but you will not admit that you have a spirit."

"I have never experienced anything which could convince me that I have a spirit."

Madame Tamvaco held up her arms with a gesture of despair. The Professor rose.

"Oh, you scientists !" cried she ; "I will have nothing to do with you. You have surrounded yourselves with an atmosphere so dense that you cannot see through it. You are caught in your own trap. You are behind the march of science, not in advance of it. When are you going again to Errington ?"

"On Monday evening at eight o'clock."

"Very well, you shall see. Now, if you were convinced, you would not be honest enough to own it ? You would be *chassé* from your society. Your fellow-scientists would shunt you. And you would not be honest, like Crookes and Wallace, for example ? You would cling on to your old prejudices ?"

"Possibly. I do not know."

"Then, why will you not rise and make a rush for knowledge and grasp it ?"

"Because," said he, bidding her farewell, "I think it best to let knowledge come of itself, and find its own way."

As the Professor departed, Mrs. Edye entered.

She was in walking-dress, and her height made her conspicuous. She gave a careless nod to one or two who had greeted her, and went straight to Graysett, standing before him and looking him through and through with her clear eyes.

"You are in trouble," she began, then abruptly

changed her tone; "we'll talk about that presently. I have just come from a lecture."

He made some inquiries with a faint simulation of interest.

"Madame is going to talk to you by-and-by," she said absently, her gaze roving round the room and resting for a moment close by, upon Madame Tamvaco and Princess Golovine, who were conversing earnestly. "You must wait a minute or two. . . . . Yes, I liked the lecture. It was in a very grand house. There were a lot of women there, and about six men besides the one who talked. And I thought the whole thing extremely funny—a phase of British life. I am going to write an article on it when I get home. Think of a man getting a friend to lend him her parlour, and lecturing in it for his own benefit. My! fancy charging a dollar and a half for that! Why, you'd get the best lecturing possible for twenty-five cents in America!"

"Was Pran Nath there?" asked the American Professor jerking back to Graysett the remark, "that's another of the Chelas, there's a whole school of them who travel about with the old lady. When is he to be here? I have got some questions to ask him."

"Oh, Pran Nath is coming back presently," said Mrs. Edye. "I left him to sit it out. He didn't much care for the lecture. There was a frown upon his brow. It was all about the beauty of wedded love, and meeting hereafter, and that kind of thing. It did not fit in with Pran

Nath's notions. My! it was odd to see him there among the women; not the right sort of thing for a Chela vowed to celibacy."

"It doesn't make much difference to the Chelas whether they are in the company of women or men," said Madame Tamvaco, interrupting her conversation with Princess Golovine for a moment. "If it did, they'd very soon be ordered back to Thibet."

"Well, it was funny," continued Mrs. Edye, with her American laugh. "Most of the old ladies were asleep; and I was just trying to dissect them as they sat in front of me. I could see one right through, inside and all round her." She paused. "Major Graysett," she said abruptly, and moved a little apart, "you have got a patient for me. You need a doctor, on the occult plane."

A sudden impulse moved Graysett. "Heaven knows," he said, "I need a woman friend, who will befriend another most unfortunate woman."

"You want me. You want a doctor," she repeated; "a doctor like me. Why, certainly! I've made the disease you are interested in my peculiar study. That old Frenchman was right in his diagnosis; but he'll never get any further than that. Your physicians had better give up trying to tackle mental disease till their own inner eyes are opened. They can cut off your arms and legs, and cure a cold or the measles; but they aren't fit for much beyond. What has your vaunted science done in all these ages for incurable maladies, which the ancients believed, truly enough, were afflictions from the gods? It is we, the pioneers in spiritual magnetism, who are destined to make discoveries for which we shall earn the gratitude of the Race."

"Tell me," he asked, "how do you know of my trouble? Who has told you of her?"

"I have seen her. I have heard her tell her wretched story. I was with you both yesterday. You believe in clairvoyance, don't you? If you doubt, the proof lies within yourself, or else I am greatly mistaken. . . . . That's how I know. I was certain you'd come here to-day; and I guessed just how you'd feel. You have been looking round and thinking what a bubble it all is; and that we are a pack of self-deceived or fraudulent idiots. You have been blaming yourself for the impulse that brought you here. I daresay you have been wondering whether it isn't all a solemn hoax. My!" and she gave her mouth a queer little twist, "I should like to hoax some of *these* idiots who come to listen and to laugh, and to tell flippant dinner-table stories of our queer ways of going on. What do they know of our real aims our true aspirations? It's phenomena they want, and I'd give them a whole bureau-full if it would satisfy them. But that wouldn't be of any use. They'd never get, in this generation, any nearer to true wisdom. That's all I care about, Major Graysett. I've come over to Europe in search of it; and I'll go to Asia, if it is only to be found there. I want to help my fellow-creatures. I want to get at their souls through their bodies. When I saw that poor young thing for the first time the other evening, though I could not quite place her then, I said to myself, 'There's a case for you.' And I'm going to take charge of her, just right away—Madame Tamvaco and I have settled it all. You, she, and I will start off to-morrow, for a high mountain place I know of, and she shall be healed. I shall keep in the background, but you will know I'm there. You may trust me. You may trust those who are mightier than I. Let the world say what it pleases. That's no business of mine. Society is a hypocrite. I like to cheat hypocrites. Major Graysett, I could see right into your heart yesterday. You are a true man. Just think it over, and make any arrangements that you like. I am ready."

She ceased; and without waiting for an answering word—only giving him a strange little nod—flitted away into the crowd.

A few minutes later Graysett felt the touch of a hand upon his arm, and turning, saw that Madame Tamvaco was by his side. Again the woman's whole demeanour had changed. Her face was grave, even sad; and her glorious eyes seemed to have borrowed the far-off lustre of the stars.

"Go," she said very gently. "Go to her whom you love. It is near the hour of your appointment."

"Madame?" he exclaimed questioningly; "you will help her? You will save her?"

"She is saved," replied Madame Tamvaco solemnly. . . . .

CHAPTER XXIV.

The fantastic, vaporous suggestion that through Madame Tamvaco's lips, Destiny might give forth her utterance, had drawn Esmé Colquhoun also within the magic circle of the Sibyl's presence.

Repulsed ; passion burning in him like living fire, and yet with his brain cool and steady to scheme and to will, he walked away from the door.

The carriage which contained Princess Golovine passed him. She kissed her hand to him. The flashing vision seemed a gleam from his heaven of sensuous ecstasy ; and the beauty of this foreign woman, a symbol of that heart-cherished loveliness there enshrined. His brain revelled in alluring imagery. He was intoxicated with his poetic dreams. Their realization seemed dimly foreshadowed. He felt himself a conqueror.

His private hansom had been slowly following him. He signed to the driver, and jumped in. "To Baron's Gardens—Mrs. Borlase—and be quick."

Christine's French maid knew him well. In days not so long back, her mistress's secret had been no secret to her. For Esmé Colquhoun, the forbidding edict set forth in the artist's firm writing, "*Engaged till six o'clock,*" had never been put into operation.

A few diplomatically worded inquiries elicited the information that Madame had no sitters that afternoon, that a model had been dismissed early, that Madame was weary, indisposed. She was resting upon her couch. But Monsieur Esmé Colquhoun had doubtless, as formerly, the privilege of *entrée.* Madame should be informed.

"On no account." Esmé was imperative. As Pauline was aware, Madame had always accorded him the honour of entering her presence without formal announcement. He would step softly into the studio, and, should Madame be reposing, would withdraw so noiselessly, that she could suffer no disturbance—and—a *douceur* did the rest.

Pauline ushered him into a drawing-room opening off the hall, which, notwithstanding the traces of Christine's admirable taste shown in its furniture and decoration, had yet the look of stiffness an unused room must inevitably possess, and then closed the door behind her, leaving him alone.

He lingered for a minute or two in this ante-chamber, gloating on the marks of her handiwork, recalling tender associations, hugging, as it were, his passionate delight, and, voluptuary-like, intensifying by voluntary delay the divine thrills of anticipation. He passed into the conservatory, a mass of flowers and greenery, where two pyramids of roses in bloom guarded the veiled doorway that led into Christine's sanctuary. It was very silent here, and there was in the air the dreaminess that comes with heavy perfume. He could hear the bees murmuring, as they drowsily crawled out of the drooping yellow hearts ; and a light breeze from the garden caused the heliotrope clusters and the drooping passion-flowers to whisper tenderly to each other.

Esmé stood in the gallery. His hand was laid upon the heavy folds of the inner curtain, and he shivered in the delicious suspense with which he waited for the sound of the step—of a falling brush—of a snatch of song, such as was wont to burst from her while she worked.

But there was no audible sign of her presence. He lifted the drapery and descended the steps to the studio. A large easel stood in the centre of the room, and upon it the unfinished portrait of his wife. Judith's face was the object upon which his eyes first rested. It seemed to project with startling vividness from the dark background, at which he saw that Christine had been working. The palette and mahl-stick lay upon the ground, as though they had been despairingly thrown aside; and Christine herself, in weariness or perhaps in grief—for he fancied, as he approached and scanned her face, that a tear-drop was dry upon her cheek—had sunk down also, and had fallen asleep.

There was something inexpressibly touching in the unconscious *abandon* of her attitude. She was half sitting, half reclining, upon a broad, shallow sofa of the old-fashioned, high-shouldered kind, her arms thrown back upon a pile of cushions and supporting her head, the chin turned upwards, the white throat showing, the mass of short curls crushed up against the pillows, and falling over her forehead.

Her bosom rose and fell, as her breath flowed, not in the regular undulations of happy slumber, but with agitation—a troubled-heaving ; and now, as she faintly stirred, with a deep, sobbing sigh.

He came near, and stood over her, his eyes clinging to her, as though they could never have their fill.

He gazed and gazed, passion tearing at his heart, and his exaltation and resolve changing into black despair. For he knew, as he studied the pale, proud face of the sleeping woman, that, however defiant she might be of conventional obligations, there was in her nature an irresistible loyalty against which his grosser love might never prevail—the loyalty to a woman friend ; the loyalty to an ideal.

He clenched his hands in silent, impotent fury, and turned suddenly from her face to the face of his wife. His eyes dilated and darkened, shooting forth deadly gleams, till his countenance seemed for the moment transformed into that of a magnificent fiend. His form expanded and reared itself to its full height, as though he were gathering in superhuman strength. All the force of his soul, all the vital energy of his being, became concentrated in a intense passion of hate. "*Die!*" said the inner voice, "*Die! Die!*" and if thought were dynamic, the murderous will must have sped like destroying lightning to the accomplishment of its purpose.

As he gazed in fierce intentness at Judith's face, the outlines of the picture faded and were blurred ; and before him there seemed to rise a thick, dark mist, in which the form of Judith shaped itself, and swayed towards him and vanished. Fear came upon him ; and, in the reaction from his guilty desire, his limbs were like water, and great drops of sweat stood upon his forehead. He staggered blindly forward. The easel fell with a great crash, awakening Christine, who rose to her feet uttering a cry of terror. But without a word Esmé passed her, and left her presence.

CHAPTER XXV.

IN strange irony of coincidence, Graysett also waited upon the threshold of his mistress's boudoir, for sound or token that should welcome him to his tryst.

This room, too, seemed very silent. The light was subdued. The perfume of dying roses filled the atmosphere.

Again there crept over him the clammy horror of his dream, icily gripping his throat, and turning him sick.

Again he seemed to hear the plaintive notes of the melody which had preluded his vision. There, at his feet, lay the bunch of withered roses ; upon a chair near him, a mantle Judith had worn. All the minute details of his dream-chamber forced themselves upon him now, as then.

He felt cold and giddy. A mist rose before him, for moment, blurring the scene ; and out of the mist, looked Esmé's face—Esmé's eyes dilated and glaring with murderous hate.

Then the dimness cleared, the image vanished. He moved dizzily forward to the window. A ray of sunlight entering through a rift in the closed venetians fell upon a mass of yellow drapery, a tense form bent backwards on the cushioned divan, an upturned face framed in golden-brown hair.

"Judith!" he cried; and, falling upon his knees beside the couch, he bent over the prostrate form.

She had not swooned, for though the face was ashen pale, with a faint violet discoloration, the eyes were wide open, brilliant and prominent.

"Judith!" he said again, in a tone of the deepest anxiety. "I am here; speak to me."

But the eyes still stared fixedly, and the lips made no movement. He had kept his tryst with a dead woman.

PRINTED BY BALLANTYNE, HANSON AND CO.
LONDON AND EDINBURGH

www.ingramcontent.com/pod-product-compliance
Lightning Source LLC
Chambersburg PA
CBHW031023120726
47905CB00007B/2023